A COUNTERFEIT COURTESAN

THE SHELLEY SISTERS BOOK 3

JESS MICHAELS

This entire series has been dedicated to Shelly Das and Jenn LeBlanc.

Jenn, your amazing creativity always boosts my own. I could not imagine doing a book anymore without playing in your playground first. And that doesn't even begin to explain how deeply I value our friendship. Thank you for mentioning sushi at that conference all those years ago because I don't know how I'd get along without you. XOXO

And Shelly, this series started as a joke about how we could get you on all my covers forever. It's turned into one of my favorite and most successful series. Thank you for being you, an amazing model, a talented production assistant and most of all, a great friend.

CHAPTER 1

Late Summer 1812

Ellis "Handsome" Maitland leaned back against the long bar, drink balanced in his hand as he scanned the wide, open room before him. It was a room he knew well, for he had hunted here at the Donville Masquerade for years. The notorious underground sex club was the perfect place for a man like Ellis to find lovers, find marks, find trouble.

Trouble had found him here, too. Not the harmless, fun kind. The *real* kind. The kind that had destroyed too many lives. The kind he had to end now in the only way that made sense anymore. There would be consequences, but there always were. This time he wouldn't be able to avoid paying them...and he had accepted that.

He slugged back his drink with a wince. A fissure of pain shot from his shoulder at the movement. He'd been injured there a few weeks before. The wound was healing but still ached. Only it wasn't just physical sensation that made him flinch, as much as he'd like to pretend it was. *Fear* ripped through his chest. Perhaps he hadn't *fully* accepted the consequences that would come. But he was working on it.

Across the room, the big double doors carved with rutting lovers opened and a woman stepped through. Not all that shocking. After all, ladies made up nearly half the occupants of the room, seeking their pleasure with as much gusto as the men here did. Sometimes with more gusto, truth be told. It was a safe place to do so. Most everyone here wore masks, which gave all the attendees freedom to explore and surrender and play to their heart's content. He wore one too and lifted his hand to touch the leather edge as he adjusted it.

What made the newcomer stand out was how little effort she put in to doing so. The ladies who came here were mostly experienced. Married women seeking what their husbands could not or would not provide, widows who refused to climb into a grave with their lost lovers, courtesans who sought the safety this club and its owner, Marcus Rivers, provided while they sold their wares for pleasure and enormous profit.

Everyone here had their role and their place, and as Ellis looked at the woman who had just entered the room, he realized *she* did not. It wasn't that she didn't try. She wore a mask, but unlike the other ladies who made a show with feathers and satin and jewels, the disguise was plain. Her gown was daring enough. The neckline dipped down, revealing the upper swell of a truly lovely pair of breasts, but it looked like she had merely altered an existing gown, perhaps removing some tulle or lace that had once offered more modesty when it was worn in a ballroom or a parlor. The gown was certainly not designed to attract in this den of sin. It had *butterflies* on the fabric, for God's sake.

And then there was her demeanor. The lady stood stock-still just past the entryway and stared into the room, mouth open in just the slightest manner as she stared around her in what appeared to be shock.

Ellis had ceased to be shocked by anything in this world when he was eight. Jaded, his cousin always used to call him. Before Rook stopped speaking to Ellis weeks ago.

He shook his head and pushed that troubling thought away. Protecting those he cared about was why he was here. Not pretty ladies who were looking around the big room at couples pawing each other, suggestively dancing, rutting against the wall as others leered.

The woman across the room shifted, looking back toward the door behind her. But she didn't run. She fisted her hands at her sides, and he watched her draw a long breath that lifted her breasts. Apparently gathered, she came farther into the room. So, there was steel in her. Courage. He respected that.

It had been a long time since Ellis had played the libertine. Once upon a time, it had been his greatest pleasure, his way to make a living. Love games were his expertise. He'd carefully chose a mark, one who needed what he provided and little more, or one whose bad behavior made his ultimate abandonment fit their prior crimes.

Then he seduced. He convinced. Ultimately, he fucked. Everyone left satisfied, at least physically, he with a heavier purse. But in the last year or so…he'd had no interest in such things. His only attempt at a seduction scheme had started and ended badly…with his cousin's now-wife, Anne Shelley. Anne Maitland, he supposed, and winced at the thought.

The only flare of *real* desire he'd felt in that time had risen at the most inopportune moment, with a woman who surely despised him. The new wife's sister, actually. Juliana. Her very name was a benediction. A prayer Ellis sometimes woke saying in the night, hard as a rock as he remembered a brief moment when he'd held her in the midst of hell on earth.

But as he shook those thoughts away and stared at the woman at the door, he realized he wanted *her*. Just *wanted* her. Not for any ulterior motive, but because she had drawn his eye.

"Why not?" he muttered as he scanned the room another time and found it still devoid of the man he was hunting. "There won't be many chances left for pleasure, after all."

Those maudlin words hung in the air around him as he downed

the remainder of his drink, set it behind him and shoved off the edge of the bar to stalk toward her.

She didn't look like she fit here, but certainly she must. Women didn't come to the Donville Masquerade unless they wanted the kind of pleasure innocents couldn't fully understand. Her darting gaze and shifting body could very well be part of a game. Something a smart courtesan might do. Play the innocent. Bring in the bees through a different kind of sweetness than that of the experienced women who were moaning and pleading in the crowd around them. Hesitance had its beauty, after all. It made a man want to chase.

If this fetching woman wanted to play games, Ellis Maitland was the perfect man for her.

He edged closer, and she turned at his approach, lifting her gaze to his. He came to a sudden stop as he stared at those eyes. Eyes that he knew. Eyes that had haunted him for nearly a month, dancing into his dreams, digging him further into a hole he would never escape.

He knew those eyes. Knew their owner even though he'd only touched her once, held her once as she trembled in fear that was all his fault. The two of them had bled together. He, after being shot trying to protect her. She, after being sliced with a knife because he had failed. Even now, he saw the edge of a scar on her cheek peeking out from under the mask. He flinched at the sight of it and the proof it provided to his mystery woman's identity.

Juliana Shelley.

But what was she doing here? What the hell was *she* doing standing in the middle of the Donville Masquerade, looking up at him with an expression of interest and fear, but not recognition?

Well, he was damned well going to figure that out. So he shrugged on a new mask, the one of "Handsome" Ellis Maitland. A persona he had come to hate as much as the physical mask that pinched the bridge of his nose as he smiled at her in false greeting.

~

Juliana Shelley couldn't breathe. She knew how to breathe, of course. She must know how, she'd been doing it all her life. But she couldn't seem to drag in air as the very tall, extremely well-favored man she'd noticed at the bar the moment she entered this place crossed the room toward her.

He couldn't be coming for *her*, of course. Not when all around her far more experienced women offered things she'd been taught all her life to withhold. She was shocked by what she saw, in truth. Men and women grinding together in a titillating display of activities she had only ever read about in a naughty book she'd found in her father's study months ago.

Being here was far more powerful than looking at those things, dreaming of them while she touched herself.

She swallowed hard because the man coming her way had stopped. He was just an arm's length from her now, and he stared at her, seeking...something. She didn't know what exactly, but she shifted under his regard.

He had a black leather mask covering the top half of his face, but she could see the almost navy blue of his eyes, the fullness of his lips, the harsh line of his jaw. His dark hair was a little too long and slashed across his forehead in a wild wave she somehow wanted to smooth.

Her heart rate increased as he gave her a half smile. Something cocksure and a little smug. She should have been turned away from such an expression, surely she had refused many a man of her class in the past because of his smirk. But that wasn't what she wanted to do now.

"Good evening," he said, his voice low and rough in the din around them.

There went breath again. She could only hope she would remember how to form coherent sentences a bit more easily.

"Good evening," she returned, and hated that her voice cracked a little.

He arched a brow. She saw the movement beneath the leather, and for a moment, she felt a sense of familiarity. But that wasn't possible. She didn't know this man. She couldn't.

"I couldn't help but notice your entry into the hall," he purred as he grasped two glasses of wine from a passing footman's tray. He held out one and she took it with shaking hands. When she did so, his fingers brushed against hers. By design, she thought, but that didn't reduce the effect of him touching her.

It was like fire under her skin. She sipped the drink to soothe her dry throat and try to regroup. "Thank you?"

He chuckled at the question in her tone. "But I can't help but wonder if you know what you came for."

She jerked her face toward him. He had a touch of mockery to his voice now. Her spine straightened in response. She had never been the one in her family to fight—that was her sister Anne—but right now Juliana felt like channeling that strength to defend herself.

"I came here for what everyone comes here for," she said, forcing herself to meet his gaze. "Perhaps it is *you* who is confused if you must ask me what that is."

She sounded far braver than she felt, and for that she was pleased. He, on the other hand, looked less than happy. His full lips pursed a fraction—was it in annoyance? She couldn't tell without a full view of his expression. And in that moment, she realized just what a dangerous position she'd put herself in. She didn't know this man or his intentions or motives. He could be of a cruel bent. He could be the kind of man who didn't accept no as an answer. Or who reacted with violence when challenged as she had just challenged him.

She swallowed hard, waiting for him to say something, do something. Then he cocked his head.

"I beg your pardon, my lady. I think I have offended you. I didn't intend it."

"You didn't offend," she said softly, carefully. She glanced around them, the spell broken for a fraction of a moment. There was a couple at a table just to her left who were passionately kissing. The woman was perched in the man's lap, grinding down on him as their tongues tangled.

She darted her gaze away as a gasp left her lips and her body jolted with awareness. Gods, what had she done by coming to this place?

"Do you mind if I ask you a question?" he said.

She turned her attention back to him, wishing she didn't feel so hot and achy when he was standing so near. She nodded. "What is it?"

"Why *are* you here?" He motioned his head toward the kissing couple. "Your shocked expression when you see them touch each other, it says to me that you aren't a bawd as you might wish to be seen."

She lifted her hand and touched her mask. It covered the scar that sliced her cheek. She couldn't feel it beneath the fabric, but she knew it was there.

Memories returned to her in a wave. Of a man who'd taken her because he thought she was her sister. As one of a set of triplets, that was a common mistake, but this time it had nearly proved deadly. The man had attacked when he wasn't given what he wanted.

And she was left...*damaged*. She saw it in the mirror every day. She knew what it would do to her future, especially when combined with the shocking actions of her sisters as they'd found their true loves in the past weeks.

"I'm here because I don't want to..."

She bent her head. This man was a stranger; she owed him no explanation. And yet with the masks, telling him some version of the truth felt easier.

"Want to?" he encouraged, almost gently.

She worried her lip with her teeth. "I want to feel something good," she said. "I want to feel something just for me."

He was silent for a long moment, holding his gaze on hers. It felt like an eternity passed by, like they were suspended in their own bubble amidst the shocking debauchery of the room around them. Then to her surprise, he held out a hand.

"Come with me to the back room." His voice was even rougher now. It seemed to dance up her spine, and she shivered against her will. "And I can make you feel something. That thing you want to feel."

She stared at his outstretched hand. Ungloved, strong, lean fingers, a scar across the top of the second and third knuckles, a fresher one on his palm. She let her stare slide up the man's forearm, hidden under black wool, to the bicep that strained against the same, to broad shoulders that spoke of strength caged beneath propriety.

And finally she let her gaze settle on his lips. This *was* what she'd come for, wasn't it? This moment where a man would choose her, would guide her to some quiet room and take her. Take the thing she had been guarding her whole life, and for what?

She didn't want her innocence anymore. She wanted to feel alive.

Still, those old habits died hard. Politeness, propriety, protection. If she took that hand, everything would change. There was a strong part of her that wanted to pivot and run from this room and its heady air of sex and passion. Run from a man who would crook his fingers and know she'd follow.

"Miss?" he said, his tone gruff.

She let out the breath she'd been holding and took his hand. "Yes."

There was a flicker of something in his eyes as she touched him. Desire, she thought. That particular emotion had never been pointed at her, but she'd seen such a look in both her sisters' husbands' expressions when the couples thought no one was looking. But there was something else in this man's gaze, too. Respect? Regret? Some combination of the two?

She didn't understand it, but it didn't matter what kind of past or pain brought this man here. It only mattered that he drew her forward, through the milling crowd, back to the entrance to a long hallway. He spoke briefly to a man standing there and then guided her farther from the relative safety of the hall. Into dimness and darkness.

From behind the doors she heard soft sighs, louder moans. People were...doing things in those rooms. Wicked things she couldn't help but imagine. Every sound put her further on edge. Made her question her decision, solidified the same decision as excitement grew in her chest. She was going to bed this man. Or let him bed her. She wasn't certain *she* knew how to bed anyone, but certainly not this man who glanced over his shoulder as he opened the last door in the hall.

Their gazes met.

"Still want this, angel?" he asked.

She tensed. *Angel*. Another man had called her angel once, not that long ago.

She pushed the thought away. She wouldn't think of *him*. She refused to acknowledge she'd thought of *him* at all over the weeks since she last saw him. Since an afternoon of blood and pain and confusion that had changed her life forever.

"Yes," she said, a bit too loudly as she tried to make the thoughts go away. "Yes."

He pursed his lips again and stepped inside the room. She entered behind him, passed him, looking around. It was a small room with a big bed in front of a roaring fire. It seemed clean, elegant even, with its sophisticated artwork and silky coverlet. Odd, for she had not pictured a club of ill repute being so fine.

The door closed behind her with a click and she pivoted to face it with her heart in her throat. The masked man was leaning against it now, watching her as she reached out a trembling hand to support herself on the back of a close-by chair.

"Changed your mind," he pressed, "now that you're here?"

"Have you?" she asked.

"You know what I'll do, don't you?" he all but purred as he stepped toward her. When she didn't answer right away, he continued, "I'll strip that gown off you. You'll be naked before me. Then I'm going to touch you all over until you're arching, until you're begging. And then I'm going to put my cock in you."

She winced at the bold language he used. And yet the soft, sensual tone of those words excited her, too. After living her life without such blunt address, she found she actually *liked* it.

"Tell me you want that," he said.

Her thighs clenched at the order, said in such a gravelly tone. "I-I think my coming with you to the room tells you that."

He shook his head slowly. "No. You're not a courtesan. I thought it before, I know it now. So I need the words. Say the words to me."

Her cheeks felt like they were on fire as she stared at him. He couldn't *really* want her to repeat those wicked things. She'd never said those kinds of statements before. "I can't—"

"Say it," he repeated.

She squeezed her eyes shut. This was her last out. She could pretend offense and stomp from the room. He was all but daring her to do so. Or she could surrender to exactly what had brought her here tonight. Give herself over to the things this man promised and change her world, only this time on her own terms.

"I want—" she whispered.

"Look at me," he interrupted.

She let her eyes open and glared at him. "I want you to strip me naked. I want you to touch me. I want you to put your...your..." She huffed out a breath because her face felt like flames were devouring it. "I want you to put your cock in me. Please."

She added the last bit out of habit. A lady always said please. But his smile fell as she did so. He drew in a long breath and set his shoulders back slightly. She had displeased him somehow, it seemed. Though she didn't know how. She'd done what he'd asked, hadn't she? She'd said what he wanted her to say.

"Sir," she began.

He jolted slightly, and then he reached up and, without preamble, tugged his mask away. Her eyes went wide, and her mouth dropped open as he did so. Because she knew this man. Knew him far too well for her own good.

And he knew her.

"Ellis...Mr. Maitland," she stammered, taking a long step away from him.

He shook his head slowly. "Miss Juliana Shelley," he said softly. "Just what the hell are you doing?"

CHAPTER 2

Juliana knew she was gaping at the man before her like a fish, stunned into silence by his being here, by his question spoken like a scolding governess, not a wicked pretender. Not like the man who had crept into her wildest dreams ever since the last time she saw him.

The man she hated herself for dreaming of. He had harmed her family, after all. His actions had led to...

She lifted a hand and let it touch the place where her scar hid under her mask. He flinched when she did so, his gaze breaking from hers at last. At least she could breathe again.

"You have no right to question me," she said through gritted teeth. The door was behind him, but he wasn't entirely blocking it. And what she needed to do right now was run. As far and as fast from this man as she could.

She marched forward, hoping she looked more determined than she felt, and started around him toward escape. He didn't allow it. He caught her arm as she passed him. Not roughly, but gently, and her mind blasted her back weeks before, when he had held her against his chest, whispering words of comfort warm and close to her ear. Even through her pain and shock and fear, she'd noticed he smelled of leather and fresh linen that day. The same scent wafted to her nostrils now. How had she not known it was him immediately?

He dragged her toward him just an inch and stared down into her eyes with that hypnotic blue stare. "Juliana," he growled.

When he said her name, her entire body twitched. She jerked her arm away and swung without thinking. Her palm hit his cheek with a crack that echoed in the room. He turned his face, his defined jaw setting as he released her.

Everything felt like it slowed to half-time as he looked down at her again. She could have run, but she didn't. It seemed he didn't have to touch her to hold her where he wanted, he just had to look at her and she was frozen. With rage, with regret, with desire that she hated herself for more than anything.

"*Explain yourself,*" he said at last, drawing out each syllable.

She turned away from him because she couldn't look at that handsome face anymore. As she did so, she lifted her own mask away. It seemed she didn't need it. He'd seen right through it, piercing the heart of her that she hadn't wanted to share. Putting himself in the middle of her pain, as well as her longing. He wasn't wanted in either place.

"I don't owe you anything," she said softly as she stared at the fire across the room.

He was silent behind her for what felt like a lifetime. Then he said, "Perhaps not, but you owe yourself. Go home, Juliana."

"No!" she burst out as she pivoted toward him. She knew her eyes were wide, her face lined with desperation. She saw him recoil from that dark emotion.

He shook his head. "Juliana—"

She stepped closer even though it went against every instinct of self-preservation she had in her body. "You will not take this from me, Mr. Maitland. Not when you have taken everything else."

He had barely reacted when she hit him, an action she regretted already. But those words hit the mark far harder. His expression crumpled slightly, his lips tightening at the reminder that her destruction had been his doing.

She took the opportunity to move past him. This time he didn't touch her. He didn't argue against her. He let her go without so much as a word as she slid the mask back over her face and ran. Away from this place of ill repute. Away from the emotions and desires it stirred in her.

Away from him.

~

Ellis followed Juliana from the back room at a distance, far enough that she might not be aware of his attention. Close enough that he could intervene if she were bothered. The idea of her going back into that room and finding some other man to take her body was…

Troubling wasn't the word for it. It was something much darker and uglier.

Only she didn't stalk a new lover. He watched as she rushed across the room, not even looking at the increased debauchery of the club around her and fled through the doors she had entered what felt like a lifetime ago.

She was gone. And he should have felt relieved, but instead he was bereft. He'd been so close to…well, a heaven he didn't deserve. He'd touched this woman only a few times. Even when she slapped him, it was far more than a man like him deserved.

He had to remember that.

And hope that he had put her off going to dangerous clubs to find a man for her bed. He squeezed his eyes shut and tried to forget the fantasy of being that man.

Then he turned and went across the room. There was a guard at the bottom of a long set of stairs.

"Is he in?" Ellis asked the liveried servant who was staring straight ahead like he was part of the King's guard.

"He don't take visitors," the young man replied.

"Tell him Handsome Maitland is looking for him."

The use of his nickname brought the young man's eyes to him, wide and, Ellis thought, impressed. There were benefits to a reputation, it seemed. Or perhaps it was past relationships. He'd known Rivers since they were children, after all. Street recognized street, even when it dressed as something else.

He waited as his message was taken upstairs, and a few moments later the servant returned and motioned Ellis toward the office above. He climbed the stairs and entered above after a light knock.

Marcus Rivers was sitting behind a huge desk, papers strewn out before him. He had a frown on his face, but as Ellis entered, he rose and a rare grin lit up his face and brightened his green eyes.

"There he is." Rivers held out a hand to Ellis without hesitation. "You haven't darkened my club's doors for what feels like forever."

Ellis shook the offered hand and forced a smile. "I've been...busy."

He tried not to think of the last year and all he'd done and destroyed. Including the woman who had just stomped off away from him, probably never to be seen again.

Rivers frown deepened, but he crossed to a sideboard, where he poured them each whisky. As he handed over the tumbler, he motioned to the chairs before his fire. They sat together, and Rivers sipped his drink before he leaned forward, draping his elbows over his knees. "You look tired. And you're injured."

Ellis shook his head. Fucking Marcus and his ability to see every damned detail. It had served him well when he was stealing for a bastard named Jack Quill many, many years ago. It served him better as a man who ran an establishment built on sin and secrets.

Ellis shifted his shoulder and tried to ignore the pain that still lingered there. A few weeks had helped considerably, but a through and through injury like the one he'd suffered took time to heal completely.

"It wasn't anything," he lied.

Rivers lifted both brows and downed the rest of his drink with a grunt. "I'd rather hoped you'd gotten out of the life, my friend. Your cousin did, didn't he? Married recently, I think. To a respectable lady."

Ellis snorted into his glass. "Oh yes, he did that. Only a few days ago, actually. The fact that it's already reached your ears..."

Rivers shrugged. "Means nothing. I hear *everything* first. It behooves me to do so."

"Well, it's done and I wish him well." Ellis sighed, thinking of the betrayal in his cousin Rook's eyes the last time they'd spoken. Rook had offered him a way out. Ellis had known he couldn't take it. Even then he'd been aware there was only one end to this. "But it's the pirate's life for me, I think. I'll keep playing my games."

"Until they kill you," Rivers said.

Ellis shifted, for that statement reminded him of why he'd really come here. "I need a favor."

Rivers set the empty glass down on the table beside him and leaned back. His dark green gaze never left Ellis's, but it was inscrutable. Then the corner of his mouth quirked up a fraction. "Don't you owe me one already?"

Ellis shrugged. "Yes. Now it will be two."

Rivers nodded slowly. "What is it?"

Ellis drew in a long breath because in a moment Rivers wouldn't be inscrutable at all. He would be livid and questioning and pushing. "Winston Leonard."

Rivers' expression went flat in an instant, all emotion leaving his entire countenance except for his eyes, which immediately lit with rage. His hand twitched at his side, pulsing into a fist that he rested on his thick thigh. "That bastard isn't allowed in my club," he growled.

Ellis nodded. "I know," he said softly. "I heard what he did."

"It took three of my men to keep me from killing him. I wish they'd failed," Rivers said. "You don't mess with women in my club."

"You've always been firm on that."

Rivers jumped out of his chair, the action sending it screeching backward across the floor. He ran a hand through his hair as he paced to the window that overlooked the club floor and glared down at his domain. Ellis heard his friend taking long breaths to calm himself.

"How could you involve yourself with such a man?"

Fuck. So Marcus knew. Ellis stood slowly. "I bolloxed it, Rivers, what can I say? I saw what I thought would be easy money."

"I couldn't believe it when I heard you were working with him," Rivers growled. "You should have known better."

"Well, I've paid the price, I assure you," Ellis said, wincing. "And so have a lot of other people who *didn't* deserve it. I'm trying to set it to rights, do you understand? I'm trying to fix what I did. But I can't do that if I can't find him."

Rivers' boot tapped against the wooden floor as he held Ellis's stare evenly. "What are you going to do, Handsome?"

Ellis shook his head. "What I should have done in the beginning."

"Maitland," Rivers said, his tone a warning and a worry at once.

Ellis shrugged. "It's better if you don't know. You're almost respectable, friend. You'll need deniability."

"Fuck." Rivers stared up at the ceiling for a moment, drawing a few breaths to calm himself. "So you want me to let him back in my club."

Ellis nodded. "If you can."

"I *can* do anything—it's my bloody club." Marcus sat down at his desk and stared at the papers. Then he grabbed for a ledger at the corner of the desk and flipped through it. He scanned the lines before him and glanced up. "He still has money on his books for membership. When I kicked him out, he demanded it back but was refused."

"Well, he's a greedy prick," Ellis said as he stepped to the window Rivers had abandoned and looked over the kingdom of seduction his friend had built for himself. "I suppose money *might* bring him around."

"It isn't the money. It's winning over me," Marcus said with a long sigh. "I'll have my man Abbott send word to his people that the remaining membership will be honored if he can control himself. I don't know if it will bring him out, but you're welcome to him if it does. Whatever you plan to do, though, I hope you won't do it here."

"I owe you too much to do that. I just need to get him out of whatever hole he's been hiding in."

Marcus shrugged. "I'll keep you apprised." He leaned back in his chair. "I saw you with a lady tonight."

Ellis groaned. "Christ, were you spying on me, you degenerate?"

"You didn't pick a room where I *could* spy on you, even if I wanted to do such a thing," Marcus laughed, though there was a glint in his eyes when he referred to the rooms where lovers could be watched. "But I saw you circling her from up here. Saw you go into the back rooms. Didn't seem like you were back there long enough for much fun."

"No," Ellis agreed, picturing Juliana's face when she'd lifted the mask away and glared at him. God, but she was beautiful. "The lady, I'm afraid, hates me."

"After so short an acquaintance?" Marcus said with another chuckle. "Smart woman, figuring you out so swiftly."

"She is that," Ellis agreed. "No, she knew me before tonight. She doesn't belong here."

"Half the ladies who attend don't belong here," Marcus said. "That's the fun for them. They love to come somewhere so low and find what they can't get up high."

"This one might hurt herself in the process," Ellis sighed.

"You care?" Rivers couldn't cover the surprise in his tone. "I thought you lived for the love games."

"I lived *on* them. But I never picked innocents." Ellis flinched as he thought of the lie in that. "Well, I *tried* to avoid them unless it was absolutely necessary. Tried to pick women who wanted what I offered and didn't care about the price. Or deserved the price they'd pay. But this one...she's neither of those things."

"Do you want me to let you know about her, too?" Rivers asked.

Ellis pivoted to face him. "How would you know her?"

"I can figure out what name she gave at the door. If she returns, I'll send for you. And have her protected if she requires it."

Ellis considered the offer. He ought not to take it. Juliana Shelley wasn't his responsibility, after all. She didn't *want* him to take care of her. She claimed she didn't want him at all. Except that he'd seen the flare of desire in her eyes, and not just when she thought he was a stranger.

Want and need were different things.

"Yes," he said. "Tell me if she returns."

Rivers stood up and extended his hand again. "Be careful."

Ellis shook the offered hand, then turned to the door with a burst of humorless laughter. "I never am."

CHAPTER 3

Juliana stared out the parlor window, down at the Earl of Harcourt's garden. Normally she would enjoy the view, for she'd always loved a peaceful garden. Today, her mind wasn't on the beautiful flowers or the finely shaped bushes. Nor was it on the conversation going on between the members of her family behind her.

No, her thoughts were lost in a back bedroom of a notorious club, with a man who had made promises about what he'd do to her and then not kept them. Of course, that man was a liar, so she shouldn't have been shocked. Or still so titillated about what it would have felt like if Ellis Maitland had actually touched her instead of pushed her away.

"Don't you think, Juliana?"

She jolted at the sound of her name and turned to find her sisters standing together, watching her with expectation. As triplets, they had spent their life as the Shelley Sisters. A unit. One she'd taken comfort in, just as she had taken comfort in sharing the same face with two people she loved more than anything.

But in the past few weeks, everything had changed. She was no longer part of the unit of the Shelley Sisters. Thomasina was now

Countess of Harcourt, and Anne had married Constantine Maitland on their way to London just a few days before. Ellis's cousin, the one called Rook.

Juliana was happy for them. She could be nothing but. Despite troubled beginnings, they were both blissful in their marriages, and she never would have wanted anything less for them. But their sudden and heavenly unions had the effect of severing the sisterhood in a way she had always feared would happen: their strongest bonds were with their husbands now.

Nothing could ever be the same.

"Juliana?" Thomasina repeated, tilting her head with concern. Thomasina had always been the kindest, the most desirous of pleasing those she cared for. Though Juliana had noticed a change in her since she'd been forced to marry and then fallen in love with the earl after a scandal had broken his engagement to their sister Anne.

Pleasing others didn't seem to be her strongest drive anymore. Thomasina was truly coming into her own.

"I'm sorry, I was woolgathering," Juliana admitted with a forced smile.

Anne exchanged a look with Thomasina, and their powerful, sisterly bond was obvious. It had to be after their shared birth and life. They'd turned to each other when no one else saw them as anything but interchangeable, including their father. Juliana could see and feel the concern for her pulsing like a heartbeat between her sisters.

And it only made her feel more like an outsider than she had before.

"You have been nothing but distracted lately," Anne said, stepping forward. "What can we do for you?"

Juliana bent her head. Anne had been known as the wild child of their threesome. Proven by the fact that she had broken her arranged engagement to Harcourt and ran away with Ellis Maitland earlier in the summer. A fact that jolted jealousy through Juliana as she glanced up at her confident sister.

It hadn't worked out, of course. Ellis had immediately abandoned her with his cousin, Anne had fallen deeply in love with Rook as they struggled to find their way back to her family and now, she was here. Changed, just as Thomasina had been, by love. Anne was...softer somehow. She no longer had anything to prove because she had everything she ever wanted.

"I don't need any help," Juliana said softly as she turned away a moment.

Her role had once been to help everyone around her. Thomasina pleased, even if it hurt her. Anne went wild, even if it destroyed everyone else. And Juliana cleaned up the messes left behind.

Only now they didn't want her to do that. No, now they pitied her. And that was the biggest change between them, even more than the units her sisters were happily forming with their new husbands. They saw this next step in their lives as freedom at last, and she? Well, she was left behind.

"Juliana—" Thomasina began as she touched Juliana's hand and urged her toward them again.

Anne swiftly shook her head toward their sister and smiled instead. "Not now, Thomasina," she said. "Father will only be gone a moment."

Juliana let out her breath in a long sigh. Their father. While his daughters' worlds had been torn apart, he only cared himself. But that had always been true, from the moment their mother died and he became their only guardian. What mattered to him were his plans, his goals. And now he had apparently left the room, which she hadn't even noticed when she was lost in thought and regret and longing for things and people she couldn't have.

Shouldn't *want* to have.

Anne turned to Harcourt and Rook, who were standing by the fire, heads together in serious thought. The pair had not always gotten along. Harcourt was suspicious of Rook's past, his connection to Ellis and the underground. But the men had made a some-what wary truce at present, in order to protect their wives. Still, she sometimes sensed what could be a bond growing between them, and she thought one day they would be friends.

And then she would be truly cut out of her sisters' lives. They would become a foursome, not a threesome, and she would be alone. Even if they invited her along as an afterthought.

"Rook," Anne said, her face lighting up as she crossed the room to him, weaving her fingers through his. "You were saying something about Winston Leonard."

Juliana flinched but pushed her shoulders back to forge past the fear and pain that name caused. "You have news?" she asked.

Harcourt looked toward Juliana with concern for a moment, but then his gaze flitted to Thomasina and she was forgotten. "Yes," he said. "Rook?"

Rook lifted Anne's hand to his lips for a brief kiss before he released it and paced across the room. "We all know that Winston Leonard is a villain of the worst kind. Duke's third son or not, he is a dangerous criminal. When my cousin and Harcourt's late brother were working together, they were fairly harmless. But Leonard only wanted to use them, so he saw them as disposable."

Harcourt nodded, his lips in a thin, grim line. Thomasina moved away from Juliana's side to go to the earl as he said, "They were fools to fall for his schemes. And even bigger fools to betray him."

"Why do you think they did it?" Juliana asked, her thoughts returning to Ellis. His actions in the last few months had clearly been born of desperation, but he hadn't seemed a desperate man last night. Perhaps that was why she hadn't recognized him right away. He'd been confident and calm and cool as he toyed with her, then confronted her. Then let her leave without touching anything more than her hand.

"Ellis thinks he can handle anything," Rook said with a shrug. "He always has. And most of the time he's right. I'm sure he thought they could do the job Leonard required, stealing that gemstone that has caused so much trouble, and get paid. Job done."

"But Leonard didn't pay them what he'd promised," Harcourt sighed. "My brother never would have let such a slight stand. Too proud."

"For Ellis, the reasons for a response would have been even deeper." Rook scrubbed a hand over his face, and for a moment, Juliana saw the weight of worry for his cousin on his face. "He's known in the underworld. To be cheated like that would put a mark on him. Make him a target if he was seen as weak. He had to fix the situation. He had to lash back. *That's* why they stole the gem out from under Leonard and launched this march to hell."

"Your brother hid the gem when it was clear Leonard was coming for them," Anne said to Harcourt. "And when he was killed by Leonard—"

"The hiding place died with him," Rook said.

"We know all that," Juliana said. "It is all we have talked about in the past few weeks preparing to leave Harcourt for London and during the trip here. You have the code that tells us where the jewel is. Wouldn't it end the danger for all of us if you had it delivered to Lord Winston? Then he can work it out himself and leave all of us out of it."

Rook flinched. "I have worked over the code for weeks and cannot break it. I doubt Winston would have any better time of it. It could serve to provoke his rage further."

Juliana took a deep breath and hoped her tone wouldn't betray her. "Then why not ask Ellis for his help?"

Rook held her gaze for a beat. "Because I don't know where he is," he said softly. "Even if I did, right now I don't know if I can trust him. He was desperate when he hatched his plan to use Anne as leverage against Harcourt. And when Handsome is desperate, he makes bad decisions."

Handsome. Juliana jolted at the use of Ellis's street name. It fit, of course. There was never so handsome a man. Damn him.

"Well, I don't know what any of it has to do with me at any rate," she said, turning away so no one would read her expression too closely.

"When Leonard mistook you for Anne and kidnapped you, you became a part of this story as much as anyone." Harcourt watched her as she paced. "Leonard has to know he's gone too far. He…he injured you. He shot Ellis. He has to assume there are consequences, and that's why he's gone to ground."

Juliana stared at her brother-in-law. Harcourt was still talking, but she didn't hear any of it anymore. "Ellis was…he was shot?" she whispered.

The room went quiet as everyone stared at her. "Yes," Anne said at last. "Don't you remember? He was shot in the shoulder in the scuffle."

Juliana's harsh breathing echoed in her own ears as the room began to wobble around her. Her mind yanked her back, far back, to a bluff on a hill. To Winston Leonard threatening her, promising her that he would see her dead before this was over.

And then Rook and Harcourt and Ellis had come. There was shouting, and yes, she did remember a shot ringing out. Then the slash of the knife across her cheek. Pain and terror were all that remained then. And the warm arms of Ellis Maitland as he cradled her close and whispered in her ear.

"Hold on, angel. I won't let you go. You stay with me now."

He'd held her gaze with his, willing her to be present with him, not to surrender to the pain of the injury as he pressed his big hand to her cheek and held her together.

The rest was a blur.

"He was shot," she repeated, pulling herself back to the present.

Thomasina nodded. "You really don't remember?"

"I'm not surprised. The shock will do that," Rook said. He met Juliana's eyes and held there. "I'm *sorry*, Juliana. I'm sorry that none of us protected you better."

Juliana shook her head. "It's—it's fine. I'm fine." That was a lie, but it didn't matter now. Ellis had seemed well when he approached her. She hadn't noticed anything about him that said he was hurt. So even though he had been shot, he was...functional.

Rook looked less than convinced at her distracted dismissal of the past, but didn't push on the topic. "We've been talking about the danger, though, Juliana. Harcourt has implemented some security measures here with my help. Until we can find a way to deal with Leonard, we want to convince your father to allow you to stay here with the rest of us."

"I think not."

The entire group turned as Philip Shelley entered the room with a glare for his daughters and their husbands. His last glance was for Juliana, and it was dismissive.

"Father, be reasonable," Thomasina said, moving forward. "You must understand that Juliana might be in danger. She was attacked not three weeks ago."

"It was a random act," their father said with a wave of his hand. "Highwaymen are terrible things."

"It wasn't a highwayman who attacked me!" Juliana burst out, pivoting to face him. She had spent her life arranging things for this man, making him comfortable and fixing his problems, and now... now he acted like this.

"That is the story I have begun to spread to explain that hideous scar on your cheek," Mr. Shelley said, his gaze darting away from her face. Just like every other person's eyes had started to do. "And that is the end of it. We have enough troubles without bringing some kind of intrigue to London to sully our name more than Anne already has. Juliana stays with me. *That* is final."

"Mr. Shelley," Harcourt said, his tone low and serious. "Your daughter is in danger."

"One of them might be, but not Juliana," Mr. Shelley huffed. "What value does she have to anyone? If someone is coming for vengeance, it will be against Anne or Thomasina, and they are your problems now, gentlemen. I will not lose my secretary just because

Anne married a former thief." Rook stiffened and Anne lifted her chin in anger. Their father didn't seem to notice. Or perhaps even care. "And now we have stayed too long. I will call for the carriage. Juliana, you will join me in the foyer after you say your goodbyes."

He pivoted without another word and left Juliana and the rest of her family gaping after him. Then her sisters were there, buffeting her on both sides, each with an arm through hers.

"I'm sorry," Thomasina whispered.

"He's *wrong*, just as he always is. And we *will* fix this," Anne added.

Juliana smiled at them in turn, though she felt no pleasure in this moment or this humiliation. "I am simply glad you two are free of him," she said, and pulled from their arms. "It seems I am expected to follow, and what other choice is there? He is right, at the heart of it. I have no value to anyone, certainly not to Winston Leonard. You should all focus your attention on keeping yourselves safe and in celebrating your happiness. You ought not worry over me. I'll see you all later."

She didn't wait for their arguments or farewells, but turned and followed her father. He was just exiting the foyer when she entered, and she trotted after him, feeling rather like an ill-favored dog with an angry master.

He entered the carriage at the bottom of the drive without waiting to assist her. That job went to a footman, who helped her up in the carriage while staring at the red line of her scar across her cheek the entire time. She fought tears as he closed her in the rig and shouted to their driver to take them home.

"Don't you get ideas in your head, girlie."

Juliana blinked as she glared across the carriage at her father. He wasn't looking at her, but at some papers he had drawn from his inside coat pocket.

"About what?" she asked, though she already knew.

He lifted his gaze ever so slightly and speared her with it. "They're all worked up over nothing, you know. Winston Leonard is a gentleman, not like Ellis or Rook Maitland. He can be dealt with as such. You have no need to go stay with your sisters and be part of their hysteria."

She gritted her teeth at how easily her father could take sides with the man who had maimed her. And he'd intended worse.

"So you said," she growled.

His gaze narrowed. "Your accident is unfortunate, but your prospects were minimal at best, thanks to Anne and her behavior. You didn't lose much in the end. So you will be my secretary, and all will be well."

She stared at him, wishing she weren't still shocked by his bad behavior, by his selfishness, after all these years. "My *accident?*" she repeated. "That is what you call my being attacked by a mad man?"

Her father grunted and buried his attention back into the papers. It was probably for the best. After years of balancing everyone's needs so well, Juliana found it was far more difficult in this moment. Emotions bubbled up in her, burning and ripping and tearing at the control she'd practiced her whole life. Her anger and her fear and her confusion were all balanced on the blade of the knife that had changed her face and her life.

In the end, she wanted to feel none of those things. She didn't expect happiness or joy. Perhaps those things would never be hers again. But she would settle for not feeling the bad things. Last night she hadn't. At the Donville Masquerade, the negative emotions had been replaced with desire and titillation and anticipation.

She straightened her shoulders. She didn't want to lose that. So she was going back there. Tonight. Ellis Maitland and his edicts be damned.

CHAPTER 4

When she'd entered the main hall of the Donville Masquerade the previous night, Juliana had been shocked by the activities around her. Her gaze had darted around the room, never fully settling on the scandalous actions and sounds that permeated every part of the room because it was all so overwhelming.

But tonight it was…different. Tonight as she entered the hall, her gaze *sought* the wicked things. Settled on them because they centered her in some way. They took her mind off far worse matters.

So she allowed herself to stare openly at a table of four men and one lady who were playing cards. Except when one of them lost a hand, they stood and shimmied out of an item of clothing. The men were in various states of undress, including one who was entirely naked. The lady was bare from the waist up, and she giggled as the naked man flicked a thumb across her nipples before he dealt the next hand.

Juliana sucked in a gasp of air and stepped farther into the hall. She wasn't ready for such things, that was for certain.

She looked elsewhere and found two ladies sitting in the back of the room at a table. Their heads were together, fingers laced as they passed a drink back and forth between them. Finally the taller woman, with dark hair and warm brown skin, leaned forward and kissed the other lady. Their connection escalated rapidly, and soon their tongues tangled in passionate display before they parted, smiling at each other with affection.

Juliana swallowed and glanced down at her feet. What was she doing here? She was a shy little sheltered mouse, it seemed, just as Ellis Maitland had said. He would laugh heartily to know how shocked and titillated she was by all this. He would think her even more of a fool than he already did.

She frowned. Why was she thinking of *him*?

"No," she muttered, and shook her shoulders to clear her mind. She was here with a purpose and she was going to fulfill it. She scanned the room once more and this time her gaze settled on a man standing along the wall, watching the actions of those around him. He did not wear a mask, as was more common with the men in attendance, and he had a nice face. Not as handsome as Maitland, but then again, who wanted beauty that could be weaponized?

She drew a long breath and slowly began to cross the room toward him. Her hands shook as he noticed her and straightened up, his eyes flitting over her with interest.

"Good evening, my lady," he drawled when she reached him.

She inclined her head. "G-good evening."

"Are you enjoying your time here?" he asked.

She shifted as her gaze darted to the great hall again. It was one thing to look at these things, but to observe them with a stranger…

"Er, it's quite…stimulating," she whispered.

"Indeed. I had heard a great many things about this place over the years," he said. "But never attended before. I suppose for a lady such as yourself, it is more commonplace."

She wrinkled her brow. "A lady…a lady such as myself?"

He nodded. "A courtesan," he said. "Only courtesans would wish to partake in such things, I think. True ladies feel no desire for such pleasures, no matter what Marcus Rivers sells to create interest in membership."

Juliana pursed her lips. There were a dozen things to be offended by in his suggestion. One was that women would not feel desire the same as men. She certainly felt it and knew her sisters did the same. No one could mistake their attraction and attachment to the men they'd married.

The second was his dismissive tone when he spoke of courtesans. After recent events, Juliana could easily imagine circumstances that would lead a lady to trade on her body for survival or even for mere pleasure. If that was the path, why shouldn't a woman enjoy herself?

"Excuse me," she said as she turned away from the man with a sniff. "I think I shall seek company elsewhere."

"Wait," said her companion, who seemed far less handsome now. "You did not even allow me to ask your price."

She straightened her shoulders. "There is no price high enough, sir. Good evening."

She pivoted then and stalked away, her heart pounding and her nerve sinking. God, but this was harder than she'd thought. One nice-looking person and he'd turned out to be an arse. And the only person who had really sparked her interest was…

She stopped in the middle of the hall as her gaze swept across the parameter and fell on the very man her mind was about to conjure. Ellis Maitland. He was wearing a mask, the same one he had worn the night before. And just like before, she recognized him. She would have recognized that casual way he stood, the strength of his fingers around the drink in his hand. The smirk on his face as he watched the crowd like a wolf.

That bastard.

She pressed her lips together as hard as she could and began to stomp across the room toward him. But before she could reach him, another gentleman stepped up to speak to him. She hesitated because when Ellis looked at his new companion, his face lit up with joy. Love. Her heart skipped at the expression. It made the man who so confused her seem…younger. Less jaded.

Who was this person who could change Ellis so much? As if in answer to her question, the newcomer turned slightly, and her breath caught. He had the same nose and jawline that Rook and Ellis shared. Another family member, it seemed. Another Maitland. He was younger than her, Juliana thought. With a bright, fresh-faced smile and an adoring gaze for Ellis. He was dressed well and had a confident air about him.

They spoke for a few moments, their heads close together. Then the younger man clapped Ellis's arm and headed off into the crowd. For a moment, Ellis only stared after him, his mouth a thin line. His gaze almost mournful, despite the mask. But then the expression was gone. Dragged back under the veneer he chose to show to the world. He straightened his shoulders and looked back over the crowd as if his relative had never approached.

But she'd seen the pain there. She'd seen the connection and the heartache. And for a moment, she wanted to go to him and give… comfort. To take his hand and ask if she could soothe whatever fleeting pain he had allowed himself.

"No," she muttered, pushing those thoughts away. Ellis Maitland might indeed be capable of love, but he was also capable of worse. And that he'd come here, that he was still intruding into her own plans, was unfair. She couldn't forget that.

Her hands shook, but she shoved them behind her back as she continued on her path toward him. At last she stepped up to him. He looked over her in one sweeping glance, one much like the one the other gentleman had given her.

Only when Maitland did it, her body reacted of its own will. Oh, she hated how treacherous her longing was. This was an enemy at her side, not a friend, damn it!

"Leave me alone," she growled past clenched teeth.

He stared for another beat, and then he tilted his head back for a laugh that revealed straight, white teeth and very interesting cords of muscle along his neck that were normally covered by a cravat. There was no remnant of the emotion he'd shown when with his companion. As if he had never felt it at all.

She blinked at how easily he covered himself. At how quickly he laughed at her. "Do not mock me."

He returned his gaze to her. "I would *never*, angel. I am laughing because *you* approached *me*. You must admit, the rules of leaving you alone are confusing at best."

She clenched her fists at her sides. He'd called her angel again. Damn him. "You're following me, aren't you? You're here because I'm here."

A faint smile twitched at his lips, but then it faded, and he seemed to grow more serious. His gaze flitted to the crowd, watching where the other man had left moments before. "No. As much as I enjoy watching you, I'm here for a much darker purpose."

Her anger dissipated a fraction at those words. "What do you mean, a darker purpose?"

He shrugged, and she noted the tension around his mouth as he did so. Pain. She recognized the expression as one of pain, a mirror of what she'd seen when he was standing with the other Maitland. She stepped closer, searching his gaze since she couldn't see his face when it was obscured by the mask.

"Were you shot?" she whispered.

He jerked at the question, and for a moment, he seemed surprised. She was proud of that fact, more than she should be. This man was jaded—being able to surprise him was a boon.

"You know the answer to that, I think," he said. "You were there."

"I was so wrapped up in myself that I *didn't* know," she explained as her fingers fluttered up to touch her scarred cheek through the mask. "Until my family told me this afternoon. Ellis…"

He turned his head. "You shouldn't say my name, angel. I'm not worthy of that."

"You were shot protecting me," she said, ignoring his admonishment.

His mouth tightened. "I was shot because I *failed* at protecting you."

Her lips parted at the choked sound to his voice. True regret, not something put on. Or if it was, this man was an actor of the highest caliber. How could she even know the difference?

"Is your wound healing?" she asked.

He shifted as if the concern was uncomfortable to him. She wondered if no one cared about this man and his wellbeing. He'd once been close to Anne's husband Rook, but she knew the two were estranged and had been for a long time, even before Anne's marriage. There was this other family member, or who she assumed to be a family member. But their interaction had been brief, if warm.

So was Ellis all alone in the world?

"I'm fit as a fiddle, angel," he drawled, and the genuine quality was gone now. He was back to the game. Back to being Handsome Ellis Maitland, a character, not a person. "Are you hoping to test that out?"

Heat suffused her cheeks at the question, not even subtle in its double entendre. "You are so confounding," she snapped.

He smiled and a dimple popped in his cheek that she suddenly wanted to trace with her tongue. "Thank you, I do my best."

She huffed out a breath. "You say I shouldn't be here, but then you try to seduce me."

"I don't *try* to seduce, Juliana." He drew out her name and inched forward, invading her space a fraction. She gasped at his body heat and the delicious leathery scent of him. "And you shouldn't play with fire."

"What I do is none of your business," she whispered. "I came here to tell you that, nothing more."

"You came here because you didn't like how your encounter with that pup at the wall went," he said, reaching out to catch an errant curl that had fallen from her bun between his fingers. He twisted it around his finger slowly and the gentle tug at her scalp made her catch her breath. "You came here because of your own dark purpose."

Her breath came short now and she glared up at him. "So you *were* watching me."

"If we're in a room together, I'm watching you," he whispered. "Am I wrong, Juliana?"

She pursed her lips in frustration. Damn this man. "No, you're not wrong. I approached that man along the wall, and he said something...something very rude to me."

"What did he say?" Ellis asked, his tone suddenly sharp as he jerked his gaze toward the young man she had approached what felt like an eternity ago.

"Something about only courtesans coming here," she said, shaking her head. "It was uncouth, nothing more."

"Ah, you didn't like being compared to someone so low," he said. "I understand."

"No!" she said, pulling back from him. "I didn't like his implication that a lady cannot feel desire. Or that desire or the control of one's own body and its needs is something to be considered low. I would *never* judge another woman for her life and her choices."

Ellis stared at her, his eyes wide beneath the mask. She felt trapped by that regard, sucked into blue depths that were brighter than the sea on a summer's day, more pure than a cloudless sky, more hypnotic than a sapphire.

He reached for her, and even though she knew she should, it was impossible to pull back. His hand closed around her forearm and he tugged her forward, closer and closer as he bent his dark head to hers.

She found herself lifting to meet him, desperate for that moment when their lips were a millimeter apart. There he paused and drew a deep breath, like he was trying to take her in or perhaps slow himself down. If she feared he would withdraw, though, he did not. His free hand lifted to cup the back of her skull, lean fingers digging into the coiled mass of her hair, and then his lips brushed hers.

She had somehow thought it would be rough when he kissed her, but it wasn't. He was gentle, just gliding his lips back and forth against hers in a slow seduction. She sighed at the pressure, at the warmth of his mouth and his breath. His grip on her forearm tightened, and suddenly she was molded even tighter.

Her softness seemed to tuck perfectly into every hard line of him, and they moaned together as the space between them vanished. When her lips parted, he traced them with his tongue, and gentle suddenly changed to something else.

She opened without understanding and his tongue moved inside, probing her, tasting her. She gasped and suddenly her hands were gripping his lapels. Had she done that? She didn't recall lifting or fisting the fabric in her hands, but here they were. She touched his tongue with hers.

And the dam broke. He crushed her harder against him, his lips and tongue more insistent, his hands tugging slightly on her bun and mixing an odd and wonderful sensation of the slightest pain with the deepest pleasure.

She wanted more. Even though she didn't fully understand it. Even though every proper word that had ever been spoken to her by every stern lady screamed at her to pull away. To run before it was too late.

She ignored it all.

She didn't want to run. She wanted to wrap herself around this man until this deep, throbbing ache inside of her was soothed. Until she didn't feel so empty anymore. She would fill herself with him. She would drown if she had to.

And just when she thought she might, just when she began to believe he might give her what she wanted, he pulled away. He steadied her before he backed up a long step, breaking all contact between them. Suddenly she heard the sounds in the room again, felt the eyes on them from those nearby who probably hoped for the same kind of show others were putting on.

Ellis stared at her, silent, his expression inscrutable thanks to more than just the mask. He didn't want her to know what he felt. What he wanted. Why he was playing a game with her.

That thought made her anger return, and she lifted a shaking hand to her lips. They felt so hot. So full. She glared at him. "L-leave me alone," she whispered, though there was no heat to the words. No truth.

"You endanger yourself, Juliana," he said.

She folded her arms. "*You* endangered me."

His jaw set as if he was gritting his teeth and his gaze left hers at last. He nodded slowly. "I did do that, yes. And now I'm going to protect you."

"I don't want that," she said, throwing her hands up in exasperation. "I don't want *anything* you have to offer."

"Well, we both know that isn't true," he said with a half-smile. "We both know you *want* a great deal. You *need* even more."

She shook her head, hating that he could see through her. Hating that he could use her body and her heart against her. She stepped toward him. "Mr. Maitland—"

He groaned and lifted a hand. "Don't. You are testing something you don't understand." He sighed. "Now I'm taking you home."

Her lips parted in shock and she fought to find some way to deny him. Only he wouldn't be denied. He reached for her hand, catching it in his as he started toward the door. And she followed, even though she kept telling herself to pull away. She followed, her heart throbbing faster, her body tingling with reaction and her soul longing for another kiss.

Even though this man was everything she shouldn't want.

Ellis looked across the carriage at Juliana. She was sitting ramrod straight, her hands folded in her lap, her gaze focused on him. She would have looked as proper as any well-bred lady should, were in not for the revealing dip of her gown's neckline or the mask still on her face.

Two things that made his half-hard cock twitch a little in his suddenly very snug trousers. The woman was a menace, plain and simple. And he'd never been able to resist one of those.

This time he had to.

He leaned forward. She stiffened but not in fear. Her hands clenched against her lap and her breath caught as he slipped a finger beneath her mask and pulled it away gently. He tossed it on the bench beside him and examined her again.

Great God, but she was a beauty. It was funny because he'd met her sister Thomasina, though not exactly under the best of circumstances. And he'd used all his seductive powers on her sister Anne to try to save himself from the dangerous situation that now threatened them all. But even though both women shared Juliana's face, he had never been drawn to either of them the way he was to her.

He couldn't stop looking at those eyes. A fascinating shade of green that reminded him of spring in the countryside. Someplace safe and warm. A place he didn't belong and never would. But it was a place he wanted to belong to, especially when he was vulnerable. Unexpectedly seeing his brother Gabriel tonight at the Donville Masquerade...

That made him vulnerable. He had gifted a membership to the club to his brother upon his eighteenth birthday. And though it was awkward to bump into Gabriel at that place of sin and seduction, he still loved talking to his brother. Having that all-too-brief connection before Gabriel went off to have a little fun.

It might be the last time Ellis saw him. And that cut down to the bone. So, of course, Juliana Shelley would come up after that. Of course she would challenge him and surprise him and let him kiss her until the pain dulled and his blood roared in his ears. She made him forget.

He had to remember now. He leaned back. "Why are you doing this?"

She didn't answer, but her fingers came up to trace the length of the scar across her cheek. He followed them in the dim light. She had only been injured a few weeks ago, so the damage was still dark red, and the skin around it was slightly puckered as it healed. It *would* heal, but she would always have a mark there.

"Because you think you're damaged," he said when she didn't fill the silence.

She let out her breath slowly. "I *know* I am," she corrected, her voice shaking. "And not just because of the scar."

He wrinkled his brow. "What does that mean?"

She turned her face, looking out the window at the darkness outside. "Perhaps a man would have been able to overlook the scar, considering my dowry. But I was already on shaky ground socially. Being a triplet makes me and my sisters…oddities. And then you did what you did. You seduced Anne and she ran away. The scandal of her broken engagement and Thomasina marrying Harcourt in her stead…" She bent her head. "*That* is what damaged me most."

He clenched his jaw. "I never *seduced* Anne."

Her gaze flitted to him. "You convinced her she could love you so that she would go with you. You wanted to have leverage over Harcourt."

He couldn't deny that, nor the guilt that slashed through him. "Yes. I thought Harcourt knew the location of this damned gem his brother and I stole. I knew a straight-laced fop like him would never give it to me outright, especially considering his financial situation. I went back to what I know."

She shifted in her seat and her head bent. "Love games," she whispered. "Seducing women for your own purposes."

He nodded. "That's what I do, angel."

"What you're trying to do with me," she corrected. "Isn't it? What is it you want, Ellis? Another way to get to Harcourt? Information you think I have? A way to punish Anne for choosing Rook over you?"

His lips parted at the last suggestion. "I want to make it clear: I *never* wanted Anne. She was a way to get to Harcourt, plain and simple. I am happy for her and my cousin. I know Rook like the back of my own hand, and he adores her. They will make a happy life together. I feel no regret in anything to do with her except that so many were hurt by my actions."

He thought she smiled ever so slightly, but it was hard to tell in the dimness of the carriage.

"At any rate," she said, and sighed, "the scar is only a final straw in a long march to ruination for me. The only benefit is that at least the mark will help everyone tell me apart from Thomasina and Anne now as I labor for the rest of my life as my father's secretary."

"Fucking fops," Ellis growled, not even trying to tamp down the rage that lifted in his chest. "If those arses could look at you, scar or not, and not want you, they are fools."

She shrugged. "Then they are *all* fools. I assure you, no one wants me. That's why I went to the Donville Masquerade. I know my future." She looked out the window and her tone went faraway. "I just wanted a taste of something more before I surrender to it. Just like I told you that first night before I knew you were...you."

He clenched his jaw at how resigned she was, and although he'd never considered himself the kind of man to comfort or soothe, he couldn't resist reaching out to take her hand. It was warm in his. So soft that he almost moaned at the feel of it. He lifted her fingers to his lips and brushed them ever so gently, and her gasp echoed in the quiet around them.

"You asked me what I wanted a moment ago, what my game is," he said, holding her gaze steady. "There is no game, not this time. I kissed you because I wanted just what you *think* you want. The difference is, I understand it."

She pulled her hand away, clenching it in her other one as she glared at him. "I understand it. I'll have you know I read a very shocking book. With *pictures!*"

"Christ." He squeezed his eyes shut, trying not to imagine Juliana bent over some naughty book, green eyes wide with desire at the scandalous images, perhaps even touching herself as she learned about pleasure.

The carriage was beginning to slow as it took the last turn toward the home Juliana shared with her father. Her lips pressed together in a thin line and her cheeks flamed before she whispered, "Do you really want me?"

He nodded. "Yes."

She looked out the window again, and desperation lit in her stare. He hated to see it. Hated more what it drove her to do. The danger she put herself in because of it.

"Don't go to the Donville Masquerade again, angel," he said softly.

She jerked her stare back toward him. "I won't promise that."

Although that wasn't the answer he wanted, he had to smile. She was a spitfire beneath that propriety. He'd never been able to resist a spitfire.

The carriage stopped and she moved toward the door as it was opened. "Good night."

"Good night," he echoed, watching as she pushed her shoulders back and strode with purpose to the door. He had no idea how she was going to explain her late arrival to her father, or if the man even cared, but she seemed unconcerned as she walked into the house and out of his sight.

He flopped back against the seat as his carriage moved again. His poor rock-hard cock was not going to survive too many more encounters with this woman. And he had just enough time before they reached his own small home on the other side of London to relieve the ache she had caused in him.

With a groan, he eased the placard of his trousers down and touched himself as he thought of Juliana Shelley and her soft, sweet mouth on his.

CHAPTER 5

Juliana sipped her tea and tried not to look across the parlor in frustration. Thomasina and Harcourt had gone out for the afternoon, and Juliana had thought she and Anne would be having tea alone. She'd actually looked forward to the moment of normalcy after the madness of her last two nights at the Donville Masquerade. But Anne had come downstairs with her husband, Rook, and the two were now standing at the fireplace, heads together, discussing something closely.

Juliana might as well have been invisible. She *was* invisible. Of course, that afforded her the opportunity to observe Rook Maitland without it being obvious.

He was Ellis's cousin and the two did have some similar features, ones she'd also seen on that mystery man at the Donville Masquerade the night before. Their noses, for example, were alike, and she couldn't help but think of Ellis's nose nudging hers as he kissed her.

Their jawlines were also close in appearance. Ellis's jaw had a smattering of stubble that had abraded her fingertips slightly when she brushed her hand along it.

Damn it. She didn't want to keep thinking of that moment when he'd kissed her. She didn't want to think of *him* at all. But she couldn't stop. She'd thought of him when she got home and lied to her father about deciding against staying with her sisters, as had been her explanation for being out.

She'd thought of Ellis as she readied for bed. She'd thought of him as she tossed and turned in the sheets. She'd thought of him when she finally snaked her hand between her legs and by touching herself had relieved some of the tension that had flared between them. Then she'd proceeded to dream of him all night.

He was an intrusive menace and she didn't want to want him.

"Juliana?"

She blinked as Anne retook her seat on the settee across from Juliana. Rook joined her and poured himself some tea. "Yes?"

Anne smiled. "I'm sorry. You looked so far away."

"There is just so much to think about," Juliana admitted with a sigh. "So many upheavals and unexpected moments in the past few months. I am trying to rediscover my place in the world."

"Isn't your place in the world the same as it ever was?" Rook asked gently.

Juliana considered him again. Once he had been a thief like his cousin. The two men had worked together, side by side. But he'd given all that up. Been redeemed by words, by deeds...by love. Was Ellis capable of such a transformation? A ridiculous question, of course, but one that popped into her head regardless.

"I think it is entirely changed," Juliana said, setting her cup down with a clatter. "When we left London, I was one of three unmarried sisters. We shared the same face, we were almost considered the same person. I knew exactly where I fit in Society, for better or for worse. But within a few short months, not one but two of my sisters have married, neither to a man that was expected. The ripples of their actions are far and wide."

Anne bent her head and her guilt was clear. "Yes. What happened was fortunate for Thomasina and for me, as we have both found love. But I recognize you've suffered greatly as a result of our passions."

Juliana stifled a laugh. Anne made it sound like that was a one-time thing. But her entire life had been spent cleaning up the messes other people made, especially her sisters. She was the one who soothed hurt feelings and smoothed ruffled feathers and fixed broken toys and hearts. Anne running away from her engagement was a large example, but it was not a new circumstance.

It was hard not to resent it, even if she loved her sisters deeply.

"I am happy for you both," Juliana said slowly. "Love is a rare commodity, especially for those of our situation and with a father so mercenary."

Anne reached across the table between them and caught Juliana's hand. "I *know* you're happy, you don't have to keep saying it to prove it. You are *also* allowed to be concerned about your own future. Or even angry about what you've lost."

Juliana shifted. Angry. She wasn't *allowed* to be angry, no matter what anyone said. "Right now, I think we must all remained focused on being worried for our lives," she said with a shake of her head. "After all, Winston Leonard is still on the loose. He could return to London at any time and decide to try to find this code you have again."

Rook exchanged a glance with Anne, and Juliana saw the concern on both their faces. It seemed even more stark than it had been the previous night. It made her wonder if something had happened. If she was being left out of this, as well as everything else.

She, who had once been at the center of the relationship with her sisters.

Rook sighed. "We're still investigating. I was thinking of seeking out my cousin. I have heard Ellis is back in London. I know he'll not wash his hands of this matter any more than the rest of us have. Too many people he cares for are endangered thanks to Winston Leonard."

Juliana stiffened. She could tell her sister and brother-in-law that Ellis was indeed in London. But then she'd have to say why she knew. Where she'd gone. What she'd done. She wasn't about to watch them first pity her for pursuing such a desperate desire, then find a way to judge and forbid her.

Instead, she ducked her head. "I have often wondered what your cousin is like."

Rook jolted, and his gaze went faraway and pained. "Er, he is… he is complicated." He pushed to his feet. "We came from such a different background than you and your sisters. Ellis's father died when he was young, and he was forced to the streets to take care of his mother. She remarried when he was eight or nine, and the new husband was…he was dangerous. Cruel to my cousin. Ellis left when it was evident he wouldn't be protected. His only tie to them is his half-brother, Gabriel. The one Winston Leonard is threatening at present."

Juliana fought not to respond, but she was sucking in these words like a sponge. She couldn't help but think of the man she'd seen Ellis with last night. The young man had shared his features. Could it have been this Gabriel? That made sense, given the gentleness of their interaction. The wistful expression on Ellis's face when the other walked away.

So Ellis presented himself as a cad and a thief and a scoundrel, but it seemed his motives were often driven by a desire to protect those he loved. His brother. His cousin.

Her. He kept saying he wanted to protect *her*. But of course, he felt nothing for her except maybe desire, if he were to be believed.

"Why the sudden interest in Ellis Maitland?" Anne said softly, her green stare locked on Juliana's face.

Juliana immediately broke the gaze. The connection she had with her sisters, that triplet bond that was so powerful, also meant either of them could sometimes read her expressions. She didn't want Anne to do that. To know.

She shrugged. "The man did save my life a few weeks ago. And his…his connection to you is what changed everything for us all."

Now it was Anne who shifted, and Juliana found herself tracking the movement carefully. After all, Ellis had explained a little about his relationship to her sister last night in the carriage. But Anne had not spoken of it much. She was obviously deeply in love with Rook...

But that didn't mean there had been nothing between her and Ellis. No matter what he said.

Anne glanced at Rook, and he smiled. Gentle, accepting. "You didn't do anything wrong. I have nothing to fear about Ellis, and I know it."

She nodded slowly, relief coming across her features. "I didn't care for Harcourt, and Ellis used that against me. But I didn't love *him* either—just saw him as a better alternative. After all, he can show himself as...passionate, engaged...fun. That is the game he plays, and he plays it well. But as for a true connection, there was never that, and I realized it the moment I made the foolish decision to run away with him."

Juliana hated to be relieved by those words, which dismissed what had been between Anne and Ellis as swiftly as those he'd spoken a few hours before. She also hated to be concerned about the *other* words. That Ellis could *pretend* to be passionate. *Pretend* to be engaged. That he could see what a person wanted and become it, if only to obtain what he desired.

If he were doing that with her, playing a game with her...did that mean the kiss wasn't real?

"Is he *ever* genuine?" she found herself whispering.

Rook nodded. "When he loves, he does it completely and whole-heartedly. That is genuine. *That* is true."

Anne smiled up at him. "I'm glad you can remember that. I know he's important to you, no matter what barriers have come between you."

"We've been through a great deal together," Rook agreed. He sighed and looked troubled. "Will you ladies excuse me? I've much to think about and I don't believe I'll be very good company while I do so."

He inclined his head as he stepped from the room. Anne watched him go, her face crumpled with worry.

Juliana shook her head. "You want to go after him," she said with a squeeze of her sister's hand. "You should. I'll be fine."

Anne nodded. "Thank you."

Without another word, she hurried from the room, leaving Juliana alone. And perhaps that was for the best. After all, she had a great deal to consider.

The picture of Ellis Maitland was beginning to become clearer to her. A man who had two sides. The carefree swindler and the loving family member. A man who would risk all for those he loved, a man who used his passions against those he could benefit from.

And he might be using her. She wasn't so foolish as to think he wasn't. But if he *was*, she had to believe his motives were, in a strange way, pure. To find Winston Leonard, to protect his brother and cousin, to atone for all he'd done wrong.

If she accepted those ulterior motives, couldn't they come to some kind of accord where they *both* got what they wanted? She could have the passion she desired, the passion she felt so strongly whenever he touched her. He, the conduit to the information she could provide.

It would be a bargain. One gone into with open eyes and strict rules and regulations. That was the only way to protect herself.

Now she just had to find a way to become bold enough to suggest it. And hope Ellis Maitland would take the suggestion without laughing her out of the Donville Masquerade.

E llis leaned back in the chair in Marcus Rivers' office and watched as his old friend poured him a drink from the sideboard. He hadn't imbibed this much in months, but who could refuse a friend? Especially one with such high-quality stocks. He took the drink and sipped, savoring the expensive whisky as Rivers retook his place behind the desk. He remembered this man as a wild, unwashed pickpocket, but here he was, every inch the polished businessman.

His business was sex, so hardly respectable, but he no longer looked like an urchin. Ellis wondered if he still felt like one. If the bite of the past still stung him like it did Ellis. If men like them could ever be free of what they'd seen and done.

"I'm surprised you aren't knocking the room over in your haste to know about Winston Leonard," Rivers said with a chuckle as he set aside his drink and steepled his fingers.

Ellis shifted. "You asked me here to give me news, and I've no reason to believe you're lying or playing with me. You'll tell me in your own time."

Rivers nodded toward Ellis's leg. Ellis followed the gaze and found his foot was bouncing. A tell. God's teeth, when was the last time he'd allowed himself a tell? He was getting soft, weak. Playing from a position where there was so much to lose rather than his usual higher ground of never risking anything he cared about.

It was a dangerous game.

"I won't torture you any longer." Rivers moved a pile of papers on his desk and came up with a sheet. "The message to Winston Leonard that his case had been reviewed and the club has decided to honor the remainder of his membership term was delivered. We chose to send it to the London estate he keeps first, as that seemed the least suspicious choice to make."

Ellis nodded. "I agree. Sending a note out to his country home or trying to find him with more verve would only serve to perk up his ears. They're high enough already after the problems we've encountered with the man. He'd be a fool not to be suspicious."

Rivers shook his head. "I'd still like to know more about that, but my place is not to push."

Ellis smiled. "Except you will, I know that. You'll just do it in your own way."

"My way is the right way," Rivers said with great certainty. "At any rate, because one doesn't send a pup to deal with a volatile tiger, I sent my man Abbot to deal with the situation personally. He had a few observations."

"Which were?"

Rivers didn't answer, for at that moment there was a light knock on the door. "We're ready for you," he called out.

The door opened and a tall, thin man with brown hair and eyes stepped into the office. He held himself ramrod straight, rather like a soldier, as he closed the door behind himself.

"Mr. Paul Abbot," Marcus said with a slash of his hand toward the intruder.

Ellis glanced at Rivers. "Did you...did you plan the timing of this?

Rivers chuckled. "I plan *everything*, Handsome. Abbot, will you share your report about Lord Winston's home with our guest?"

Abbot inclined his head and then focused his attention on Ellis. "I delivered the missive about the club myself yesterday afternoon. I found the household in some upheaval. They were clearly preparing for something."

"The return of Winston Leonard," Ellis breathed as he pushed to his feet and moved toward Abbot a step.

Abbot nodded. "That was my guess. When I mentioned Rivers' name and the club, the butler suddenly took great interest and said he would deliver the note to his master the moment he returned. I didn't get any other information about when that would be, but based on the state of the house? I'd say no more than a week."

A week. Ellis sank back into the chair as the air left his lungs. It seemed like a lifetime to wait. And it seemed like nothing more than the blink of an eye. In a week, this would be resolved at last. The way it always should have been. And everything would be over, the bad and the good.

Regret washed over him, but he shoved it aside.

"You don't look as pleased by this news as I thought you would," Rivers said.

"I am," Ellis said softly, and glanced up at Abbot with a grateful nod. "I appreciate your intervention more than I could express. I realize this puts you both out."

Abbot's forehead wrinkled. "Doing my job doesn't put me out, Mr. Maitland, I assure you. Is there anything else you require, Rivers?"

Marcus motioned him to go and he did so, leaving the two friends alone again. Marcus leaned across the desk, his dark green eyes holding Ellis's without letting go.

"What are you going to do, Handsome?" Ellis flinched before he could stop himself, and Marcus's expression fell a fraction as understanding dawned. "You're going to kill him."

CHAPTER 6

Ellis had been formulating the plan for weeks, since the encounter back in Harcourt when Juliana had been injured. But this was the first time it had been said out loud and those words rang in his ears like a gunshot.

He could have denied the charge. He could have told his friend to bugger off. He could have lied. But he didn't do any of those things.

He shrugged his good shoulder. "I don't have a choice."

Rivers was silent for what felt like a lifetime. Then at last he said, "Why?"

Ellis shook his head. "I knew exactly what Leonard was when he approached me. I'd heard the same rumors everyone else had. But he offered easy money."

"And your worst impulses kicked in."

Ellis nodded. "They always do in the end. I've never been able to stop them from doing so. When he double-crossed me, I had to retaliate, or risk being seen as weak. More than that, I wanted to make him pay. I wanted him to fear someone else for once. I decided to...to steal something Leonard wanted. My partner and I—"

"The previous Earl of Harcourt, Solomon Kincaid," Rivers interrupted.

Ellis stared at him. "That's well known?"

"Only by me," Rivers said. "I always know everything. It's my business."

"Jesus, you should have been a spy. Well, Kincaid was reckless, inexperienced. And..." He trailed off as he pictured Kincaid's blank eyes that horrible day when his life had been ended. "And a good friend. When Leonard came for us, I realized what a calculated mistake we had made, but Kincaid *refused* to return what we'd stolen. He thought it could be handled in a gentlemanly manner. He didn't believe someone of his own rank could be so vicious. Because he's never lived like you and me and seen these toffs at their worst. He hid it before he died and I'm still trying to figure out where."

"Fuck," Marcus grunted. "No wonder Leonard is out to get you."

"Not just me," Ellis said. "*Everyone* I love. He threatened my cousin, he's been following my half-brother, he injured—" He cut himself off. There was no reason to bring Juliana into this mess. Not even with Rivers. "Leonard *won't stop*. Even if I can find the item we stole, he might still exact revenge just because it pleases him. And if I can't find what he wants? He will absolutely destroy my world, and any innocent in his way, to punish me."

Marcus's mouth was a thin line. "The tales about his violence are widespread."

"I swear to you, I tried to reason with him, Rivers. Back at the beginning." Ellis sighed. "I tried to manage. I tried to give him what he wanted, at any cost. But now I realize there's only one way out of this for my family, for the ones I care for. And it's for Winston Leonard to die."

"He's the third son of a duke," Rivers breathed. "You'll...be transported. Or...or hanged."

Ellis nodded. There it was. The consequence he'd been trying to ignore. The one that rose up in his nightmares. The unavoidable end to his worthless life.

"I know," he whispered.

Rivers' jaw flexed and his gaze left Ellis's. He said nothing as he took the glass of whisky and downed the rest of it in one long swig that showed no respect to the expensive quality of the drink. "Can I help?"

Ellis sagged a fraction at the question, at the kindness being offered through it. "You already have. Leonard attacked a few weeks ago. It went badly for him. That's why he's been in hiding. You helping me bring him out is enough. And as I said, I would never take care of the problem in these halls. I just need to find where he is so I can do it elsewhere."

"I don't like this," Rivers said softly.

"You and I ran the streets for a long time, friend. Most of the men out there have some kind of code. Leonard doesn't. He's a sadistic brute, rabid with violence and power. He's a dog that needs to be put down." Ellis replied. "And since I'm the one who set this dangerous animal loose on my family, on innocents who don't deserve the consequences, it's my job to end it."

Rivers ran a hand through his hair, but Ellis could see he wouldn't argue. Because Ellis was right and they both knew it.

"Are you putting your house in order then?" Rivers asked. "With all those people who you say you love enough to protect?"

Ellis froze. *That* was a question he'd been trying to avoid as much as the others. By one means or another, his life would be over in a matter of days, maybe weeks. And he did have things he'd left unsaid and undone. Ends he recognized he should tie up, because once he made his move, he wouldn't survive it. When he'd seen Gabriel in the crowd, he'd felt it even more powerfully. And their meeting, while brief and casual, had been tinged with all the love he felt for his brother. And the knowledge it might be the last time they spoke.

"I know I need to," he said.

Marcus got up from his desk and came around to where Ellis sat. He leaned against the edge of the desk and looked down at him, his expression drawn with worry and sadness. "Then do it, friend. Say what you need to say if this is the only way. And do it fast."

Ellis pushed to his feet and the men stood staring at each other for a long moment. What felt like an eternity. Then he extended a hand. "You were a friend to me and to my cousin when we needed one," he said softly. "And you've done more than be a friend now. Thank you, Marcus."

Rivers' mouth turned up in the slightest of smiles at the rare use of his first name. He shook the offered hand. "It's always been a pleasure, Ellis."

Ellis sighed as he stepped away and pushed this connection aside. "And now I'm going to go drink myself utterly stupid in your club, lose all my blunt and find a woman to tup."

"Ah, that's the real payback then," Rivers chuckled. "The woman you've been stalking through my halls the past two nights?"

Ellis ducked his head at the mention of Juliana. At the memory of her mouth on his. "I don't think she'll be back."

Rivers arched a brow and tossed a glance over his shoulder. "She's down there right now."

"What?" Ellis snapped, racing to the window to look down over the debauchery below. His gaze narrowed as he instantly found the figure of Juliana Shelley in the crowd. He ground his teeth together. "That woman *never listens*," he grunted before he pivoted on his heel and headed for the door.

Behind him, he heard Marcus's laughter echoing as he called out, "Sounds like she's your perfect match then, mate."

Ellis ignored the jab as he clattered down the backstairs and stalked across the room toward her. He saw the moment she realized he was there. Saw it in the way she straightened ever so slightly, the way she veered toward him as if she were a divining rod and he water. Her eyes went wide under that plain mask she wore, and she took half a step back as he reached her.

He ignored the retreat and caught her elbow, guiding her across the room without speaking. He motioned to the man at the entrance to the private hall and he nodded, holding up four fingers to indicate which room they were to take for their "fun."

"Ellis," she whispered but didn't tug against him as he hauled her into the room, slammed the door and locked it.

He glared at her as he raised a finger for her to wait. She watched, brow wrinkled as he crossed to the opposite side of the room. There was a screen there that he pulled down and latched before he spun around to face her.

"Juliana—" he began, trying to modulate his tone.

She cocked her head. "What was that? What did you do on the wall there?"

He gritted his teeth. Her innocent question proved his point that she shouldn't be here. And it set his body on edge as he growled, "Some people who come to this establishment like to watch others in their private fun. Some like to *be* watched. A fine combination, so the rooms are rigged for such things. I closed the screen so no one could spy on us."

Her full lips parted and she stared at him, then the wall, then back at him. "To watch?" she repeated.

He glanced up at the ceiling and took a slow count to five. "Yes, angel. Fucking is a spectator sport for some. It's rather invigorating. What the hell are you doing here?"

She swallowed hard as his voice elevated, grew sharper. But she didn't back down. Instead, she lifted her chin. "I don't know why you think I wouldn't come back. I haven't gotten what I came for."

He shook his head slowly. What she'd come for. Sex. The ridding of that pesky virginity she and her ilk put so much value upon. She'd come here to be…God, he could think of so many things he wanted to do to her. For her. With her.

And he couldn't do a damned one of them. He wasn't worthy of what he'd already taken, let alone more.

"You want this?" he asked, forcing his tone to lower, slowing it, narrowing his gaze as he held hers. "You want what you see out in those halls? You want what you read about in some sad little book your father hid? You want to be debased and debauched and ruined?"

She didn't flinch, but instead her pupils dilated. "Yes," she whispered, her voice rough. "You say those things to frighten me, as if you think I'm some fool who doesn't understand them. I may not be so versed in the ways of the world as you are, Mr. Maitland. I may not be jaded and experienced. But I know what I want. You can't scare me away by shouting and blustering and trying to name it. Naming it only makes the ache..." She dropped her chin. "Worse. *You* only make the ache worse."

Ellis was on fire. His blood burned, flowing through his body like lava. He wanted this woman so badly it physically hurt.

"Juliana," he whispered as he stepped toward her. She trembled as he did so, looking up at him through those stunning pale green eyes. With a sigh, he hooked his fingers beneath her mask and pulled it away, tossing it aside.

"You are..." She was struggling to find the words, but she never backed down. "I know you only give if you can get something in return. You bargain and barter when it comes to...to this."

He flinched but didn't deny her. After all, that was a good summary of the transactional nature of most love games he'd played over the years.

"I'm not expecting to be different," she continued. Her voice was shaking, her hands were shaking, but she didn't stop. That strength drew him in. That strength made his own knees quake.

"No?" he pressed. "What *do* you expect?"

"You're determined not to see me do what I want to do with the strangers I might encounter in this place," she said. She drew a long breath before she continued. "So I...I'm asking to do it with you. I want *you* to be the one to give me what I need. And in return I'll... give you something you need."

∾

Ellis had been standing so close to Juliana, but the moment she made her offer, he backed up, spun around, paced to the fire. His back was still to her and she saw his shoulders lifting as he took deep breaths. Was he offended? Amused? Shocked?

She had no idea. How she hated that he was so good at hiding all reactions and emotions unless it suited him to show those things.

She folded her arms and waited, determined not to beg for what she'd already asked for. The clock ticked on the mantel, taunting her with each passing second as they collected and mocked her.

At last he faced her. His handsome face was still unreadable. "What do you think I *need*, Juliana?"

"In the carriage, you said you wanted me," she whispered. " there is that, though I don't have any illusions that you couldn't satisfy your desires with a dozen other more experienced women."

"A dozen women," he said with a half-smile. "You overestimate my prowess."

She clenched her teeth. "Mock me all you want, you know what I meant. I'm just saying that if my body isn't enough to tempt you, I could…" She pushed her shoulders back. "I know you're still looking for Winston Leonard. So are Rook and Harcourt. I can share their information."

Ellis's eyes went wide, and for the first time since she'd met him weeks ago, he actually looked…surprised. Was it possible she'd shocked the most jaded man she'd ever met? It seemed so.

He moved toward her. "You would betray the husbands of your sisters just so that I'd open your legs?"

She flinched at the crude way he put it. "It isn't a betrayal. The three of you are trying to find the man for the same purpose, to stop his threats against all of us. To bring him to justice for what he's done and what he's capable of doing still."

Ellis's lips thinned, and for a brief but powerful moment, she saw sadness in his eyes. A heartbreak so real and so pure that it made her own chest ache at the sight. She moved toward him. "Ellis, what is wrong?"

He stared at her. "You've never called me by my given name before."

She swallowed. She always referred to him as Ellis in her head. In her dreams. But she'd kept herself from being so informal when in the same space with him. To be so felt…dangerous.

Just as everything about this man was dangerous.

"Do you want me to stop?" she whispered.

He chuckled, and the sound seemed to enter her bloodstream and wend its way through her entire body. How could he affect her so without even touching her?

"No. Ellis is better than Mr. Maitland, by far," he said. "And there is nothing wrong. You're right, we all have the same end in mind when it comes to that bastard. To see him pay for what he's done."

"Then I won't be hurting anyone by sharing what I see and hear and know," she said, repeating the way she'd justified this plan in her head on the way here.

"Only yourself," he murmured.

"How will I hurt myself?" she asked. Suddenly she felt so damned tired. Too tired to dance around the subject. "I'm ruined by the actions of my sisters, ruined by the scar on my face. My father has no intention of bringing me out again—he's all but vowed I will be his hostess and secretary until he gives over his life. By then, I will be a spinster who will be forced to depend on the kindness of family. I am resigned to that, Ellis. Please don't make me give up this one last chance I have to feel…to feel…"

"You cannot even name it," he whispered. "Don't you see what a problem that is?"

"I want to feel good," she said, glaring at him. "I want to feel that dam of pleasure that builds when I touch myself at night. I want to feel the shivers of release like I do then. But I want to feel them with another person. I want to feel them with *you*. And if you won't do it to slake your own desire, or to get the information I can provide, then I suppose I must remind you that you owe me."

"I owe you," he said. "How is that?"

She turned her face, flashing the scar that marred her skin. "You know why."

It wasn't a fair accusation, at least not entirely, but Ellis flinched at it regardless. He seemed to ponder the request...well, not a request, really. She was ordering him, wasn't she? Forcing him through rather underhanded methods, truth be told. And she fully expected for him to put her in his carriage again and drive her home again and tell her...*again*...not to return. That was their game, after all, or it had become that in the past few days.

If he denied her this time, she would probably follow that directive at last. Coming back here over and over without getting what she wanted was too difficult. This was her last chance.

He moved forward, and she braced herself for some kind of playful, gentle denial. He reached for her, his rough fingers sliding along her jawline, his thumb pressing her lower lip as he stared down at her with those bright blue eyes.

"Then I owe you," he said softly, hypnotically. "And the bill has come due." He nodded slowly. "Very well."

She didn't have a chance to respond to the unexpected capitulation. He bent his head and, for the second time in their brief acquaintance, he kissed her.

For a moment, only their lips touched. He wasn't holding her, he wasn't pressed against her. It was just his mouth on hers, gentle, lips closed.

He was holding back and her frustration ratcheted up. This wasn't what she wanted. Well, it *was*. Even this chaste kiss was... lovely. It was lovely, for his full lips were warm and soft against hers, the brush of them sending little crackles of awareness through her.

But she didn't want crackles. She wanted lightning bolts and explosions. She lifted up on her tiptoes, winding her arms around his neck as a rough sound exited his lungs. She recalled how his mouth had opened the last time they kissed, so she did the same, drawing her tongue across his closed lips.

"Fuck," he muttered against her mouth. His hands settled on her hips, and he tugged her a fraction closer as he tilted his head for a better angle. His tongue met hers and the world spun off its axis as she drowned.

He delved into her with great gusto, tasting her like she was a fine meal and he a man starved. He dueled with her tongue, sucking and swirling around it. And all the while, he inched her closer and closer, molding her body to his until there was no space between them.

Her heart pounded as she clung to him, a hard, powerful rock in the midst of a sea of desire. He was both the cause of her need and the salvation she would find from it. Assuming he wouldn't deny her again.

She couldn't take it if he denied her.

But he seemed to be in no hurry to do so. He slid his fingers into her hair, cupping her scalp as pins pinged on the floor around their feet. Her hair fell around them and he pulled back, panting as he stared down at her.

"So lovely," he breathed, wrapping a long strand of hair around one finger. He lifted it to his nose and took a long whiff. "Vanilla and lemon."

She smiled. "My soap," she explained.

He leaned closer, to where their lips nearly touched. "Let's find out if you smell that way everywhere."

Her eyes widened, but she didn't get a chance to question that statement, because his mouth was on her again, silencing her questions as he backed her toward the bed in the middle of the big room. She expected him to toss her on the mattress, lift her skirts and do what he would do. She was shaking with the thought of it.

But he didn't. They stood beside that bed, inches from where all her problems would be resolved, and he simply held her. His arms were warm, his mouth gentle as he just kept kissing her like he could live that way forever.

She was shaking with anticipation and she drew back to look up at him. He smiled down at her in the soft light of the room. "You know, I've never had a lady scowl at me while I was attempting seduction. You are very unique."

She hated that she wanted to laugh at that quip. This was serious business. He ought not to be joking around at a time like this.

"You are *not* seducing, though," she pointed out. "You're just standing here kissing me."

His smile flashed wider for a moment. "Always a challenge. You don't like it when I kiss you?"

She shifted. "I-I like it very much. It's all I've thought of since the last time it happened. But I know full well that this…" She waved one hand around them. "…this isn't just about kissing. If you're going to do what I want, I'm just wondering *when* you're going to do it."

His brow wrinkled. "While I applaud your singular dedication, this entire thing is going to be much more pleasurable if you let the person with experience manage it. I realize that's difficult for you."

Her lips parted at that offhand comment. "It—it's not difficult. I'm not so controlling."

"I think you are because you've had to be." He tilted his head and she felt him reading her. "All your life, it seems. Always having to take care of everyone else, always having to tidy up after the outbursts."

Her breath came faster. He was deconstructing her whole existence with just a look and a few words. She hated that he had the power to do so. That he did it with a casual flare.

"Ellis—" she whispered, flinching when her voice broke.

He nodded. "I see. Well, I am not a man to be managed, Juliana. I don't need to be taken care of. And since we have agreed that I owe you something, I think you ought to let me simply settle my debt."

He leaned forward and pressed a light kiss to the tip of her nose. "Agreed?"

She stared at him for a long moment. This man of experience, a riddle, a liar, a charlatan. A man she dreamed of, a man she wanted so badly that her legs shook. He made this so hard. And yet he also somehow made it easy. Like it wasn't the most overwhelming thing in the world.

He smiled like it was fun. When was the last time she'd just had fun? She couldn't remember. It wasn't that she didn't have fun. She loved to laugh and tease with her sisters and their small group of friends. She enjoyed a ball and had always enjoyed dancing.

But this kind of fun felt...different. This was a step away from the day-to-day obligations of her life. If she said yes to him, that would be surrendering control. Trusting that he would take care of her, at least physically, for the short time they shared in this room in the back of a wicked club.

Could she do that? Knowing what he was? Knowing what he'd done in the past?

But then again...perhaps that made him the perfect person to give herself to. He would certainly know how to do this.

She licked her lips and his pupils dilated slightly, his hands stirring at his sides. Those hands that would...

She swallowed hard to interrupt the line of her thought. Then she managed to slowly nod. "Fine," she whispered when she could find her voice. She could only pray she wouldn't come to regret it. "I will...trust you to...to manage this."

CHAPTER 7

For a moment after she capitulated, Ellis simply stared at Juliana. Like he couldn't believe she had agreed. Like he had been trying to test her and she had not reacted in the way he'd hypothesized.

But then he smiled. That broad, real, dangerous grin that seemed to tug between her legs because it was a smile filled with such dark promise.

"Excellent," he laughed at last. "Then let us begin. Turn around, please."

She wrinkled her forehead and was about to question him, but he arched a brow and met her gaze. Ah, yes. Her agreement that she wouldn't manage. It seemed he meant to hold her to it.

She huffed out a breath and turned her back to him, uncertain of what he would do. She recalled an image from that naughty book of a lady bent over a table with a man taking her from behind. Perhaps that was his intent.

He pushed her hair forward over her shoulders, revealing the back of her dress. Her breath caught as he leaned in and his mouth brushed her neck. She jolted toward him, her hips bumping his. He let out a strangled chuckle but continued to suck gently on the flesh along the column of her neck.

Air touched her skin, and she jumped as she realized he had unfastened three of her buttons without her even being aware of it. She glanced over her shoulder, and he leaned around to kiss her mouth yet again.

She pressed back, opening to him. He flicked the remainder of her buttons open and the dress gaped. Warmth from the fire, warmth from his body curled against her bare skin, for she hadn't worn a chemise beneath the dress. It was one of Anne's old gowns, adjusted to reduce modesty, and the chemise showed too much to wear.

"Surprise after surprise," Ellis purred as he glided his fingers down her exposed spine.

Juliana gripped the edge of the bed as the shock of sensation that light touch created ricocheted throughout her body. Every nerve ending in her body felt alive now, her sex pulsed, and she felt very wet between her thighs. Her nipples were hard and rubbed against the silk of the gown. Her body was not her own anymore. She didn't control all its reactions.

And she wanted more.

Slowly she turned to face him, but he didn't step back. She was wedged between the hard chest of a very focused man and the soft edge of the bed. He held her gaze as he grasped the fluttering edges of her short-sleeved gown and tugged.

The entire contraption floated away at his insistence, exposing her from the waist up. She swallowed, fighting the urge to fold her arms over her naked breasts. No man had ever seen her like this.

This one stared like he was trying to memorize every line of her body. He didn't speak as he reached out. The back of his hand caressed her collarbone, then he slid it down, holding eye contact as he stroked one nipple with his knuckles.

She gasped. She'd touched herself like that before, grazing brushes when she dressed or bathed. It had never tingled like it did when he touched her. And that tingle had certainly never spread heat from the point of contact down between her legs.

He smiled at the sound and brushed again, this time a little harder. She gripped his forearm with one hand as she tried to find purchase. This was what she'd come here for. It was what she wanted. And yet she was completely overwhelmed by it. By him.

"Ellis," she whispered.

His expression softened a fraction. "Too much?"

"No. I-I don't want you to stop." She licked her lips. "I just feel...I feel a little...dizzy."

"Hmmm." He tilted his head as he looked her up and down. "Well, we wouldn't want that. Especially since it's all going to get so much more pleasurable. So..."

He reached out and tugged her dress. It slid over her hips and pooled at her feet. Now she was naked, and she jerked her hands down to cover the space between her legs. "Ellis!"

He shook his head. "This is what you wanted, isn't it? Are you telling me you've changed your mind?"

Her lips parted. He was...*baiting* her. Trying to taunt her into admitting she wasn't ready or strong enough for what she'd said she desired. And the worst part was, he might be right. She'd felt the dizziness of desire before, when she looked at that dratted book she'd found.

But it had *never* been as intense as this. With this man. She didn't want to let that go. She didn't want to regret giving up what would happen here.

She drew in a long breath and backed away from him. She pushed up on the high edge of the bed and scooted back so that she was propped up on the pillows. Then she met his gaze with as much haughty elegance as she could manage when she was so utterly conscious of being naked. "There, that's better. And I think you need me in this position, at any rate, to do the...er...the taking. The claiming? The taking."

The dimple that popped in his cheek revealed his amusement. "You are patently incapable of letting go of control, aren't you?"

She worried her lip. "When I do…sometimes bad things happen."

His expression softened and he nodded. "I see. Well, angel, let me tell you this: nothing bad will happen tonight."

She wanted to believe him in that moment. She wanted to fully trust him. That was folly, of course, but it didn't change the desire that rose up in her to give herself to this man in every way, not just this one.

Instead, she nodded.

He pressed a hand into the mattress, bowing it with his weight as he joined her on the bed. He crawled up the length of her body, picking carefully where he set his hands. Never touching her but coming oh-so-close. At last he pressed one hand on either side of her head and leaned down. She lifted to meet him, and he was kissing her again.

Her mind emptied at last as she surrendered to the kiss. Now that she didn't have to focus on somehow remaining upright, she could feel everything else a bit more. She tasted a faint hint of whisky on his tongue, along with the bite of mint. She felt the gentle abrasion of the beginnings of whiskers on his chin. And when he drew his mouth away from her lips and began to kiss her throat, she let out a long, low sigh of final surrender to the pleasure she so wanted to find.

When Juliana let out a low, soft sigh, Ellis lifted his head to look at her. Her face had gone relaxed at last, her eyes fluttered shut, and she'd stopped bracing so hard against the bed. It was something to see that act of submission from a woman who kept herself in tight control.

Better still was to be the man who had inspired such a surrender. He didn't deserve it, of course. He'd never deserved or expected it.

But he wanted it, he wanted *her* for as long as he could have her. And because he was a bastard, he would take her when he knew he shouldn't.

He lowered his mouth to her flesh again and licked a gentle pattern along her collarbone. Her skin was so soft. Had he ever had a lover with such soft skin? He couldn't recall one. Actually, in that moment, he couldn't recall another lover at all, despite having a good many in his past. But right now it was only Juliana. If he would likely die soon, she would be his last lover and that was something beautiful.

He moved his mouth lower still, until he scraped the beginnings of stubble against the swell of her breast. She gripped at the coverlet with a sharp intake of air, and he smiled. She was very responsive. He liked that. He liked making her arch up and sigh and gasp with pleasure. He wanted to do that more and more. Until she was begging and moaning and shaking with release.

He recalled how she had reacted to the touch of his hand against her nipple and smiled as he brushed his lips there instead. Her hands came down, for a moment he thought she would push him away. But instead she dug her fingers into his hair and held there, a silent demand for more. So he gave it, darting his tongue out to trace the raised nub of her nipple. He swirled around the exquisitely fragile flesh, tasting her, nibbling her and at last sucking until the skin shone and her nipple stood at full attention.

"Ellis," she grunted, her hips lifting against his chest.

"Mmmmhmmm?" he muttered without lifting his head. He scraped his teeth gently against the sensitive nub. "Do you need something?"

"Yes." The word was a broken sigh, and he glanced up her body once more. Her face was twisted with pleasure, her eyes squeezed shut. He had barely begun and she was already on the edge. It was going to be so easy to just push her over when he was ready. When she was ready.

He smiled at the thought as he dragged his lips to her opposite nipple, licking and laving there until she writhed on the silky sheets and gripped at his hair with incoherent sounds of pleasure.

He could have stopped there, he supposed. He knew in some deep part of himself that wasn't utterly ruined and debauched that he ought to stop. She was a lady, after all. She was desperate. It wasn't right or fair to take advantage. But she was sprawled out so prettily beneath him. She was moaning and panting for release that he knew he could give.

And goddamn it, he wanted to forget everything except what her orgasm tasted like. Not just for her and this foolhardy idea she had about last chances for pleasure. He needed to know for himself. He needed to forget all the darkness that was about to come after his conversation with Rivers.

They both had their needs, and this night would fill them. Was it really so very terrible to do exactly what they both desired?

He knew the answer and it in no way absolved him, but he ignored that as he slid farther down her body. Her skin was sweet, and he feasted as he licked a slow path along the apex of her body. He swirled into her navel and she gasped. His fingers gripped her hips and she surged against him with a cry. He inched lower with his mouth, lower still, scraping his teeth against that sweet line where her leg met her hip.

Her legs parted a little as he inched between them and rested a hand on each thigh to push them a bit farther. She had been panting above him, reveling in his touch, but the moment he opened her, she stopped. He looked at her and found she had pushed herself up on her elbows and was staring down at him, watching through a hooded gaze. She was holding her breath.

He stroked his fingers on her inner thighs, massaging gently. "I can stop."

She shook her head. "N-No. I don't want you to stop. I just want to see it when you...when you do it."

"Do what?"

"Take me," she said, darting her gaze away from his with a blush.

"I want to see it when you take me. Though I don't know how you'll do it fully dressed."

He tilted his head. "You are very focused on me fitting myself inside of you." When he said the words, his entire body twitched with anticipatory pleasure, but he ignored that and the deep throb in his cock that told him to do just that, and as quickly as possible. "Are you not enjoying the rest?"

"Yes, very much. But I know it isn't the most important part."

Ellis pursed his lips. "I disagree. I have, as you know, done this very thing with a great many women."

He thought a shadow crossed over her face, but then it was gone, and she nodded. "Yes. That's why you must be the best one for the job."

He choked out a laugh. "I wouldn't call it a job. It's not a chore, that's for certain, to be perched here between these very pretty legs getting ready to do such wicked things to you."

She shifted, and bright pink entered her cheeks. "Thank you," she whispered.

He smiled. "But because I *have* done this with a great many women, I can tell you that this part is my favorite."

"That cannot be true," she insisted.

"But it is. I could press a willing woman against a wall and rut with her any time I like. And there is value in something hot…" He accentuated the word by licking his finger and gliding it across the crease of her entrance. "…and fast." He repeated the action as she hissed out her breath. "But doing this…watching you flush and writhe and hearing your breath hitch with pleasure…angel, *that* is the best part of my day."

She gave a shaky laugh. "Well, I wouldn't want to deny you the best part of your day."

"So kind," he teased as he settled on his stomach between her legs and smiled up at her with all the wicked intent he could muster. "And now I'm going to try to give you the best part of your day."

"You're very certain of yourself," she gasped as he peeled her open gently.

"Always," he agreed, and then he bent his head and stroked his tongue over her. She was as sweet as he'd known she would be and he drank of her, memorizing every nuance of her flavor because he knew this was a night that could never, would never, be repeated.

So he was going to enjoy every damned minute of it.

CHAPTER 8

Juliana's vision actually blurred as Ellis ducked his head between her legs and stroked his tongue against her sex. When he touched her, it was like magic. But this…this was something more. This was something…she couldn't even describe it, probably because he stole her breath and her reason as he spread her flesh wide and feasted on her like a man starved.

He teased with his tongue, flicking her sex, gentle and light. She found herself aching for more, reaching for it by lifting her hips toward his mouth as she dipped her head against the pillows with a shuddering sigh.

He ignored that wordless demand, continuing to tease her with those gentle yet focused licks. Her body's reaction was a ricochet of pleasure that started at the point of contact and worked its way through her entire being. This was more powerful than when she touched herself, but built to that same crescendo she so longed for.

"Please," she groaned, hating herself for begging this man but unable to stop.

He glanced up at her, though he continued to lick. His blue eyes were dark with purpose, with desire. And they were entirely focused on her, as if there was nothing else that mattered in heaven or earth more than making her tremble. That powerful intensity that only made the pleasure between her legs all the stronger.

He gripped her hips tighter, tugging her flush against his mouth. Everything became more forceful then. He sucked her, tugging her flesh between his lips, nipping and nibbling to mix pleasure with just the slightest hint of pain.

She surged against him, grinding on his mouth as her back arched almost against her will. He held her tighter, pressing her hips against the bed so she couldn't guide her own release, toying with her as he swirled his tongue around the bud of her clitoris, then darted away to penetrate her with the tip of his tongue. Back and forth he moved, tormenting and torturing with the sweetest rhythm that seemed to go on forever.

After a while, she heard herself moaning, a sound unlike any she'd ever made before. Something that came deep from within her soul. Was that truly her who begged without words? She who never asked for what she wanted? She who had always been the one to give, not receive?

But in this moment, she was utterly selfish, and she reveled in it. She wanted more, and this time when Ellis returned his lips to her clitoris, she gripped him tighter with her thighs, trying to hold him in place.

He chuckled against her body, and the vibration shot through her. "Very well, angel," he whispered, blowing gently on her clitoris. "Ready or not..."

He sucked her as he trailed off, focusing all his attention on the bundle of nerves at the heart of her pleasure. She could focus on nothing else, either. She dug her heels into the mattress and ground against him. Sensation built within her, a storm, a waterfall, and unrelenting force that could not be denied. And he didn't deny it. He swirled his tongue harder, faster, flicking at her as the sensation peaked.

And then she was falling, her body rippling with deep, powerful waves of release. She cried out, thrashing against the pleasure, rolling with him as he drew out her release longer and harder. Until she was weak with it, until the pleasure was almost too much to bear.

She collapsed back on the pillows with a gasping cry. He stroked her a few more times and she twitched. Her breath came short, her legs shaking, her body quaking. She almost didn't notice when he kissed her gently, this time with closed lips. Almost wasn't coherent enough to recognize as he crawled up the length of her body and pressed a more heated kiss on her mouth. She tasted her release there, salty and sweet, and her body jerked once more.

He smiled down at her and she braced herself for what would come next. The claiming, one she didn't fear now that she was humming with release. But he didn't remove a stitch of clothing. He didn't move to take her.

She blinked up at him as he continued to smooth tangled locks away from her face.

"When will you...when will you..." She trailed off as he flinched and shook his head. In that moment, she felt him pull away, and her heart sank as he got to his feet and backed up from the bed. He continued to look down at her, his expression one of longing and regret. Perhaps a bit of pity.

The pity was what broke her.

Her hands shook as she gathered a handful of silky sheet and tucked it around herself, covering her body so that she was no longer as physically exposed as she was emotionally. She drew a few breaths, trying to remain calm, trying to remain cool.

But her voice was shaking as she asked, "You aren't going to take me, are you?"

Ellis heard the rejection in Juliana's voice as she asked the question. Heard the pain and embarrassment. He looked down at her, temptation embodied lying on those silken sheets, her blonde hair tangled around her shoulders, her body ready for more, her cheeks pink from pleasure, darkening the scar that marred her flesh.

And she thought he didn't want her. He had never wanted any woman more in his life.

"I won't *ruin* you," he corrected, hoping that the distinction helped her. It didn't help him, because he wanted nothing more than to strip out of his trousers and delve deeply within her, to forget everything but the pulse of her around his cock for a while.

But that was a pleasure he hadn't earned and never would. Not after the filth of his life.

She gritted her teeth, and there was no denying her frustration as she glared at him. It lined her once-relaxed face and brightened her green eyes. "I already told you, Ellis, I want it *all.*"

He shook his head. Christ, she would kill him at this rate, because she had no idea what those words did to him. He was trying not to be an utter bastard, and that was difficult enough. It went against everything he'd been doing these past few years, both for survival and pleasure. He was fighting his nature with all his might, then she whispered about need and desire and stared at him when he still had her taste on his lips?

He let out a long sigh and perched on the edge of the bed. He brushed a lock of hair from her face, reveling in the softness of her skin against his rough fingers. "No," he said. "You don't, angel."

"Ellis—" she began, her determination written in the wrinkle in her forehead, in the strength in her tone as she readied herself to launch into an argument.

One she might win if he let her.

"You feel lost right now," he interrupted, and watched all the color exit her cheeks. "And I understand that…more than most. But you don't want to make any rash decisions."

She'd been clutching the sheet around her breasts, but now she folded her arms across them instead. The sheet slipped a fraction, revealing the hint of curves he'd already worshipped. How he wanted to touch them all over again. He'd never stop if he did. He would do exactly what she thought she wanted and they would both regret it. But the moment of surrender?

Fuck, but that would be sweet.

"Says the king of rash decisions," she grumbled.

He couldn't help the smile that curved the corner of his lips. She was a spitfire. Accustomed to managing every outcome, used to knowing what was best for everyone, even if they didn't. She marched through life with certainty and he was so drawn to that, it was scary. Not only was this remarkable woman out of his sphere, but he was about to sacrifice himself. There was no going back once he did that, one way or another. He couldn't give in. He had the memories of what they'd shared, and that had to be the end of it. For both their sakes.

"You don't want to be like me," he said.

"No, I want to be *with* you," she insisted.

He groaned as he got to his feet. "I'm trying to be a better man, Juliana. Help me out."

"If I wanted a better man, as you put it, I wouldn't have come here," she huffed.

Ellis had been practiced in controlling his reactions over the years. He never allowed anyone to see his true feelings unless that was what he wanted. Unless those feelings drew him closer to a goal.

But right now it was an effort not to flinch at that barb, thrown in anger. Still he managed it and turned back to her with a practiced smile.

"Then you got what you came for," he said. "In more ways than one. I would suggest you be happy with it and let go of this notion of endangering yourself for pleasure."

Her bottom lip trembled slightly, and she bit it to stop the motion. He fought a groan because damned if he didn't want to bite that pretty little lip himself. Instead, he reached down to grab her wrinkled dress from its forgotten pile on the floor. He held it out to her. "Get dressed, Juliana. I'll take you home."

She slithered down off the bed, struggling to keep the sheet around her as if he hadn't just worshipped every inch of that amazing body, and snatched the gown from his hand.

"Fine," she ground out. Suddenly she sounded like the haughtiest of ladies of the manor, upset at the lack of performance of a servant. Not the worst comparison, actually. "If you insist on being difficult about this, I *refuse* to argue. Please turn around."

He arched a brow at the modesty. "A bit late for that, isn't it?"

She pursed her lips. "You don't want it, so you don't get to see it. Turn around." She swallowed hard. "Please."

He did what she asked, mostly because he recognized that it wasn't her body she didn't want him to see—it was her vulnerability. In her mind, he had rejected her. It was better that way, no matter how wrong she was.

Because all he was capable of doing was compromising her. And tonight was a glorious, blazing, erotic mistake he had to ensure was never repeated. The first step to that was to stop thinking of all the ways to put her on her back.

If that was possible.

Juliana leaned forward, trying to stay as far away from the warm hands that were buttoning her gown. It was to no avail. Ellis brushed her skin with his fingertips every time he fastened her and her entire treacherous body lit on fire when he did it.

She stepped away from him when she was covered, wishing her hands weren't shaking quite so obviously, and pivoted. He was staring at her with a tight smile. It wasn't real, that was obvious. Nothing about the way he was looking at her was real now. This was all the act, all the show that was Handsome Ellis Maitland, seducer of women and expert player of the game.

She hated to think she'd been just another piece on his chessboard tonight. But then, perhaps she hadn't been. After all, he had pleasured her, given her what she wanted...almost. And hadn't taken anything in return.

"And what thought is creeping through that pretty head of yours?" he asked as she picked up pins from the floor around them and carelessly fixed her hair.

She shrugged. "I'm only trying to determine what part of you is the real man and what part of you is the act."

He stilled and the expression in his eyes darkened. He bent his head. "If I ever figure that out, I'll be certain you are the first to know. Now come. This room will be required by others and it's late."

He held out a hand as he spoke, and she stared at it. Those lean, strong fingers had moved over her body so intimately. They had traced every curve of her, coaxed pleasure from her unlike anything she'd ever experienced.

She blushed as she took the offered hand and let him lead her from the chamber where she had been forever changed, even if it wasn't in the way she had wished to be. He said nothing as he guided her down the dim hallway toward the larger, brighter main hall. Already the laughter from the bigger room echoed toward them. Mixed with moans.

She understood the moans a great deal more now, and her body twitched with reaction.

Damn him for half-waking this thing inside of her. It was almost worse than knowing those desires were there sleeping but being unaware of how to fully unlock them. Perhaps if she said the right thing...perhaps then he would understand and do the rest.

She stopped as they reached the end of the hall and tugged on his hand. "Ellis."

He stopped. His back was still toward her and she watched him drag in a long breath before he faced her. The brighter light behind him outlined his broad-shouldered body but partly obscured his handsome face. A perfect metaphor for the man of shadow and light that he was.

"Yes?" he whispered, and she heard the strain in his voice.

She recognized that he still longed for the same thing she did. That he was holding back, perhaps out of some twisted sense of honor that a thief might not typically exhibit. And that meant there was a chance for her, for *them*.

She swallowed, uncertain how to proceed. She hadn't exactly seduced a man before. Certainly not one with so much experience in the world and in the bedroom as Ellis Maitland.

She searched for the words, but before she could find them, she caught a glimpse of a man in the crowd just past Ellis's shoulder. Her lips parted at the profile of him. A profile she'd seen before, studied even though she hadn't wanted to do so.

Winston Leonard. The man who had kidnapped her thinking she was her sister just a few weeks prior. He had terrorized her, then slashed her face in the struggle that ensued. He was the one who had shot Ellis in the shoulder.

But that couldn't be right. The bastard had been hiding since the attack. She was seeing things, that was all. Brought on by the intensity of her feelings tonight. By the fear that still haunted her dreams.

As if he sensed someone's eyes on him, the man turned his head. He scanned the room, then glanced toward her. God, did he see her? No, it didn't seem so. They were in the darkness of the hall, which protected them from his seeking gaze. But she knew then that she wasn't dreaming. She wasn't wrong.

"Ellis," she hissed, clinging to his hand tighter.

His expression softened, filling with concern. "What is it?"

She struggled for breath. "It's...it's...it's him! It's Winston Leonard."

CHAPTER 9

Ellis pivoted and dragged Juliana behind him as he looked through the crowd for his quarry. The one he had been distracted from finding thanks to the woman shaking behind him, clinging to his hand so hard that her nails pressed into the skin.

He was almost ready to dismiss her words as imaginings brought on by the strain of the past few weeks when his own gaze found Winston Leonard in the crowd. Everything slowed to half-time when he did and the boisterous sounds of the room around them faded.

Leonard was an unassuming figure. He was of average height, average build, had a soft jawline and watery gray eyes. If one didn't know what a threat he was, if one didn't know to be afraid of him, well…that made him all the more dangerous.

And yet his reputation had been made through a great many misadventures so that even here, in this den of debauchery, those around Leonard gave him a wide berth and whispered as he passed by.

Rage boiled up in Ellis's chest. That was yet another emotion that he had learned to control in his life, but now it threatened to overtake him. This man, this bastard he had been fool enough to involve himself with, had destroyed so much that mattered.

He had killed Ellis's friend, the Earl of Harcourt's brother Solomon. He had threatened Ellis's half-brother and his cousin, the only people he truly loved. He wanted nothing more than to cross the room in a few strides and kill the man right here and now. His promise to Marcus Rivers be damned.

"Ellis."

He jerked at Juliana's small voice behind him. In his rage, he'd all but forgotten she was right there with him. Her face was turned toward his, tears filling her eyes and brightening the green to an emerald color. His eyes flitted to her scar, which had been brightened by the fact that the color had drained from her cheeks. Leonard had done that too and the fear that lit in her now, extinguishing all other brightness, was palpable.

He returned his gaze to Leonard and found the man had turned. He faced the hallway firmly now, and it was clear he could see Ellis. Their stares met, and Leonard tilted his head to one side with a big grin.

"It's him," Juliana whispered.

She was peeking around him now, her eyes as locked on Leonard as his were. Ellis looked back just in time to see the man slipping through the crowd.

"Damn it," he grunted, and lunged forward a step. He had to follow him. He had to finish this, because now that Leonard knew he'd been spotted, he might go underground again.

Or worse, he might move on those Ellis loved.

But Juliana's hand was still locked in his. If he followed Leonard, he endangered her. Again. So he stopped and huffed out his breath.

"Ellis," she repeated.

"I know," he snapped, perhaps more harshly than he meant. She flinched and pulled her hand away, lifting it to her chest as she stared up at him. He shook his head slowly before he repeated, "I know. At least you're wearing your mask. But this is all the more reason to get you out of here. Did you come in your own vehicle?"

She shook her head. "A hack."

He squeezed his eyes shut and refused to lecture her about the dangers of such a thing. "Come on."

He guided her through the crowd, keeping an eye out for Leonard, but there was no sign of him as they exited the building. He motioned for *his* carriage, and in a few moments they were safely inside with his driver heading to Juliana's father's home across town.

Juliana was silent as she looked out the windows into the inky darkness, but he could read her reaction like a book. She was trembling, her hands clenched in her lap.

It was fear. No, not just fear. Terror.

His own frustrations at not being able to pursue Leonard faded, and he leaned forward in his seat and caught her hand. "Juliana."

She didn't respond or even seem to recognize he had touched her.

"Juliana," he repeated, this time sharper.

She jolted from her distracted state and glanced at him. "Yes?"

He hated to see her fear. Hated that his actions had been the root cause of that fear. She never would have become involved with someone like Winston Leonard were Ellis not such a fool.

"He can't hurt you, angel," he said. Hoped it would be the truth. Knew he had to make it the truth no matter the cost to himself. "He *won't* hurt you," he corrected. "I'll make sure of it."

She nodded slowly, then her hand lifted up. She tugged her mask off and slid her fingertips across her scar. He tracked the movement and felt an answering sting in the injury on his shoulder. The marks of war. A woman like her never should have received one.

"But he *did* hurt me," she whispered. "Seeing him brought it all back, like I was right there again."

Ellis shifted. He knew that feeling. Too well. How a smell or a look or a sound could jerk a person to the worst moments of their life. How a memory could flash through the mind and feel as real as the moment that had first created it.

"Do you...do you want to talk to me about it?" he asked. "Would it...help?"

She worried her hands together in her lap. "I don't know. I haven't spoken of it much, truth be told. My sisters both get so upset when the topic comes up, as they feel responsible for that day, as do Harcourt and Rook. My maid clucks her tongue and tells me it's better not to think about it."

"But you still *do* think about it," Ellis said, smoothing his thumb across the top of her hand.

She nodded and blinked at the tears that sprung to her eyes. "I do."

He drew in a long breath. Here he'd been telling himself all night that he needed to separate from this woman. That backing away was his best way to protect her, to protect himself. That was still true. But in this moment, it was also impossible.

"It's my fault he found you that day," he said softly. When she sat up straighter and made to argue, he lifted a hand to silence her. "I brought him into your life. You and your family never would have gotten near him but for *my* actions. My failings. It only seems fair that I hear what you need to say, Juliana. So say it if it would help. I'll take it."

She stared at him for a long moment. This woman had been willing to share her body with him, but to share her heart? Her mind? Her past? He could see she was trying to decide if he was good enough to do those things.

And he found himself longing for them even more than he had longed to bury himself in her not so long ago.

At last she let out her breath in a shuddering sigh. "Anne and I were looking for Rook," she said softly, her voice strained and cracked. "She was desperate to find him. I knew she loved him then, more than she had even admitted. And I feared for her to love a man like that. I didn't know him at that moment, of course. Just what he seemed to be."

Ellis flinched. Rook, had been his partner in crime once. They'd run the streets together for years before his bad behavior had pushed his cousin away. He was happy for him now, to be settled with a woman who loved him as fiercely as Anne seemed to do. For him to be out of the life for good. Not many got out alive.

But Rook was the better of the two of them. And if Juliana had hesitated about him, Ellis knew what that meant in the long run when it came to how she felt about *him*.

"Rook had gone looking for me," Ellis said.

She nodded. "Yes, but we didn't know that. We came into Harcourt's study and there was…" Her voice shook and she cleared her throat. "Winston Leonard was there. He was looking for the treasure you and Solomon had stolen. He mistook me for Anne because I was dressed more extravagantly. Because she was dressed simply, he thought her to be Thomasina."

"The confusion of being triplets," Ellis said, hoping the interruption would help her. "I would always know you, Juliana."

She shook her head. "Well, I'm scarred now. It's a bit of a cheat."

"I'd know you with your back turned," he whispered, and it wasn't a lie.

She blushed, but then gathered herself. "Anne tried to tell him the truth of our identities, but he didn't believe her. He was determined to take me, thinking it was her, and exact his revenge. When he threatened to kill who he thought was Thomasina, as revenge on Harcourt, I told him Anne was actually…that she was me. After all, *Juliana* Shelley would be too unimportant to anyone to kill. He agreed, and that worked in our favor."

He jerked his gaze to her at that statement. Was that how she saw herself? As unimportant? How that cut him, even though it shouldn't have. He hardly knew her, after all, stolen moments at the masquerade aside.

She shivered. "He didn't kill her so she could deliver his message to Harcourt and Rook, and he took me."

He pressed his lips together, trying not to think of the part of this story he knew. About him and Rook arriving at Harcourt's estate to hear that Juliana had been taken. At the stricken looks of her sisters. Of the terror all had felt that she would be killed. At the awful moment when Leonard had slashed her face and she'd looked toward Ellis for help. When he'd held her trembling body and felt the stirrings of something he had no right to feel.

"What did he do?" he asked, forcing himself to consider her needs in that moment, not analyze his own.

Her gaze went unfocused, and for a moment, he saw her relive those terrible moments. She swallowed hard again. "He put me on his horse. He was rough and cruel, he didn't care if he hurt me. He seemed to *like* hurting me."

Ellis squeezed his eyes shut. The harshness didn't surprise him, but still put red rage in his vision.

"While we rode to the hill where we were to meet Rook, he talked." She shook her head and her voice dropped to a whisper. "All he did was talk. He talked about being double crossed by you and Solomon Kincaid. He talked about killing Solomon and how much he enjoyed it. He talked about my sisters and how foolish we were to involve ourselves with such men. And because he thought I was Anne, he talked at great length about how he would kill me in front of Rook to watch him suffer. Or kill him in front of me for the same reason."

She recited the words, quietly and calmly. But the moment they were said, she bent her head, placed it in her hands and shook with silent sobs. The kind of crying that had been held in for a very long time and now couldn't be contained.

He couldn't let her weep without comforting her. It wasn't his place and it didn't matter. He slipped to her side of the carriage and cradled her into his body, holding her as she cried it all out, wishing with all his might that he could take that past away.

Knowing he couldn't. All he could do was make sure those terrible moments weren't repeated in her future. By destroying Winston Leonard before they could be. And by resisting her so she wouldn't encounter even more danger by linking herself, even briefly, with a man like Handsome Ellis Maitland.

He pressed a kiss to her temple as her tears slowed and then subsided. She sucked in a long breath. "He tied me up when we arrived and we waited. It felt like a lifetime. He kept going on and on like he had on the ride, but I just kept thinking of the sea. I kept picturing the waves rolling in and out. I refused to listen to him. Refused to hear his cruel pleasure in what he was doing. It kept me calm until...until the end. When he called you and Harcourt from the brush and the struggle began...I knew I would die."

He caught his breath. "Juliana."

She shrugged. "Who would protect me? Harcourt was for Thomasina. And Rook would die for Anne. But I had no one. And then you were there, and you put yourself in harm's way for me."

"Some good it did," he whispered, letting himself trace her scar for the first time with his fingertip. She caught her breath at the touch, and perhaps also at how close they were in the dim carriage.

"He would have killed me and I'm alive," she said, shivering as he dropped his hand away. "You helped me."

"I should have done more," he said. "You *never* should have been hurt in the first place."

A tiny smile tilted her lips. Ellis was shocked to see it there, but in that moment this woman, this sheltered, upper-class woman, almost seemed like she knew more than he did about the world.

"Should, should, should..." she mused. "If we could have a farthing for every should, you wouldn't have to play your games anymore. You'd be the richest man in London."

"I *like* playing my games," he said in what he hoped was a teasing tone. Right now he couldn't quite control it.

She shrugged. "I suppose my point is that I can't live in what should have happened. I have to live in what did. And you *did* help me, Ellis. When you had me in your arms, right after I was slashed, do you remember what you said?"

He stared down at her. And he lied, because he knew if he told her he did remember that it would only create more confusion and pain for her in the future. "No."

There was a flutter to her lips. "Well, you said something to me that comforted me. It might not have meant much to you, but it meant the world to me. So I thank you."

Ellis shook his head in shock. This woman had every right to blame him for what had happened to her. He knew a part of her *did* blame him. And yet she had enough grace to be able to see some good thing in him. Enough that she trusted him with her story, trusted him with the offer of her body.

He had never been that good a person or man. He'd learned early and hard to take a person at face value. To never look for deeper goodness once he had seen a hint of danger. It was part of survival.

And yet when he sat next to Juliana Shelley, stroking her hand in his, he felt shame for that dismissal. He felt small in it. He felt like he wanted to be…more.

He'd been a villain since he was ten. Running the streets, stealing what he needed, playing love games starting at fifteen. He'd told himself he could never be more.

And in this moment he wished he could. That there was change in his future like there had been in Rook's. That he could somehow endeavor to one day deserve a woman who looked at him like Juliana was looking at him in this moment.

Except doing that would destroy her. Dragging through the mud with him, linking herself any deeper than she already had? She would sink in it, sink with him.

So if he wanted to be good, to be decent, he realized he had to be bad. He had to push her away to protect her. Not weakly like he had before, but truly. Before Winston Leonard got her back in his sights.

Before Handsome Ellis Maitland ate everything good and beautiful and decent in her and spit her out a shell of what she'd once been.

Even if it broke his heart, that cold, black thing he'd once thought didn't exist…he had to do it. Now.

E llis tugged his hand away from Juliana's and eased himself back on the carriage seat across from her. She felt the change in him. The rig felt colder as he looked at her with a gaze that held… nothing. Not even a hint of anything at all.

"Well, I'm pleased some meaningless platitude I recited was helpful," he drawled. "As I said, I don't recall what I said."

She flinched just as he had done the first time he'd said he didn't recall his words. What had been so important to her meant nothing to him.

"Here's your father's home," he said, motioning toward the window, where the townhouse was rising larger in the distance.

"Thank you for the escort," she said, watching as he examined his nails with a bored expression.

"I suppose it's the least I could do, considering the pretty little gift you gave to me tonight," he said, lifting his gaze to hers. His tone was mocking.

She gritted her teeth. "Will I see you again?" she asked. Hated herself for asking when he was obviously so driven to get rid of her.

He arched a brow as they came to a stop on the drive. "This isn't for you, Juliana. I am not for you."

He swallowed hard, as if saying those words was difficult, and for a moment she saw a glimpse of the man who had asked her about the day she'd been taken. The man who had pleasured her so sweetly. The man who teased and played and made her smile.

"Ellis—" she whispered.

He lifted a hand to silence her. "We both got what we wanted tonight. So go inside and forget me. Forget tonight." The door opened, and he smiled. "I will."

She caught her breath as a servant offered her a hand to help her down. She narrowed her gaze at Ellis, but he held her stare firmly, his expression flat and bored and cold. She shook her head and exited the carriage with as much dignity as she could muster.

The moment the door was closed, she heard him rap on the carriage wall and it drove on into the night. Away from her like nothing mattered. Was that real? Did he truly not give a damn? Was all his talking and smiling and offering comfort a game? The same one he'd played with dozens of women before her?

She had no idea. And that stung more than anything else.

She pushed her shoulders back and moved to the door. It opened and revealed her father's butler, Maxwell. The man took her wrap with only a sniff of disapproval. She ignored it and trudged toward the stairs. It was very late, too late for the hot bath she longed for. But she could at least curl up in her bed and try to sleep away this long and confusing night.

She was almost to the stairs at the opposite end of the foyer when she heard the sound of a clearing throat from the closest parlor. She froze and turned to find her father standing there, a drink in hand, staring at her.

"Father," she began, trying to think of some excuse for why she was coming into the house alone at such a late hour. She could think of none, so she simply sighed. "I thought you were spending a late evening with some of your associates at the club."

"I can see you did," he said with a shake of his head. "What have you been up to, girlie?"

She squeezed her eyes shut. Her entire life had been spent placating this man, soothing his upsets and angers, protecting her sisters from his wrath when it was incurred. Making things easier for them all. Tonight she could not find the energy for those machinations.

"I find I am not in the mood to talk, Father," she said. "Please just let me go to bed and we can discuss it in the morning."

His grip on his drink tightened and his scowl deepened. "Come into the parlor, Anne."

She glared at him. "Juliana," she corrected. "You would think you'd know me since I am the only daughter left under your care."

"I simply mixed up your names," her father said with a wave of his free hand. "Come into the parlor...now."

She clenched her fists at her sides and marched past him into the room. Her heart was throbbing in anticipation for the showdown she feared would come, but she fought to keep that reaction from her face. She had to be more like Ellis. Not show weakness.

Not show anything. Did he feel anything at all?

"Juliana!"

Her father's sharp tone yanked her back to the room and she frowned at him. "Yes?"

"I asked you a question. Where were you?"

She shrugged. "I went out to see a...a friend in need."

The words seemed foolish as she said them, and it was clear her father didn't believe her as he slowly shook his head. He downed the remainder of his drink in one swig before he said, "I don't know what is wrong with you, Juliana. I can only imagine what trouble you were getting yourself in to. But you must not get ideas in your head. Your future is..." He trailed off and the heat seemed to go out of him as he turned away.

Her lips parted. Was that *pity* in his expression? Her heart ached. "What is my future, Father? Say it."

He poured himself another drink before he faced her again. "It is set now. We both know that. But you needn't fear. You will be a great help to me and that will provide meaning to your life. You'll always have a place here, as long as you behave in a way that allows me to offer it."

Her breath caught and her throat felt like it was closing as she stared at him. He'd talked about her being his secretary several times since the attack on her. Mused that he hadn't lost much because she was so good at managing his household. He was always hushed by her sisters when he brought it up.

Now they were alone and she saw the full truth of it. He wanted what he wanted, saw the situation in only his own terms, but that was nothing new. Their father had always been desperately selfish.

What was different is that he now saw *her* as pitiable. This was a bone he threw to what he perceived to be an injured dog. The best she could expect given the scandals her sisters had created, given the mark on her face and her character. She was broken in his eyes and he was trying to find some altered use for her.

"Father—" she gasped out.

"Do not reach too high, daughter," he grunted. "Or there will only be further to fall."

Anger she rarely allowed herself rose up in her chest as she gaped at this man. How many times had she considered his comfort above her own?

"Like you have, you mean," she snapped out, and then clapped a hand over her mouth. She had never spoken to him in that fashion, and for a moment they just stared at each other.

Then his face twisted in rage, going purple as he set his drink down with a loud clink. "One of my daughters married an earl," he growled. "I choose to focus on that success rather than my useless second son-in-law."

"Who Anne loves," Juliana argued, and she realized she was nearly shouting now. "And is as kind a man as any I have ever met."

"Perhaps," her father said with a dismissive shrug. "Perhaps his underground links will play out as useful to me at some point. But I can't focus on him or on *your* failings."

"Because I shall never marry. No one could want me now, at least in your eyes."

"No one of value. Do you disagree?" he scoffed. "It is a shame, really. You were my true prize. I thought I would leverage you for much more than either of your sisters. But what is done is done. I have decided it is best to remain kind to you."

"This is what you see as kindness?"

"Careful now. It is not something every woman in your position would receive from her family. But do not mistake me, Juliana." He stepped closer, and she found herself retreating an equal distance. "I expect you to behave yourself. You shall not bring any more shame on this house than you and your sisters already have. If you do, there will be consequences."

She swallowed and all she could taste was bitterness. Her own. His.

"My entire life is nothing but consequences," she spat. Then she turned on her heel. "Good night."

He let her go without responding and she marched up the stairs with her hands shaking. When she reached her room, she flopped herself on the bed, pressed her face into her pillow and let out a scream she felt like she had been holding in forever. Once she had made herself hoarse, she rolled over and stared up at the ceiling.

She didn't *want* this life. And yet it was the only choice left. Either her father was right and no one else would want her, or he would create that very future by refusing to take her out on the marriage mart anymore. Whatever hopes she'd once had for a life of her own choosing, a life with love in it, were fading. It didn't matter how she got to that spinsterhood future, all paths now seemed to lead there.

Except for one. And that was the one she'd been trying to guide herself down with Ellis. Only *he* had rejected her too.

She pushed to her feet and paced her chamber. Her thoughts kept returning to Ellis. His face as he pleasured her, that same face as he all but pushed her from the carriage and told her she wasn't wanted. But mostly she thought of his expression when he saw Winston Leonard in the crowd at the Donville Masquerade.

That expression was a cacophony of pain and regret. She might not know what else was real when it came to Ellis Maitland, but that moment had been. And she knew that because she had felt the same combination of emotions. So many times in her life.

They were the same in some ways. No matter what he said to try to make her go away.

She folded her arms and looked at herself in the mirror. Yes, she had a scar. Yes, it drew the eye. And yes, she was changed from the terrible actions that had brought that scar about. She was stronger now. She was more aware of what she wanted.

And she was just stubborn enough not to give up on it.

"We can help each other, even if he resists that out of fear," she said, forcing herself to speak it out loud so that she could hear it. Her voice shook, but it still strengthened her resolve. "I have spent my life fixing things and I *will* fix this. For me. For him. For everyone."

Now she just had to figure out how.

CHAPTER 10

"He bloody saw me, Rivers," Ellis shouted as he paced Marcus's office the next night. "He looked me in the eye and every fucking thing I had planned was dashed in a goddamn second."

Marcus had been listening to him rail for at least a quarter of an hour, leaned back in his office chair, arms folded. Silent, of course. He offered no advice. Ellis wasn't certain if he should be pleased or upset at that fact.

"Why didn't you follow him?" Marcus asked at last, but his tone was so flat that it was clear he already had a theory about why.

It was probably on the mark.

"Because of the woman. Are you happy now?" Ellis ran a hand through his hair and sank down in the chair across from Marcus's.

Rivers shrugged. "I have no opinion on the matter."

"You have an opinion on *every* matter," Ellis grumbled.

Rivers let out a laugh. "That may be true. Very well, I have no opinion to *share* on the matter. I think in situations such as this, it's best to allow you to find your own way. I will say I don't think I've ever seen you choose a mark over your own plans."

Ellis jerked his face toward his friend. "She isn't a mark."

Rivers' eyebrows lifted. "Ah, I see. Well, a lover then."

"She isn't exactly that either." Ellis bent his head. "Almost, and not without a lack of trying on her end. I didn't follow Leonard because it would have put her in danger. And I've already done that more than enough."

"You realize it might have been your only chance," Marcus said softly. "Since he saw you."

"Yes," Ellis acknowledged, and got to his feet. He walked to the windows overlooking the main hall below and stared with unseeing eyes at the writhing crowd. "It may have been. But at least I have more focus now. I recognized my failing the moment it happened. I have ended things with the young lady in no uncertain terms. She won't be a distraction again, and I can refocus my efforts. Leonard may not come back here, but he's somewhere in London. I'll find him. And when I do, I won't have to worry about anyone but myself."

"Hmm. You're certain that's all then. You ended things and she won't pursue you again?"

Ellis glanced over his shoulder and found Marcus had also stood and was looking over the crowd. "Yes, why?"

"Because she just came into the room," Rivers said, and pointed.

Ellis followed his motion. There was Juliana, standing by the entryway to the great hall, hands clenched before her, cheap mask balanced on her exquisite face. She was looking around the room, just as she always did when she came here.

He ground his teeth in frustration. "She is, by far, the most stubborn wench I have ever had the pleasure of…"

He trailed off, for he'd had quite a few pleasures with her. Even now, aggravated as hell by her, he also couldn't stop looking at her. Wanting to touch her, wanting to claim her.

"…the pleasure of knowing," he finished with a shake of his head.

"Then your perfect match, it seems," Marcus said, laughter thick in his voice. "Stubborn and stubborn."

"She's *not* my perfect match," Ellis said, sharper than he intended. "She's a damned menace. You need to ban her."

Rivers leaned back. "*Ban* her? That's a very serious action to take. For what reason?"

Ellis rolled his eyes. Damned Marcus would make him spell out every single thing he didn't want to consider or feel. "As a personal favor to me. And to her, though she might argue that. No, she *would* argue that because she is, as aforementioned, *stubborn*."

Marcus pressed his lips together. "Hmmm. Another personal favor. Is that three now?"

"Too many to count," Ellis said softly. "But I'm still asking."

"For her protection," Rivers clarified.

"Yes."

Rivers stroked his chin as if thinking. "Even though she keeps coming back. Looking for you."

Ellis flinched. "Will you do it or not?"

"I will if it means that much," Rivers said. "But I will ask a question before I have it done." Ellis shrugged to get him to continue. Rivers met his gaze evenly. "Do you *really* want to walk away from this woman?"

Ellis shut his eyes. He could see Juliana perfectly, green gaze turned toward him, full lips slightly parted. He could see her arched back in pleasure. He could see her vulnerable with confession. He could see her shaking as he kissed her. He could smell her, he could taste her.

And all that amounted to nothing but trouble for them both.

"No," he admitted softly as he looked at his friend. Rivers looked surprised at that answer but didn't interrupt. "But my entire life has been about what *I* want, what *I* need. Now I must do what's right for everyone else. Even if it hurts them."

"I see," Rivers said.

Ellis forced a half-smile, trying to find that Handsome persona that had always been his shield. "I know it's not natural," he said with a humorless laugh.

Rivers didn't respond but walked to the door. He rang a bell, and soon his right-hand man, Paul Abbot, appeared at the door. The two spoke quietly in the entryway for a moment, heads close together. Ellis turned away from them and looked down over the crowd.

Juliana had come farther into the room, gliding through those around her, pausing to look at the powerful pleasures being shared. He marked what she stopped to see, learning what aroused her, even if he knew he'd never use that knowledge. He couldn't. He had to keep reminding himself of that truth.

"It will be done," Rivers said as he shut the door.

Ellis's shoulders rolled forward, though he couldn't have said if relief or defeat was more prevalent in his mind and body. He was doing the right thing. He was protecting Juliana because she was too upset and broken to protect herself.

But it didn't feel very good to crush the one dream she had. To take away the need that drove her and kept the nightmares from catching up to her.

He turned away from her at the window and glared at Rivers. "Thank you. Now I need to go. I have quarry to hunt and I—" He broke off. "I just need to go."

Rivers didn't say anything, just stepped aside to clear a path for him to leave. As he passed by, his friend murmured, "Don't throw away everything, friend. Please don't."

Ellis ignored him, pretended he didn't hear as he moved down the stairs and around to the back exit where Juliana wouldn't catch sight of him. No matter what Marcus thought, no matter what he wanted, he had nothing left to throw away.

Only his life. And that wasn't worth anything anyway, except to trade for the safety of those he cared about.

Juliana's gaze darted around the main hall of the Donville Masquerade, taking in the overwhelming sight of everything around her. There were the lovers, of course. Impossible to ignore because they were here to play out every fantasy for the world to see. She shivered as she hesitated to watch two men grinding against a woman, their bodies all writhing together.

But as she broke away from staring at what made her tingle, she also sought out other things. Winston Leonard, for one. She needed to know if he had returned to Donville, not just for her own protection, but to alert Ellis when she found him.

Because, oh yes, she had every intention of finding him. He would argue and try to tell her that he didn't want her, but she didn't believe him. He had pleasured her and taken none of his own. If he were truly using her, he could have ruined her and never thought of her again.

Instead, he'd taken care of her, soothed her, listened to her tale and her fear. Those weren't the actions of a man who didn't give a damn. So she refused to let him pretend he didn't.

She turned sideways, edging between a tightly packed group of patrons gawking at a woman dancing on an elevated stage in the back of the room. Just as she managed to pass through and turned to walk normally again, a tall gentleman with extremely straight posture stepped into her path.

"Good evening, miss," he said, all formality, almost like a military man.

She didn't know the man but felt immediately comfortable with him. "Yes?"

"I'm Paul Abbot. I manage the daily activities of the club. Will you step away with me a moment? I need to speak to you." He motioned to a quieter corner where none of the commotion and scandalous activity was happening. It was well lit, though, and still felt safe.

"Certainly," she said, following as he took her aside. When they were away from the others, he turned and smiled. Almost apologetically. Her heart thudded.

"Miss, I am afraid I must ask you to leave the club," he said, kindly but without room for argument.

Her brow wrinkled. "I-I'm sorry, you want me to leave? I don't understand."

He nodded. "I realize that. And I do apologize, but we have determined that you must be asked to leave tonight. And not return. I do not think you have a long-term membership."

She shook her head, still confused. "No, I have been paying my nightly entry fee each time I came here. Is it...is that not allowed? I will pay for a membership if that is required."

"It is not," he said. "Ladies who wish to attend can pay a nightly rate, as you have been doing, or a membership fee. It isn't the money that is the issue, I'm afraid. It has simply been determined that you are not a good fit for the club."

She couldn't help but lift her hand to where her scar was hidden beneath her mask. She felt the heat of embarrassment fill her cheeks as she stared at the gentleman before her. He was so kind about all of this, but that didn't make her feel any better about it.

"Why?" she asked. "Do I not deserve an answer as to why?"

He drew a breath, and his gaze darted toward the stairs at the back of the hall. The ones that led up to the office where Marcus Rivers, the notorious owner of the club, kept his watch. Everyone whispered about the man. He was more legend than human.

She shifted. How would a man like that know anything about her? Why would he care enough to ban her? Unless he had been told something about her by...

She jerked her face back toward Mr. Abbot. "Mr. Rivers is a friend to Mr. Maitland," she said, recalling when Ellis had told her the same.

Abbot's expression didn't change. "I do not speak about the patrons here, miss. You understand."

"That bastard," she grumbled, clenching her hands at her sides. "How dare he. How *dare* he!"

"Miss, making a scene will not change anything," Abbot said, still kindly, but more firmly. "Let me escort you to your vehicle. I will return tonight's entrance fee to you with our apologies and have you on your way."

"I want to talk to Marcus Rivers," she said, folding her arms and widening her stance a little.

He leaned back, and for a moment Abbot looked almost impressed. Then he gave a small smile. "I'm afraid that is not possible."

"You seem the kind of man who can make anything possible," she retorted, glad that her shaking hands weren't so obvious when they were tucked away. "I assume your job is to do exactly that. I want to speak to him *now*."

Abbot took a deep breath to argue, but before he could, another deep, rough voice interrupted from behind her. "I will discuss the matter with the lady if she wishes. Thank you, Abbot."

She pivoted and found herself staring at a very tall, very intimidating, very handsome man. He had a calm, unreadable expression and the darkest green eyes she'd ever seen. She swallowed, intimidated by his size and his presence.

"M-Mr. Rivers?" she stammered.

He inclined his head. "At your service." He leaned closer. "It would be best if we have this conversation in my office, don't you think? My appearance in the hall tends to attract attention, and I think you might not want that."

She glanced around and found every nearby head had indeed pivoted to watch the club owner as he spoke to her. She swallowed, praying she would not be recognized despite her mask, and nodded. "Yes. Lead the way, sir."

He did so, guiding her through the crowd, which parted almost magically for him. They moved up a small staircase in the back of the hall, and he motioned her into a tidy, organized office at the top of the stairs. She moved to the bank of windows that overlooked the debauchery below and shook her head. "You watch over your domain very carefully, Mr. Rivers."

He didn't speak until he shut the door. "I must, Miss Shelley."

She gasped as she turned to face him. "You—you know who I am?"

He smiled, albeit faintly. "It's my business to know everything. I'm very good at my business."

She glanced at the door and then back to him. "I assume you must be. But I will tell you that I have...I have no desire to —to—to—"

His eyes widened a fraction and then he shook his head. "I'm not interested in seducing you. Lovely as you are, I don't pursue my pleasure in these walls. And our mutual friend wouldn't be happy with me if I tried." He chuckled. "He might kill me for it."

She drew in a long breath. "Our mutual friend. I think you mean Ellis Maitland." Rivers inclined his head slightly. She glared in response. "He isn't *my* friend. He's made that very clear. Doubly so considering I think *he* is the reason you are attempting to ban me from your club. Do you deny it?"

Rivers folded his arms, and his look was stern but for the slight twitch of his lips as he watched her. "I do not confirm or deny anything, my dear. It's better that way."

She fisted her hands at her sides and huffed out a breath as she paced away from the distracting view at the window and crossed his office. She stood staring into the fire for a moment and then glanced at him again. "How do you know him?"

Rivers was silent for what felt like a very long time. Then he shifted slightly. "I've known him almost all my life. We were on the street together."

"Oh," she whispered, surprised by his candor. Then she tried to picture what that would be like. She had been so very sheltered all *her* life, she knew that. A life like Ellis's felt so strange when she tried to imagine it. "So, you really are friends."

"Yes. We're friends." Rivers sat at his desk. From any other man, it would have been rude to sit before she did. But when he did it, it felt like a kindness. He was less intimidating when he was seated.

Though his focused gaze still watched her. "He doesn't think this is the place for you."

She shook her head. "There are ladies aplenty here. Some from my sphere, even."

"Indeed, there are," he said. "But *you* are an innocent."

Her cheeks flamed and she took the seat across from him with a thud. "He told you that."

"No." Rivers leaned back. "I can just see it. Innocents…" He looked off past her, and for a moment he looked very pensive and far away. "He isn't wrong that you don't belong in these walls."

"So he gets to choose what I do?" she asked. "You think he has that right?"

"Not at all," Rivers said. "But it's more complicated than he merely wants to spoil your fun, isn't it? I can see it in his eyes when he looks at you. When he talks about the stakes."

Her anger dissipated a fraction at that observation, so quietly given and so powerfully felt. "Perhaps it is more complicated," she admitted. "What do you think of that?"

"I can't tell yet," he replied. "I don't have enough information. I do know him. But you…you are an interesting one. What is it you want from him?" She felt the heat burn into her cheeks and folded her arms. Rivers smiled, and this time there was less hesitation in it. "Besides that."

She bent her head. "I want to…to help him. I want us to help each other."

"Hmmm." He seemed to consider that a moment, and then he nodded. "Perhaps that is something he needs, after all. Especially now. You know he has a place here in Town, do you not?"

"He does?" she asked, and then felt foolish. Of course Ellis had a place to stay here. She'd viewed him as transient when she pictured him anywhere but in a bed beckoning to her or out on the street playing some kind of swashbuckling criminal.

Rivers stifled another smile as he withdrew a small sheet of vellum from the top drawer of his desk, wetted a quill and scratched something out on the paper. He blew on it, waving it to dry the ink. As he did so, he said, "You can't stay here."

She pushed to her feet, opening her mouth to argue.

He waved the paper at her to silence her instead. "I promised him. And even if I hadn't, I tend to agree that this place is not...not for you. But if you want to encounter him, there are safer places to do it. Later, perhaps. A day or two. When you have both had some time to let cooler heads prevail."

He held out the paper and she stared at it, knowing it would provide a much more intimate connection to Ellis Maitland. "You would do that?"

He nodded and pushed the paper even closer. She took it without looking at the address and folded it.

"Be careful, Miss Shelley," he said, his gaze suddenly more intense. "Not necessarily of him. He's no monster, no matter what he tells himself in the dark. But this world..." He shook his head. "It is far more dangerous than perhaps you understand."

"And I have seen more danger than you know," she retorted.

He looked at her through eyes that had seen a thousand pains and threats. He shrugged. "Perhaps you have at that. Now let me arrange for your carriage to be brought around and escort you to the safety of it."

She nodded, and he left to make the preparations. She sat back down in the chair and closed her eyes. Whatever happened next, she was diving far deeper into this world. And no matter what she said to Ellis or Rivers about it, it was a place she knew she didn't belong.

But there was no going back now.

CHAPTER 11

Ellis sat on his mount, peering through the spyglass at the fine home across the park. His stomach churned at the false veneer of decency and value there. One that had given power to a man who lived to damage everyone around him.

"So he has not returned to his townhouse for three days?" Ellis asked.

The man on the horse next to him glanced at him like he had gone daft. Golden Mitchell was one of Ellis's network and had been for years. He'd left the Royal Navy injured and been all but abandoned by King and Country. He'd gone underground with Ellis and was the best man to gather information.

Well, second best. Rook had always been the best.

Ellis flinched at the sense of loss that internal caveat caused and glared at his partner. "I asked a question, Golden."

"Aye, I heard you," Golden grunted. "But I guess you didn't hear my answer not three minutes ago, so let me say it slower. He ain't been seen by anyone since that night you spied him at Donville. He ain't come home. Servants are tightlipped as fuck about it, too."

"He's gone to the wind again," Ellis muttered.

"Perhaps," Mitchell said. "Don't know why you didn't go after him when you saw him. Could've had it all done before sunup."

Ellis didn't respond, but continued to stare through the spyglass at the unassuming home. Mitchell didn't know about Juliana. No one in his circle did. Mitchell also didn't know what the plan was when it came to Winston Leonard. He thought Ellis intended to rough him up a bit, frighten him and that would be it.

It was better that way. When it was over his little motley crew would either stay in formation and choose a new leader from their ranks or disband and disappear into the underground to pickpocket another day.

"Track everything," Ellis said softly as he handed the glass back over. "Any information, even something small, should be brought to me."

"Aye." Mitchell looked off at the house. "Your cousin is searching too, you know."

Ellis shook his head. "Of course he is. He still thinks a man like Leonard might be bargained with. Hanging about with too many fops now that he married into the upper crust."

Mitchell nudged him with a lewd grin. "But the woman is comely enough, eh?"

Ellis scowled. When anyone discussed Anne in that tone, they were, in effect, also discussing Thomasina and Juliana. He found he didn't like that so very much. But there was no use causing a tiff, so he ignored the opening. "Have you had any luck with the code?"

He scowled as he thought of it. Rook had found a coded message that could lead them to the gem Leonard wanted desperately enough to kill for it. But his cousin had always been rubbish with code. Ellis knew he could break it if only he could get his hands on it.

If he had the gem, that meant he had the power. He could lead Leonard right to him then and end this with one strike.

But Rook had partnered with the Earl of Harcourt now. Both men wanted to do this the gentlemanly way. Whatever that meant.

Danger. That's what it meant.

"Naw," Mitchell said with a laugh. "Been trying to find a way in to that Harcourt stronghold for weeks now. Rook's still crafty. Don't know where he has it or what he's done with it."

"Well, I might have to take care of that part myself, it seems," Ellis said. He wasn't looking forward to that encounter. He hadn't spoken to Rook since the afternoon Juliana was attacked. His cousin had been enraged with him.

He'd known their long friendship, their bond, was broken. And that broke *him* in ways he didn't want to consider.

He turned his horse toward the road. "Keep me apprised on Leonard. His father fears him, so keep a close watch on the duke and his other children, too. Thank you."

Mitchell grunted a response, and Ellis sighed as he rode off. None of this was going according to plan. In fact, that had been the problem with this entire mess since the beginning. He'd always been a strategist. Always known exactly the path he had to take to remain safe and dry and rich.

But the moment Winston Leonard had been allowed into his circle, this fancy fop with his promises of money and security and access to a whole new level of mark…

Well, from that moment forward, it had been anarchy. Leonard wasn't about strategy, he was about pleasure. Not in sex, not in fortune, but in pain. He took because he liked to cause pain. He broke because he liked to watch things break. He killed and threatened because the fear gave him power. Ellis and Solomon had discovered that too late.

Solomon was dead. Ellis was running. And everyone in their lives was in danger. He was the only one left alive to take the responsibility for this debacle.

And what did he do? Well, he got himself distracted by a woman with green eyes and a spine of steel hidden beneath a soft, delectable body. And distraction was a killer. It would just be a sweeter death than the one he was sure to face with Winston Leonard.

He shook his head. Christ, he had to stop doing this. He had to stop longing for something that wasn't his. It was over now. He would never see Juliana Shelley again.

And he had a job to do.

~

Once again Juliana was surrounded by her sisters and their husbands in the Earl of Harcourt's London home. Once again she sat to the outside of their foursome, watching as they talked together. Watching as the couples exchanged little meaningful glances or brushes of hands. The separation between them felt so stark now even as she tried to pretend that it wasn't.

She sighed and got up, walked to the sideboard across the parlor and freshened her tea. She felt so out of sorts, she almost didn't recognize herself anymore.

It had been three days since she had been banned from the Donville Masquerade. Three days where the address Marcus Rivers had given to her had all but burned a hole in her gown pocket. She kept fingering the fine paper, daring herself to look at it. But she hadn't found the nerve yet. Once she did, she would have to decide if she would go there.

If she could face a man who had so firmly dismissed her. If she could face herself and the desires that burned in her chest.

"Juliana?" She turned and found Thomasina at her elbow. Her sister's expression was concerned as she slipped an arm around her waist and squeezed. "What is it?"

Juliana wrinkled her brow. "What is...what?" she asked, trying to sound light and unaffected and perfectly fine when she was anything but.

Thomasina pursed her lips. "Come now. You have been distracted for days. I've watched you disappearing into your head here and at Father's. Won't you talk to me about it?"

Juliana forced a smile. Usually she was the one wheedling out the truth from her sisters. It was rather annoying being on the opposite end of that equation.

"I adore you for worrying," she said. "But I promise there is no need."

She moved to step away, but Thomasina caught her hand and tugged her back. Now Thomasina's gentle expression was lit with anxiety. "I don't believe you. Please."

Juliana bent her head. There seemed to be no hiding the truth, and perhaps she shouldn't at that. After all, there was danger to more than just herself.

"I...saw...Winston Leonard," she admitted with a quick glance toward Anne, Rook and Harcourt across the room. They were smiling. That would end soon enough.

Thomasina released her hand and staggered back, away from Juliana. "You what?" she gasped out, loud enough that all the other heads turned.

Juliana shook her head. This was happening. "Yes," she said so that everyone could hear. "I saw Winston Leonard."

Rook and Harcourt launched toward her side by side, with Anne right behind them.

"Where?" Rook barked. "When?"

"A few days ago," Juliana admitted. "Here in London."

"Where in London?" Harcourt asked, his irritation at her lack of specificity clear. "Juliana, why didn't you tell us?"

She chose to focus on the second question rather than the first. "You are all in wedded bliss," she said softly. "Two happy couples starting your lives together. You've hardly had time for anyone else, have you? If you are planning, it is without me involved. I had no chance to inform you and I was in no hurry to cause extra strain in already difficult circumstances."

Both her sisters drew back a fraction at her tone and she saw them exchange a glance. Even without the special connection they shared as triplets, she could read their expressions. Pitying. Perhaps guilty because they knew she was right. Juliana was being left behind as the only sister without true love panting after her heels.

She couldn't even get a man known for love cons to seduce her. It was rather pathetic when she thought of it in those terms.

"Juliana," Harcourt said, his face twisted as if her pain were an anathema to him. "I-I'm sorry if you feel you've been left out. That was never our intention. I have been trying to convince your father to allow you to stay with us for a while. For your protection if nothing else."

She shrugged. "He doesn't care about my safety, though, does he? You will not win that argument, my lord."

Anne arched a brow. "Well, he will not like it when I take over."

"Still," Harcourt said. "I wish you had told us about Leonard when you first saw him. Are you certain it was him?"

She lifted a hand to her scar and felt the tingle like the knife was just slicing there. "As if I would ever forget that horrible face."

Both her sisters sucked in a breath, but Harcourt ignored it. "Where was he?"

"I just...saw him at a gathering I attended," she muttered. "It doesn't matter. What matters is that he is here."

Rook's brow was wrinkled as he observed the exchange. He stepped forward and covered Anne's trembling hand. "Juliana is correct. Wherever she was, for whatever reason she is keeping it private, what truly matters is Leonard. Harcourt, if he's here, he could be drawn out."

The two men stepped away, their heads going together as they hashed out a plan. Anne and Thomasina remained at her side, each holding her hand.

"I'm sorry," Thomasina whispered, and there were tears in her eyes.

Anne nodded. "So am I."

Juliana bent her head. Now that they were apologizing, she felt silly for bringing up her feelings of separation and exile. She knew why her sisters were so focused on their husbands. She'd felt the thrill of desire herself recently and understood it far more. What she didn't understand was what went beyond the physical. Her sisters loved their husbands. They were loved by them.

Who wouldn't want that?

"I'm—I'm being foolish," Juliana said with a shake of her head. "Churlish." She looked over at the men and her sisters did as well. She felt them both vibrating with their need to cross to them. "You'd best see what they're talking about."

"No," Thomasina said. "I won't leave you."

Juliana tilted her head and looked at her sister. "You won't be. I'm standing right here."

Anne was already leaning toward Rook, but she had the grace to glance back at Juliana. "Are you sure?"

Juliana waved them off and saved her sigh until they were far enough away they couldn't hear her. She was out of sorts. She hated herself for it. It signaled such a lack of control. *Everything* she'd done recently felt like it was driven by a lack of control.

She dug into her pocket as she paced to the window. The paper with Ellis's address was still there, wrinkled now, worn from her fingers brushing it. At last she drew it out. She cast a quick glance over her shoulder, but all were engaged in heated discussion. They didn't notice her.

She unfolded the paper and read the address. She recognized it. It was a middle-class neighborhood not so very far from Harcourt's London estate. She could walk there in half an hour. A carriage would only be a few minutes ride. It was wrong, though, wasn't it? To go to a man who so evidently didn't want her around?

Except she already knew she was going to do just that. She could only hope Ellis could be convinced of what her own family could not.

That she still had a place in this world. That she could have a place at his side in this fight.

~

Ellis stormed into the foyer of his London home and tossed his great coat to the waiting butler. Reginald had once been a pirate, but had retired from the life when the heat got too high. Of course, he'd also been an inveterate gambler and lost his fortune. And so to work for Ellis he'd gone.

Now he snatched the coat with a glare. "What's got you in a snit?"

Ellis glared at him. "No news about Winston Leonard?"

Reg shook his head. "Naw. Nothin' new. You do have some chit here. Demanded to see you. Pretty thing. I left 'er in your parlor." He executed a ridiculously overdone bow. "Milord."

Ellis rolled his eyes at him. "Oh…go find something to do." Reg chuckled as he strolled off to take Ellis's coat God knew where. "Something legal!" he called after him.

From the distance he heard a snort. "Oh, you're no fun."

Ellis shook his head as he stared at the closed door to the nearby parlor. He didn't receive female visitors here at this place. When he had a mark, he'd always pursued them at a place like the Donville Masquerade. Or their own homes if he felt particularly daring. None of those women likely considered his existence outside of where they shared a bed.

But he knew one woman who might. One woman bold enough to figure out where he lived when he wasn't being *Handsome Ellis Maitland*. One woman who might come here and demand his pirate butler let her in for tea.

"Juliana," he muttered beneath his breath.

The very idea of it had his body on fire, both with arousal and frustration. The mix of those two things was confusing, indeed. If it really was her in there, he wanted to shake her for being so utterly reckless…and kiss her because he hadn't seen her for days and his hands shook at the idea of being near her.

"Enough," he grunted, and strode to the door. He drew a cleansing breath and pushed it open.

She was standing at the mantel, fiddling with a little miniature there. She hadn't noticed his entry. He took the opportunity to stare at her. Her dark blonde hair had been spun up on her head in an elaborate style he wanted to take down piece by piece until he was surrounded by vanilla and lemon. Her gown was a spring green, fitted perfectly, not too revealing like the one she always wore to the Donville Masquerade, but more of a hint at all the lusciousness beneath. It was very fine.

She was very fine. And she did not belong in his parlor. Or in his arms. Or in his bed. Looking at her here was like seeing a tiger in a ballroom. Beautiful, yes. Did it belong there? Most definitely not.

He cleared his throat and she turned. His lips parted without him meaning for them to. God, but she was lovely. Too damned lovely.

He shook his head and forced himself to go stern. He had promised to be the villain to protect her. He couldn't go back now.

"How the hell did you find me?" he asked.

She jumped in surprise. As her wide gaze flitted over him from head to toe, he thought she might just run away. Her eyes darted to the door behind him and her hands clenched together.

But then she looked at him. Really looked at him. She pushed her shoulders back.

And he realized this was war.

"It doesn't matter," she said. "I did."

He crossed to the sideboard and poured himself a hefty splash of whisky from a bottle there. He held it toward her, but she shook her head. He recorked the bottle and took a long swig of the drink.

"Yes, it does," he finally said as he tilted his head and examined that beautiful face further. He tracked every twitch, every movement as she held his stare. "Let me see, the only two people you have any connection to who would know my address are Rook and Marcus."

She folded her arms and her gaze narrowed. "Why do you need to know so much?"

"Knowing who betrayed you always matters, angel," he drawled. And hated himself because he was playing a game with her now. Just toying with her because he liked when the high color entered her cheeks.

Seemed it wasn't so hard to act the bastard after all. He was one. One without control when it came to this woman.

"Rook wouldn't do it," he continued. "For a great many reasons. Anne would kill him is the biggest one."

A tiny smile tilted the corner of her lips. "That is true. I wouldn't be so unfair as to ask him to do that."

"Marcus Rivers then," he said.

"I confronted him when he had me banned from his club on your orders." She arched a brow. "If you wish to talk about betrayal."

"I told you, I didn't want you around anymore," he said, and nearly choked on the lies. " I don't know why you're here. I don't know why Rivers wasted revealing a secret to someone who means so little to me."

Her jaw set, but it didn't seem to be out of upset. Instead she looked determined. Unwavering. God, but she had a strength to her. Like steel through the wings of a butterfly.

"I think your old friend was worried about you," she said softly. "And so was I."

He shook his head. He was trying to protect her and she would not allow it. She would force him to be cruel. She would force him to be everything he'd been his whole life. And he hated that. He hated her, a little, for creating a situation where he had no choice but to hurt her.

"You shouldn't be," he scoffed. "Because I don't give a damn about you. I'm done, Juliana. I said it in the carriage, but perhaps you didn't hear me. I am finished with this. Finished with you."

"Are you?" she whispered, and instead of backing away she moved closer.

His breath hitched as he stared at her. He'd been trying to erect an invisible wall, but she glided through it.

"Juliana," he growled. A warning. A plea. A prayer.

"Are you, Ellis?" she whispered again, and now she was right in front of him. Her trembling fingers lifted and brushed against his jawline, gentle. Powerful.

He squeezed his eyes shut. He'd faced off with many a powerful adversary in his life. He'd won a great many of those battles. But today this slip of a woman was armed only with all of her beauty and charm and gentleness, and she was destroying him.

He was destroyed when she touched him. When she said his name. When she challenged him not just to be a better man…but somehow believed he already was.

"Look at me," she demanded. His eyes came open and he stared down at her as she inched even closer. Her body brushed his. Her gaze never wavered. "Tell me again that you're finished."

She didn't allow him to respond. She merely lifted up on her tiptoes, wound her arms around his neck and drew his mouth to hers.

His mind briefly screamed at him to resist. To push her away. To end this. But the moment passed and then all that was left was desire. Need. And a draw that he'd never expected, but which had become as important to him as air or water or food.

He wrapped his arms around her, moaned against her lips as surrender. And he kissed her back.

CHAPTER 12

Juliana had expected Ellis would give in the moment his gaze had flickered over her from head to toe and she'd seen his desire for her. It had been a triumph to recognize he wanted her. That she had some power over this powerful man. And when she kissed him, she had expected him to be swept away.

Only he…wasn't. He held her, cradled her like she was something worth her weight in gold. His mouth moved over hers and it was so infinitely gentle. Almost reverent as his hands fisted against her back and his tongue breached her lips.

She shivered, and he cupped her closer, molding their bodies until there was no space between them, no breath between them. She clung to him, tilting her head to allow him deeper.

Some small part of her shifted as he tasted her. As she tasted him. She was not going to make it out of this unchanged, no matter what happened next.

As if she'd said that out loud, he cupped her waist and pushed her aside gently. He stepped back, his breath coming short. "Don't do this, Juliana."

"To myself or to you?" she asked, her voice shaking as hard as her body.

He met her gaze, and there was a desperation there. "Both," he whispered.

Her lips parted at that one word, spoken in a tone that broke her heart. He was trying so hard to be cruel, to be cold. To push her away and be the villain he'd been his whole life. But it wasn't real. He was vulnerable.

And she realized in that moment that she would not walk away.

"You need me," she said softly.

He shook his head even as his gaze moved over her again. "No, I don't. I don't need *anyone*, angel."

"Liar," she said, without heat. Without cruelty.

He nodded. "Yes. Absolutely. I tell lies to beautiful creatures like yourself, and all of them believe me. They give me what I want and it *means nothing.*"

She saw the truth of him now and so the harshness no longer stung her. She placed her hands on her hips and arched a brow at him. "Then what did you get from me?"

His brow wrinkled. "What?"

"You said you only trade on what you get. So what did you get from me?"

His jaw set. "Fun," he ground out, his angry tone belying the meaning of that one little word.

She smiled. "Good. I want that fun, too. And in return, I'll help you."

He jerked back and she almost laughed, for he looked truly confused. "Help me?" he repeated.

"Yes, I want to help you," she said. "It means to render aid. Be of assistance. And I'm doing it so you might as well stop arguing with me, you great oaf."

L ooking at Juliana Shelley, hands on her hips like an angry governess, green eyes flashing, absolute certainly on her utterly beautiful face, all of Ellis's act slipped. How could he pretend to be cold when she was so...so...so utterly mystifying?

"I know what the words mean," he said. "I just...you want to help me? How do you think you could possibly do that?"

She clucked her tongue. "Come now. You're supposed to be some great underground lord, aren't you? You must see what use I could be to you. Winston Leonard isn't just some everyday villain. He is a duke's son. *Lord Winston*. And I have access to parts of his world that would be far more challenging for you to breach. That means I can find things you cannot."

"Juliana," he gasped, and reached for her. He caught her wrist and tugged her a fraction closer. "That would be very dangerous."

She covered his hand with hers and stroked her fingers across his skin. "I'm not afraid of dangerous, Mr. Maitland. Or haven't you figured that out yet."

"You should be," he snapped even as he staggered back from her temptation. "You have no idea what you're getting yourself into."

"Perhaps not," she said and smiled at him. "Certainly, I would be much safer if a man from that world was protecting me and helping me, just as I am helping him."

"God, you are relentless," he barked as he paced away from her. "You are out of control."

"I *am* relentless," she said with a chuckle. "My poor sisters would tell you the same. But I'm very much in control, perhaps for the first time in my whole life. I'm *taking* control."

He pivoted back toward her. She was the most frustrating and fascinating woman he had ever encountered. Part of him applauded her singular focus on what she desired. The other part was absolutely terrified of what that focus would expose her to. Dangers far deeper than just him.

"In addition," she added softly. "I also have access to the plans Rook and Harcourt are hatching. I *know* you want access to those."

He froze. He did, indeed, want to know what his cousin was planning. And where he had put the code that would lead to the treasure Leonard sought so desperately. If Ellis had that, drawing out his quarry would be far easier.

But was it worth putting Juliana in danger...again?

He shook his head. "Just stay out of it."

She held his stare. "No."

Lunging forward, he caught her arms. There was a ripple that worked through her when he did. She trembled against his chest. Was that fear? Was that desire? Was it both?

"Stay out of this," he managed to repeat, grinding the words past clenched teeth. "You aren't wanted in this. I don't want you in this."

She leaned up and brushed her lips to his again. Then she pulled free of his grip and stepped away. "You either want it all or you want nothing. And whatever you say, I know you don't want nothing." She stepped toward the door. "I'm not giving up, Ellis. Think about it."

Then she turned on her heel and left the parlor. He heard her exit the house, and he threw up his hands in frustration.

"Fuck!" he barked, picking up the glass of whisky and hurtling it against the back wall. He gripped his hands against the sideboard, his heart throbbing as her carriage jangled by merrily, taking her back to God knew where.

The woman was truly unstoppable. And as much as he admired that, he also feared it. In this situation, it might get her killed. And to what? Protect him? He didn't deserve that.

So he was going to have to take the next step. And he was very much not looking forward to it.

E llis had broken into the home of many a fop in his long and illustrious career as a thief. It was never as difficult as those who inhabited the places likely thought it should be. And the house of the Earl of Harcourt was no different.

With a flick of his wrist, he managed to pry the window open and slid inside. He shut it behind him and turned, only to find his cousin, Rook, leaning against the door that led to the hallway. Glaring at him.

Ellis jumped despite himself and returned the glare with his own. "What the hell? How did you know I was here?"

"I heard the dogs barking," Rook said without moving. "And then I watched you from my bedroom window as you crept in from the garden. You're getting sloppy, Handsome. Distracted?"

"Yes," Ellis grunted, and then shook his head. "No."

Rook pushed off the door and took a long step toward him. Ellis hated that his reaction was to shift into a fighter's stance. This was how far they'd fallen. And it was all his own fault.

"What the hell are you doing here, Ellis?" Rook growled, his hands fisting at his sides as he brought himself up short.

"I'm breaking into Harcourt's house," Ellis barked back. Rook's jaw tightened and he folded his arms. Ellis felt his shoulders roll forward. "I needed to see you," he admitted softly.

There was a flutter of emotion that moved over Rook's face. All the love that the two cousins, nearly as close as brothers, had ever felt. And then it was gone, hardened and erased in a moment. Ellis hated the loss of it and hated the pit it caused in his own stomach.

Caring about others was exactly the distraction Rook had mentioned earlier. And it was endangering everyone.

"See me," Rook said. "Well, here I am. What do you want?"

Ellis drew a breath. He had been rehearsing this on the ride from his home. The words still didn't come easily. He paced away so his cousin wouldn't see his face when he said it. "Juliana."

There was a long, heavy pause, and then Rook took a step

toward him. "What. About. Her?" He ground out, accentuating every word.

Ellis pivoted to face him. "She is endangering herself."

Rook shook his head. "You must be desperate to drag her into this. To lie."

"It's not a lie," Ellis snapped. "She's been sneaking out of her father's house. Going to—" He broke off. Juliana would never want her family to know where she had gone. That betrayal would be far worse than getting her banned. And yet he had no choice if he was going to protect her. "She's been going to the Donville Masquerade."

Rook's eyebrows lifted. "Juliana Shelley? You're certain?"

"Yes." Ellis bent his head. "*And* she…she came to my house here in London this afternoon."

"Wait…so she came to the Donville Masquerade and you two interacted?" Rook said in disbelief.

A flash of Juliana arching beneath him, crying out with pleasure, ripped through Ellis's mind. He pushed it away with great difficulty. "Yes. We interacted."

"She spoke to *you*, the man who all but kidnapped her sister, the man who set in motion all the events that led to her family's scandal and her own injury."

Ellis jerked away from those very true words. The accusations he made against himself every time he saw her. They were worse coming from Rook's voice.

"She did." He gripped his hands at his sides, gathered himself and faced his cousin again. "She is altered by everything that happened. She's looking for a way to feel something. I think we both understand that."

Rook flinched and then nodded. "I suppose that makes sense. Thomasina and Anne have both commented on the change in her. They've tried to speak to her, to comfort her, but she feels outside of her own family now."

"Perhaps because she's been *left out*," Ellis said.

"Fuck you. You don't know anything about it."

Ellis shrugged. "She came to me. *That's* how desperate she is. So I think I know a little more than you do, *cousin*. You can hate me all you want, but don't dismiss me and endanger her."

"I don't hate you," Rook said softly.

Ellis walked away from him. He stood at the fireplace, watching the flames lick at the logs. For a moment, all was silent between them, though not comfortably so. All the unspoken anger and hurt hung there like a wall. Insurmountable. His making.

"I don't want to hurt her," he said at last. "I don't want to betray her like this and humiliate her. But she needs intervention. She needs a reminder that I'm dangerous, and none of mine seem to break through that marvelously thick skull of hers."

Rook snorted out a laugh and Ellis turned to watch his cousin scrub a hand over his face. "Shit. Anne is going to be livid."

Ellis smiled then. "I don't think there's much room for her to talk when it comes to making bad decisions."

"With you," Rook added.

"Yes. I suppose. Though her heart was never in it. And neither was mine. Anyone can tell just by looking at her that she is in love with you. Foolish girl."

Rook laughed a little and the tension between them faded a fraction. "They like the bad ones, those Shelley sisters. Even Harcourt isn't as straitlaced as he might seem."

A ripple of jealousy tore through Ellis before he could control it. He and Rook had been best friends as well as family. Rook had been his right-hand man for years. Now he was pulling away, separating. It was better for him, but it still stung.

"Well, then you've found a new place for yourself," Ellis said. "One with far less trouble. So why don't you let me take care of the trouble still here? Give me the code. I know you still have it."

The softness to Rook's expression dissipated in a moment and he clenched his teeth. "All this pretending to care about Juliana's well-being and what you really want is the code. Why are you so set on getting the gem, Ellis? To enrich yourself?"

"No!" Ellis burst out. "You really think that when its very existence threatens you, threatens my brother, threatens—"

He broke off because if he said Juliana's name, it would be clear he cared about her. After all, the other people he'd listed were the only ones he'd ever loved. While he didn't lump Juliana Shelley into that category—he would never be that foolish—he certainly could admit he had a stake in her well-being. The woman had all but forced him to.

"I want to take care of Winston Leonard," he said softly.

"He's back in London," Rook said with a groan. "Shit, Juliana saw him at the Donville Masquerade, didn't she?"

Ellis drew back at that revelation. "She told you she saw him?"

"Reluctantly," Rook said. "And she refused to say where. I understand why now. What is between you, Ellis?"

"Nothing," he said, and heard how unbelievable the words were.

"Liar," Rook drawled, repeating the same slur Juliana had thrown at him earlier in the day.

"I'm trying to make it nothing," Ellis said. "She doesn't make it easy."

Rook threw up his hands. "She's suffered enough."

"I know!" Ellis lunged forward and caught Rook's arm. "Because of me. This is all because of me. So let me fix it."

Rook yanked away from him and looked him up and down. "Your desperation has always been dangerous. It's what started all this mess in the first place. So we're going to do this Harcourt's way."

"The gentleman's way," Ellis sneered.

Rook's gaze flickered, but he nodded.

"You know he'll still come," Ellis said. "He'll threaten your wives and my brother and Juliana because it entertains him to do so."

He saw Rook knew that. That he understood the truth even if he wasn't ready to do what needed to be done about it. He sighed. "Well, we'll face that if we must."

Ellis backed away. "She's changed you," he said, softly and with disbelief. It wasn't meant as an insult. Just an observation that made him long for…

Well, a great many things he shouldn't long for.

"I'm glad she has," Rook said.

"So am I," Ellis admitted. "But you are wrong, even if you refuse to face it." He let out a long sigh. "Just talk to Juliana. Help her. Because I can't. I am poison, and I will destroy her if she keeps pushing. I won't be able to stop myself."

He turned and walked away. Returned to the window he had come in and stepped out. He heard Rook say his name, but he ignored it. He moved out into the night. The only place he belonged. He just had to remember it and act accordingly.

CHAPTER 13

Juliana sat on her bed in her father's house, scribbling in her diary. It wasn't her usual type of entry, which was heavy with reflections on her life and cheeky descriptions of those she knew. Today she was making a list. Things to do to make Ellis see her worth and accept her help in his grand scheme, whatever that was.

There was a knock on her door and she answered without glancing up, "Come in." When the door opened, she said, "Mary, do you think you could lay out my blue silk for tonight? The one with the gold gathering?"

"It isn't your maid."

She jerked her face up to see Thomasina and Anne standing at the entryway to her chamber. For a moment, she was pleased, because despite the fraught feelings in their current situation, she was always happy to see her sisters. Especially now when they were so often parted.

But the seriousness of their expressions sucked the joy from her chest. Replaced it with anxiety when Thomasina ducked her head and Anne pursed her lips.

"I did not expect you two," Juliana said carefully as she closed her journal and slid it beneath her pillow. She got up and smoothed the front of her gown. "To what do I owe this pleasure? And why didn't you have me come to the parlor where we could have tea?"

Anne shut the door behind them as they entered. Thomasina flinched at the sound of it closing and said, "We wanted to talk more privately. I do miss our chats at night in our bedchambers."

Anne glanced at her. "She is too clever not to see past *that* lie, love. Rook and Harcourt are downstairs discussing something with Father. I think it's best they don't hear what we have to say."

Juliana's heart rate doubled at both the look and the tone. "That doesn't bode well."

"Sit down," Thomasina said, taking her hand as she led her to the chairs before the fire. Three of them, just as there were in each of their rooms so they could commiserate together.

Juliana did as she'd been told, buffeted on each side by her sisters, and held her breath as she waited for whatever was going to be said.

She wasn't surprised when it was Anne who spoke. "We know about the Donville Masquerade."

Suddenly it seemed the room was thrust underwater. Everything sounded tinny as her blood rushed to her ears. Her sisters stared at her, but there was no doubt in their eyes.

"I-I don't know what you mean," she said after what felt like a lifetime. Of course, she knew they would never believe her. They had always been able to root out the lies in each other. "I don't even know what that is. Donville Masquerade? That sounds like—"

"Juliana," Thomasina interrupted gently.

She cut herself off. There were two choices before her. She could continue to prevaricate and shift and try to get her sisters to change the subject. An unlikely outcome, considering how certain they seemed of the accusation.

Or she could tell the truth and face the consequences of what she'd been doing behind their backs. In a way, that option felt like a relief. She'd never been particularly good at subterfuge.

She folded her arms and straightened her back. "Fine. You've caught me." Both her sisters and she ducked her head. "How did you find out? Did someone see me there? Did the driver report my activities even though he was paid so very handsomely to look the other way?"

Anne shifted now, as if she were uncomfortable with the answer. Thomasina's cheeks were bright with color.

"How do you know?" Juliana repeated.

"Ellis told Rook," Anne said at last.

It was as if the floor beneath Juliana had opened up and now she was falling. Falling forever as humiliation brought fire to her cheeks and tears to her eyes. Of all the answers to her question, that Ellis had betrayed her was the last one she'd expected.

Yes, he had been trying to stop her from entering his life and his world. Yes, he'd had her banned from the Donville Masquerade. But this was different.

By telling her family, he'd had to have known what it would do to her. By telling her family, he was not only embarrassing her but opening up a world of consequences that would truly separate them.

"Breathe," Thomasina said softly. She reached out and took Juliana's cold hand between her warm ones and squeezed gently. "And please, *please* talk to us."

Juliana shut her eyes as she leaned against the chair back with a long sigh. Her time was up. Confession was the only way.

"You must understand that my entire life has changed in the past few months," she began. "I realize your lives have also been altered, but in good ways. You've both found love, and of course, I am deliriously happy for you. But it's not the same for me."

"Because…" Thomasina trailed off and touched her own cheek at the place where Juliana's scar would be.

Juliana shook her head. "No. Well, yes, but not just that. My identity is gone. I've always been the sister who fixed things for you. The one who could be depended on. And now you have husbands to share your troubles with. Even if I'm pleased for you both, it is a change that happened so swiftly and unexpectedly that I felt... washed away on the tide of it."

Anne's expression softened and she took Juliana's other hand. "Oh, love. I knew you felt left out, but I didn't know you had gotten so low."

"I'm on the outside looking in now," Juliana said. "But I have also lost my future, not just my place. I've spent my life under the assumption that Father would match each of us. If I were lucky, it would be to a man I could like...perhaps even love."

"You still could—" Thomasina began.

Juliana cut her off with an arched brow. "He's said a dozen times that now I'll just be his spinster secretary. That I'm so damaged both physically and by scandal that he won't even consider sending me out on the marriage mart anymore."

Anne rushed to her feet with a growl of displeasure. "Damn him. He is the most selfish person. I swear, if Harcourt does not arrange your coming to stay with us, I will take care of it myself and Father will like my solution less."

"Are you planning to kidnap me?" Juliana said, unable to help her smile at Anne's frustrated desire to go to war for her. It did help to know she still mattered.

Anne pivoted to spear her with a meaningful glance. "If I must. I'm sure Rook would help."

"Anne, we must focus now. We can kidnap later," Thomasina said gently. "We understand your feelings, Juliana. But how did that end you in the Donville Masquerade?"

"I saw you both so happy. Heard your whispers about pleasure, thought of that book of Father's with all the naughty pictures." Juliana sighed. "If I were going to be saddled the rest of my life planning Father's dinner parties, I just decided I wanted something for myself first. Just one little thing."

"You wished to surrender your virginity," Thomasina breathed.

Anne ducked her head and color flooded her cheeks. "I-I understand that. I had something of the same desire in Scotland after I realized I had ruined my own future. But *Ellis*, Juliana? How in the world did you align yourself with a man like that?"

Juliana's hackles rose at the dismissive attitude of the question. She understood it after Anne's shared history with Ellis, but she still sought to defend him.

Even though he had betrayed her. She was a fool, she supposed.

"I know you have good reasons to dislike him, after what he did. After what you…you shared."

Anne threw up her hands. "We *shared* very little. I know I was not his true prize, and in the end what I thought I felt for him was more a terror at marrying someone I didn't love. He led me to Rook, so I have to…forgive him on some level. But he *is* a villain."

"He's more than that," Juliana insisted, and frowned as her sisters exchanged a meaningful look. "I was frightened at the very idea of him for so long. But when I met him that terrible day I was taken, I was shocked at how much a man he was. Just a man, not a monster, handsome and funny and flawed. He had me in his arms at once point and it was…comforting. He looked into my eyes and suddenly much more about that book made sense to me."

Anne's eyes went wide. "Juliana."

"I hated myself for it, of course," Juliana gasped, getting up and pacing away. "I hated myself for feeling attracted to a man who had caused so much pain to those I loved. I hated him for doing those irresponsible things that destroyed so much. But the body and the heart…"

Thomasina nodded. "They want what they want," she finished.

"Yes," Juliana said. "I went to the Donville Masquerade, hoping to purge those wants. I never expected it would be him who approached me."

"What did you do?" Thomasina asked.

Now it was Juliana's turn to blush. She wasn't so bold as Anne, so saying these things out loud felt very difficult. Especially about a man her family hated, no matter how passionately she defended him.

Anne stared at her for what felt like a long time as Juliana struggled. Then she crossed the room and slid an arm around her. "It will help to say it. You won't be judged."

"He…" Juliana caught her breath. "He did things with his mouth."

"Oh," Anne and Thomasina said with secret little smiles that let Juliana know she was not alone in what she had experienced.

"Yes, *oh*. And it was…amazing. Far better than anything I'd ever hoped or dreamed about." She sighed. "But he wouldn't do anything else. He never took me, no matter how I cajoled or begged like a fool."

Thomasina tilted her head. "Was he…trying to *protect* you?" she asked, voice filled with incredulity.

"That's what I tell myself to feel better," Juliana whispered. "Only now I…I must doubt it. After all, he went to Rook. He crowed about his conquest. He made sure you all knew about it because he knows I'll be stopped from pursuing him further. He…he truly doesn't want me."

When she said the words out loud, it was like someone had dug a pit in her stomach. One that rolled and burned. Heat filled her cheeks, and she backed away from her sisters so she wouldn't feel the full weight of their pity. It was quiet in the room for a moment, with only the tick of the clock to ripple through her mind.

"I could not be a judge of what that man wants," Anne finally said softly. "Not a fair one at any rate. But I do know what *I* want. Harcourt and Rook are convincing Father that you should stay with us, at least for a few weeks. Please come."

Juliana looked from one sister to the next and slowly folded her arms. "I assume this is to give you the ability to lock me in a tower. Keep me from being more of a fool than I've already been."

Thomasina crossed to her. "No," she said, reaching up to touch Juliana's unscarred cheek. "It's so we can be together. We can protect each other."

Juliana bent her head. She wanted to believe she didn't need protection. That she could make her own decisions. But Ellis had turned her in to her family as if he were the guard with a reticent child. It was as clear a message as one could receive.

And with that rejection, she could see she had been reckless. She had endangered herself. So maybe she needed the governing her family would require. At least she would be with her sisters, where she wouldn't be crowded or judged as her father did to her.

"Father isn't going to know about the Masquerade or about Ellis, is he?" she gasped.

"No!" her sisters said together with just as much horror.

"God, we wouldn't do that to you," Thomasina insisted, a hand to her heart as if that were the worst accusation in the world.

Juliana flinched. Her sisters wouldn't do that. Of course they wouldn't. But Ellis had. He'd said what he said, not caring what it caused for her. He only wanted the result: that she would be gone from his life. A nuisance taken care of with a few well-placed words.

"Very well," she whispered, her shoulders rolling forward as she conceded defeat. "I'll go if he allows it. I'll...I'll do whatever you like."

Anne stepped forward and her concern was plain on her face. "Juliana, if you—"

She held up a hand and forced a smile. "I should put together some things. Why don't you and Thomasina go down and make sure things have gone smoothly with Father and your husbands?"

She could see they wanted to argue, but they didn't. They simply moved to the chamber door.

As they exited, Thomasina turned back and met her gaze. "Despite all the chaos caused by Ellis Maitland for our family, I only hate that man for one thing," she said, her normally sweet and calm voice filled with tension. "And that is making you look as defeated as you do now. For that, I shall never forgive him."

She pivoted then and left Juliana to her packing. But as she rang for Mary, what she thought of instead was how in the world she could go back to what she had been before Ellis had touched her. And if she couldn't, who she would be now.

CHAPTER 14

I f her sisters had vowed her time at Harcourt's estate was not to be a prison, three days in their company had led Juliana to believe it was at least a variation on the theme.

Oh, everyone was very kind. They were gentle with her, almost to the point of treating her like glass. But she was hardly ever left alone. Walks in the garden were with one sister or the other. Or both. She'd played so many games of whist, she thought she had caused herself a wrist injury. Rook danced around the subject of his cousin. Harcourt spoke loudly of *anything* but Ellis or Winston Leonard and smiled at her until she feared his cheeks would crack.

And when she entered a room that was already occupied? Conversation almost always ended abruptly as she was met with false smiles and boisterous welcomes.

She thought she might go mad with it all. And mad with the thoughts of Ellis that haunted her at night. She relived their final conversation over and over, their last kiss. She relived the moment when she realized he had told on her.

She clenched her fists at her sides as she exited her chamber and walked down the hall toward the stairs. She was so torn in her emotions toward Ellis. Hate and desire. Frustration and longing.

How a man could be so many things at once was truly unfair. And so was the fact that she couldn't get him out of her mind no matter how hard she tried.

She walked down the staircase and into the parlor, where she found her sisters and their husbands breaking their fast together. As usual, their conversation stopped as she entered the room.

"Juliana," Harcourt said with a falsely bright smile that did not reach his worried eyes. "You look lovely in that shade of green."

"As does your wife," Juliana said as she moved to the sideboard and pursued the selection of breakfast delicacies. "And Anne."

She glanced at the couples at the table. Perhaps the time had come to simply be direct. As difficult as that prospect was considering she'd always tried to be the peacekeeper.

She sucked in a long, shaky breath and said, "I appreciate all your loving support, but can we *please* stop pretending that everything is normal."

Anne frowned and exchanged a look with Rook. The connection she had once shared exclusively with her sisters was now one she shared with her husband. In fact, it was even more powerful. Juliana gaped at what she couldn't ignore. And flinched at the jealousy it engendered in her. She didn't want to feel this way about Thomasina and Anne.

She stepped away from the sideboard and faced her family. "I would like to take a walk." Both her sisters scrambled to their feet, but Juliana held up a hand. "Oh please, please don't."

Thomasina cocked her head. "Don't what?"

Juliana let out a long sigh. She motioned her sisters back to their seats and took her own with a thud. "I adore you all for wanting to make things easier for me. I truly do. Harcourt, your home has been a refuge for me from my father, and I know that was a hard-won battle to allow it even for a short time. But I am stifled by all your attempts to protect me and convince me that everything is fine and normal."

Anne and Thomasina exchanged a look, and then Anne

surprised her by slowly nodding. "I can...understand that," she said. "I suppose we have been a bit overly effusive. But you know, neither of us has ever been as good as you are at putting others at ease. At fixing broken wings."

Juliana smiled at the statement. "I love that you want to. But... but perhaps some wounds just need to heal on their own. And we can't pretend them away."

Harcourt reached out and briefly covered her hand with his, surprising her by squeezing gently. "I have sometimes felt the same. I apologize for my part."

"As do I," Rook added. "So what would *you* like to do?"

Juliana considered the question for a moment. Then she said, "I'd like to take a walk in the park. I need some air and a little time alone. Obviously I'll have Mary with me."

Harcourt's lips thinned. "And a guard."

Juliana stared at him. "You—you think that is necessary?"

Thomasina nodded. "We all know Winston Leonard is likely still somewhere in London."

Juliana shuddered. "I suppose you are right. I doubt he would have an interest in me, for I have nothing to offer him. But I would not want to tempt that fate considering my last encounter with that monster."

Anne swallowed hard. "We told you that you weren't a prisoner here. I think we must follow through on that. Though when you return, I would very much like to have tea with you. Just us sisters. Just like old times."

Juliana let her breath out in shaky relief. "Yes. I would love that."

And she meant it. She *wanted* the normalcy that afternoon tea with her sisters would bring. And her walk would help her clear her mind to do her own part in that gathering. The rest of her family said their farewells as she slipped from the room.

It didn't take long for her to speak to Mary, get ready and exit the home. A man from Harcourt's household trailed behind them as they strolled down the street and into the park across the way.

It was not the biggest park in London, but it was a nice little escape from the busy roads and loud commotion of the street. Juliana began to relax as she and Mary strolled, talking quietly of the blooming flowers and the sunny day. She would have felt normal except for the quick glances of those they passed. They were greeted by many who were partaking in the beauty of the park, but she also felt eyes on her scar.

Felt the judgment that came with both her name and her face. A judgment she would face for the rest of her life now. The only place she hadn't felt it lately was with Ellis. When she was with him, she felt...normal. Like herself, though it was a new self. She also felt as if she could take time to discover who that new self would be.

She shook her head to clear her thoughts of Ellis. He didn't want her. Why did she keep forgetting that? She had to accept it if she were to move on.

She and Mary rounded the corner of the path and she staggered to a stop. There, standing on the little bridge that crossed a small creek cutting through the park, was the Duke of Coningburgh, the father of Winston Leonard. He was standing on the bridge with his daughter, a young woman named Lydia who was just a few years younger than Juliana.

She stepped forward, hands shaking as she neared them. "L-Lady Lydia?"

The young woman jolted at her name being said and glanced around her father toward Juliana. Her gaze flickered over Juliana's scar and then darted away. "Miss Juliana Shelley," she said. "How lovely to see you."

Juliana fought to keep her smile as Mary stepped away to give them privacy. Juliana's entire life she had wished on so many stars that people might one day see her as separate from her sisters. That she might be identified on her own merit. Well, she had finally received that desire. Just not the way she had wished.

"And you," she said with a slight curtsey for Lady Lydia and her father. "Good afternoon, Your Grace."

The duke gave her a slight nod and his gaze lingered on her face a moment, as well. He seemed uncomfortable and cleared his throat slightly. "Miss Shelley. Many felicitations on the marriages of both your sisters," he grunted. "Your father must be... er...pleased?"

She pursed her lips at the tone of the question that implied Thomasina and Anne had not made good marriages. Of course that would be the gossip considering all the circumstances, but she refused to participate in the speculation.

"We are all deliriously happy for them. It is not often there is not one, but two, love matches in a family, and so close together," she said with a genuine smile.

Lady Lydia looked a bit wistful. "That is wonderful."

Juliana shifted slightly, darting her gaze to the duke once again. "And how is your family? Are all three of your brothers in Town?"

Lydia's cheeks paled a fraction and her smile fluttered as if it were an effort to hold it. "Yes, indeed. My eldest two are busy with their duties and the Season and—"

"Only the elder two are in Town," Lord Coningburgh interrupted with a shake of his head. "My daughter is mistaken."

Juliana's heart leapt. He was lying. And not doing a very good job of it, based on the sticky sweat on his brow and the shifting of his weight. He looked...frightened.

And Lady Lydia appeared confused. She glanced at her father and almost seemed as though she would correct him. Then her lips pursed and she pivoted away from him. Juliana recognized her expression. It was one of a woman who was always left to pick up the pieces. It seemed she and the lady had more in common than she had thought in their brief acquaintance.

Juliana feigned bored politeness. "So Lord Winston has not joined you? That is a shame. What is it that tempts him away from the pleasures of the Season?"

Lydia arched an almost challenging brow at her father and he glared at her in response. "Business in the country," he grunted.

"Come now, Lydia. We must be off. It was a pleasure seeing you again, Miss Shelley."

"And you, Your Grace," Juliana said softly. "Lady Lydia."

Lydia shot her an apologetic look and then trailed after her father, who had headed across the park at a swift clip. Juliana watched them closely and saw how upset Lydia looked as she spoke to her father in the distance. Saw the duke cast a quick, furtive glance back at Juliana.

Once again, his fear was palpable. It caused a ripple effect through her body. The Duke of Coningburgh was a powerful man. Everyone knew that. He had maneuvered through the world using his position and his vast wealth to get whatever he wanted. And yet he was afraid of his youngest son. Deeply afraid.

Which made Juliana sharply aware of how dangerous the situation was. She faced Mary with a shake of her head. "We should go back," she said.

Mary wrinkled her brow. "But we've only just arrived. Did you not want to walk?"

"Something has come up and I need to speak to my family," she explained. "Come along."

Mary followed, uncertainty lining her face, as Juliana all but ran back to Harcourt's. She burst through the door, past the confused-looking butler and down the hall toward the breakfast room. The others were still gathered there, though their meal was almost finished. When she burst through the door, they all pivoted and stared at her in surprise.

"You're back early," Thomasina said. "Is everything all right?"

Rook pushed to his feet, his gaze narrowing on her. "What happened?"

She caught her breath. He could read her the same way Ellis could. A fragment left from the street, she supposed, where every tiny nuance had to be evaluated.

"I just spoke to the Duke of Coningburgh," she declared.

The rest of her family jumped up and a cacophony of responses echoed in the room.

"Juliana, I thought you were going for a walk!" Anne snapped above the rest. "And you go to put yourself in danger again?"

"I didn't go to put myself in danger," Juliana said back with a glare for her sister. "I entered the park and almost immediately saw him with his daughter, Lady Lydia, on the bridge. It was an opportunity I would have been a fool not to pass up. Of course I approached them."

Harcourt ran a hand through his hair. "This is exactly why we have all been watching you so closely since your arrival. You have been so reckless, Juliana."

She folded her arms. "As if any of you have any ability to discuss recklessness. Don't you want to know our conversation?"

Anne stepped forward. "Of course."

"He lied to me about Leonard being in town," Juliana burst out, and waited for them to recognize the importance of that statement.

Instead, Thomasina rushed forward, her cheeks pale, and caught Juliana's hands in hers. "You spoke to him directly about Leonard?"

"Reckless," Harcourt added.

Juliana shook her sister's hands away and backed up. "I didn't just go to him and say, 'Please tell me where your criminal son is because I want revenge after he scarred my face.' I'm not so much a fool as you all seem to believe."

That settled the room a fraction and Anne drew a long breath. "What *did* you say?"

"He offered felicitations on the marriages of my sisters," she said. "And that allowed me the opportunity to ask after his sons. And if you would stop screeching at me over my supposed irresponsibility, you would understand what I discovered. He lied and said Leonard wasn't in Town."

Rook had been very quiet during the exchange, but now he stepped forward. "He might not know the truth, Juliana."

"He did," she insisted, frustration at not being heard rising up in her. "Lady Lydia at first tried to say all three of her brothers were in London, but he interrupted and contradicted her, then he all but fled the park. He looked *afraid*."

"Then he is more intelligent than you are," Harcourt snapped. "God's teeth, Juliana. Coningburgh has separated himself from Leonard for years, protecting him but hardly associating with him. The lie could be as simple as not wanting to face embarrassment."

"Or it could be for some other reason," she gasped. "You will not even consider it? Or that Leonard's family could be a quick conduit to finding him and handling this mess?"

Rook stepped closer again. She could see he was more open to what she was suggesting, but when he took her hand, there was pity in his eyes. She tried to jerk away from it, but he held fast.

"I know you want to resolve this issue," he said softly. "I cannot blame you, for you have perhaps suffered most from consequences of actions that were not your own. Harcourt and I are not ignoring your instincts, Juliana. But truly, you cannot involve yourself in this. You've gone through enough."

She did manage to pull herself free of him then and glared at those in the room. "I am not made of glass," she hissed through clenched teeth. "Stop treating me as though I were."

With that, she pivoted on her heel and stalked to the door.

"Wait," Thomasina called after her. "Where are you going?"

"Back to my prison cell," Juliana said as she exited the room, and was pleased the tears in her eyes didn't thicken her voice. "It seems to be the only place you think I belong anymore."

CHAPTER 15

Ellis threw the papers in his hand on his desk in frustration and downed the remainder of the whisky in his glass in one burning swig. Days and days of trying to find Leonard had produced nothing. His entire network was silent. It didn't seem the bastard had left London, but he also hadn't come out again since that night at the Donville Masquerade. Rivers hadn't seen him. *No one* had seen him.

It was infuriating. Ellis had almost had the murderer. Winston Leonard had been five feet away, looking right at him. A well-placed pistol shot in the alley and he could have taken care of this problem. Except...

Well, he'd chosen to protect Juliana instead.

He didn't regret that part. He didn't regret anything except that she had made no effort to contact him since he'd told Rook the truth about her whereabouts. That silence spoke volumes about what that betrayal had caused. What her feelings were about the subject.

Ellis knew she was staying with her sisters now. That was something, at least. Rook would keep an eye on her. He would keep her safe, and that allowed Ellis to focus on matters at hand, as he should have from the very beginning.

Not that he was doing a very good job of that. He had dreamed of Juliana every single damned night since the last one he'd been with her.

"The woman is a menace," he muttered beneath his breath as she pushed the papers on his desk around as if he would possibly find the answers he sought by doing so.

The door to his study opened and Golden Mitchell entered the room without knocking. "Boss," he said as he stepped up to the sideboard and poured himself a drink.

"Make yourself at home," Ellis grumbled, more irritated with himself than Golden.

Golden shot him a glance and then inclined his head. "Will do."

"What's your report?" Ellis said on a sigh as he returned to his seat. Golden had been following the Duke of Coningburgh the last few days. Ellis had no hope Golden's report would offer any leads. None of the others had. He was beginning to lose hope. And gain fear.

He knew Winston Leonard wasn't hiding because his pursuit of vengeance and pain was through. He was only making plans. Ones that might involve injury to Ellis's cousin, to his brother...

"Toff went to the park today with his daughter," Golden said, and drew Ellis's attention back to him.

Ellis rolled his eyes. "*Please* don't give me a report on silk gowns or I shall sack you."

Golden chuckled. "No silk. But they *were* met by someone *you* might have an interest in."

Ellis jumped up. "Leonard?"

"Naw, he's still below ground." Golden arched a brow. "How about that little chit you like so much? Juliana Shelley."

Ellis's lips parted at the shock of that statement. "Juliana met with Coningburgh?" he repeated.

Golden shrugged. "Might have been a chance meeting. Didn't

last long. But that pretty little thing was certainly interested in the pair long after they left."

"Was she with my cousin or her sisters?" Ellis asked. "Or the earl?"

"By herself. Well, almost." Golden took another swig of his drink. "There was a guard on her. Not one of Rook's, one of Harcourt's." Ellis could tell Golden was disgusted by that piece of information. "Oh, and that comely maid of hers. They marched right over to the duke soon as they saw him. Miss Shelley might be your better spy, Handsome."

Ellis ran a hand through his hair. Golden was repeating, almost verbatim, the suggestion Juliana had made herself a few days before. But he hadn't wanted to involve her in the danger. He'd thought Rook would protect her, so he'd betrayed her.

And yet here she was, running around with only some fop's inept guard and a lady's maid. Directly speaking to a man whose interest Ellis hadn't fully determined.

The Duke of Coningburgh was both protector and victim of the dangerous man he'd sired. He'd helped Winston Leonard out of many a jam over the years, helping to create the untouchable veneer that shone over that bastard.

But he'd also been attacked and fleeced by the man. And had occasionally lamented his son in public spheres.

Was Coningburgh helping Leonard now? Well, Ellis didn't have the kind of connections that made finding that answer easier. He rubbed a hand over his temple. "Is she still with Rook at Harcourt's?"

Golden nodded. "Coningburgh went home and *she* walked back to Harcourt's estate. Hasn't left according to the man I put on the house." He opened his mouth and then shut it again.

Ellis arched a brow at the hesitance. "What?"

Golden held up his hands. "Don't know. Just haven't ever seen you so flummoxed by a chit before, that's all. Not sure I won't step in it."

"Fucking step in it," Ellis grunted. "What?"

"I wonder what she said to him, that's all," Golden said. "His face was dour as he got in the carriage. His daughter was angry. She sparked a reaction, that's all. Makes me wonder how."

Ellis chuckled despite the dire situation. "Just by being her lovely, wonderful, utterly frustrating self, I would wager."

Both of Golden's eyebrows lifted, and he said, "Should I put someone on her? Once she moved to Rook's protection I took them off, but—"

"No," Ellis interrupted. "If you put someone on her, Rook will catch on. I'll go myself and speak to her."

"And how will you keep Rook from knowing *you're* there?" Golden asked.

Ellis shrugged. "I just have to give the dogs a bone."

Golden wrinkled his brow at the reference he didn't understand. Then he said, "Anything else?"

"Just keep on Coningburgh," Ellis said with a sigh. "He seems to be all we have right now."

"Will do." Golden slugged the remaining liquor back in one shot and then cracked the glass down on the tabletop with a satisfied *ahhhh* before he exited the room with a false salute.

Leaving Ellis to ponder the fact he had just agreed to go interrogate Juliana Shelley. And he wasn't sure if that would end in tears or something far more pleasurable. It all depended on how much control he could muster.

Juliana sat at her dressing table, staring at herself in the mirror as Mary stroked the brush through her hair. Since her excursion to the park and unexpected encounter with the Duke of Coningburgh, she had locked herself in her chamber, stewing. Then reading. Then stewing again.

Her sisters had tried to reach out, both individually and

together, but she had not been in the mood. Currently she was in the mood for very little except a good book and then a night's sleep that she prayed would clear her spinning mind and let her decide what to do next.

Did she let go of her involvement in the pursuit of Winston Leonard as her family and Ellis so desperately wanted her to do? Or did she just hurtle herself into danger and find a way to break out of their intense rules?

"You are far away, miss," Mary said as she set the brush down.

Juliana shook her head. "It was a long day," she admitted.

Mary glanced at her in concern. "Will you need anything else before you take to your bed?"

"No," Juliana said with a pat on her maid's hand. "Thank you."

Mary gave a little nod, then slipped from the chamber, leaving Juliana alone at last. She sighed as she tightened her robe around her waist and stepped from her dressing chamber to her bedchamber. She moved to the bed, happy that her sheets were already turned down and all she had to do was slip into the coolness.

Of course, she would likely stare at the canopy for a few hours. Stewing again.

"That is not the expression of a lady prepared for happy dreams," came a voice from the darkest corner of her room.

She turned toward it with a gasp, knowing the owner of said voice even before he rose and stepped into the light.

"Ellis," she whispered, letting her gaze roll over him. Dear Lord, but the man was handsome. She always told herself he couldn't be as beautiful as she remembered, and he always was.

Tonight, his crisp white shirt was rolled to the elbow, revealing muscular forearms. He was not wearing a cravat and his dark hair was slightly mussed. Perhaps from whatever method he had used to sneak into her chamber.

She blinked as the situation became clearer. He was here. Why was he here?

She hardened herself as she recalled his actions of a few days ago and folded her arms across her chest in a flimsy shield. "What do you want?"

He lifted both eyebrows. "A cold greeting."

"Do you think you deserve a warmer one?" she asked, lunging toward him even though closer was more dangerous. "You told Rook about...about the Donville Masquerade."

How she hated that her voice broke. That heat filled her cheeks. He would see that. He would know his power. Not that he already didn't.

He arched a brow and lifted a finger to his lips in a shushing motion. "If you bring the household running by shouting, we won't be able to speak."

She tilted her head. "You arrogant arse. Do you think I *want* to speak to you?" She asked the question, but she had lowered her voice and they both knew it.

"I told Rook about your activities because you are so stubborn that I feared for your safety," he explained, and for a moment she saw the pure exhaustion in his eyes. "Juliana, I *feared* for you."

"You *humiliated* me," she corrected softly, trying not to think of the confrontation with her sisters when they'd told her what he'd done. "And by doing so, you made it very, very clear that you don't want me or my help. So, I repeat my question, *why are you here?*"

He held her gaze evenly. "You spoke to the Duke of Coningburgh today."

Her eyes went wide at that statement, made with such certainty and without hesitation. How would he know that? "Rook told you?"

He blinked. Once again, the mask he wore slipped and she saw the true pain at the mention of his cousin. "No," he said softly. "Rook has made it patently clear I have no place in his life."

She wrinkled her brow. "Then who?" He hesitated, and her jaw dropped as the only other explanation became clear. "You have people following me?"

He shook his head. "Not *you*, angel."

She turned her face. God, she was such a fool, to think he cared enough to track her movements. Of course he didn't. None of this had ever been about her.

"Once I was sure you were here with Rook, I knew you would be protected," he explained. "Or thought I knew. No, I've had men on Coningburgh for days. I think he might be the conduit to Leonard."

She nodded, and for a moment her tangled feelings were forgotten. "That's what *I* said to Rook and Harcourt and my sisters, but they refuse to listen. They can only focus on what I did. They only wanted to scold me for endangering myself."

"Which you did," he interjected.

She glared at him. "I saw the man in a public park and I have a passing acquaintance with his daughter, as we are of an age. It wasn't untoward for me to greet them. Nor to ask after their family. In fact, it would have been rude not to do so."

The corner of his lip quirked up and the dimple in his cheek made itself known. "That's how you did it. Clever girl."

She blushed at the compliment, given without fanfare. She blushed further at the way his gaze flitted over her again. With desire. She knew it. She felt it, regardless of how angry she was at him. How frustrated she was by everything else happening around her.

"*You* are the only one who thinks so," she said, turning away from him with a shrug. Breaking eye contact seemed to be the only protection from the feelings he stirred deep in her stomach. Lower still.

He laughed softly. "They *did* scold you."

"I assume you are here to do the same," she said, facing him.

He seemed to ponder that thought for a moment. Consider the benefits and disadvantages of doing just that. Then he moved closer. "No. I just want to know what he said."

She frowned. Her body reacted of its own accord, softening and wanting. But her mind? That stayed clear and it saw the truth. Ellis hadn't come here for *her*, no matter how he sauntered and smiled.

That was all his act. His love game, he called it. One he had played dozens of times and with dozens of women.

Juliana was a mark to him. He wanted something she had. Not money or jewels or whatever else he had seduced out from under those women he'd slid into his bed. No, she had information. And he expected her to give it over because she was so enamored with him.

Once she did so? She was certain he would then lecture her about her safety again, push her away "for her own good," and *she* would be left out in the cold. Just as she was left out by her family.

So, even though it was almost impossible to resist him, she shook her head. "No."

His eyes widened. "No?"

"Have you never heard that word before from the women you use that...that...that *ridiculous* smile on?" She folded her arms and put on a false voice, "*Oh, I'm Ellis Maitland and I'm so handsome. I'm Ellis Maitland and I can do magical things with my tongue.*"

"Magical," he repeated, stifling a smile at her mocking instead of being offended by it as she had intended.

She threw up her hands. "Let's not toy with each other. We *both* know what you can do. But it's a weapon, Ellis. And you think by snaking over to me so seductively that I'll just faint onto my bed and let you kiss the truth out of me on your terms. But I won't. I'm no fool."

He looked her up and down for a long moment. "You're definitely not that. You're not like anyone I've ever known."

"*Stop complimenting me!*" she growled. "It won't work." It *was* working, but she refused to show him that. "I didn't go talk to Coningburgh for you and your purposes, Ellis. I did it for my own." She backed away a step, no matter how hard that was. "Now go away."

The false smile and his seductive bedroom eyes faded away. His jaw tightened and once again he was something more real. There was fear in his stare, strategy, regret. And as drawn as she always was to the act that was Handsome Ellis Maitland, the truth of him moved her more. But she resisted. She had to resist.

"You're going to keep doing this, aren't you?" he said softly. "No matter whose roof you live under, no matter if I push you away to protect you. No matter if your family locks you in a tower. You will keep coming."

She didn't acknowledge the question but stepped a fraction closer. "It isn't your problem, Ellis."

There was a flicker of emotion over his face. A moment of possessive heat. Then he closed the remaining distance between them without breaking her gaze. His fingers lifted and combed through her hair. He used her locks to tug her against him.

"Somehow it is," he whispered as he bent his head and claimed her mouth.

CHAPTER 16

E llis had told himself on the entire ride over here that he would not kiss Juliana. He'd repeated that refrain all the while he climbed the side of the house to her bedroom window. He'd muttered it to himself as he heard her and her maid move around in the opposite chamber and pictured her changing while his cock throbbed.

He'd told himself, and yet here he was, closing his arms around her and pressing his lips to hers. Because she was irresistible. Because she was everything. And he wanted more.

So he took it, bastard that he was, thief that he couldn't help but be. He angled her head gently and drove his tongue between her lips, tasting her, drowning in her. He felt her stiffen but then melt, surrendering despite her outright refusal to give him what he wanted.

She still desired what he had to give in return. *That* was her weakness, one he could exploit. Unfortunately, it was one he shared, which meant he could as easily fall victim to it as she did.

He leaned back and stared down at her with her blonde locks spilling around her shoulders, in her thin night rail that was almost see through in the fire, with her eyes sparkling with need and anticipation. He'd done seduction. So many times. This felt…different. Dangerous. Unstoppable.

Could he manage it? Could he leverage it? She still wanted to give him her virginity. To have a stolen moment she was certain would never be repeated. He'd denied her that before out of whatever sliver of honor remained in his rotten chest.

That honor was waning thanks to the desperate position he found himself in when it came to Winston Leonard. And when it came to her. Knowing she still wanted his hands on her, his mouth on her, his cock inside of her…that was temptation.

Now it was time to test whether he could win through that temptation, or whether they would burn together, destroyed by it.

"I know what you still want," he said, hearing the strain in his voice.

She pushed from his arms, panting as she smoothed her nightgown and turned away from him. She was fighting this, like a colt trying not to be broken.

"No I don't," she said. "I don't want this."

"Then why did you lift into me when I kissed you?" he asked, stepping up behind her and letting his breath whisper across the bare skin on her shoulder. "Why does your breath hitch? Why did you moan into my lips when they were on yours?"

She tensed and then leaned back a fraction. Enough that she brushed against him. Her shoulders against his chest. Her hair against his chin. He sucked in a breath of vanilla and citrus. He drowned in it.

"I can scent your desire on the air," he continued. "I know it like I know my own. If I put my hand between your legs, put my mouth there as I did before, you would be wet for me. You would be ready for me. Deny it. Tell me it isn't true. Tell me you aren't pulsing for me right now, on the edge of release. Ready to beg for more."

She made a soft sound in her throat, but she didn't turn toward him. "I-I *can't* want this. Because I *know* you'll use it against me."

He frowned. She wasn't wrong. But he didn't like that she saw him for who he was. He didn't like that he was what she believed because she deserved more.

"True," he said slowly. "But I'm not lying to you about that, Juliana. I do want something you have beyond your body. I want your information. I-I need your help even if I've fought against it until now."

She turned then, her eyes wide. "You admit it?"

"Yes," he said, ducking his head though he felt his cheeks heat. "I can access a great many things and places, but not like you can. I need your help. And I will repay you not just with protection because I know you're going to get yourself in trouble, but with what you came to the Donville Masquerade for in the first place."

Her lips parted. "I want to be clear."

"In these cases, that's probably best," he drawled.

She didn't smile at his teasing. Her face was entirely serious. "Are you saying that if I help you, if I work with you, then you will... you'll..."

"I'll *fuck* you, Juliana," he said, emphasizing the curse that made her flinch. "I won't make love to you sweetly like a knight in some fairytale that made you swoon as a girl. I won't be cruel, but I won't be gentle. I will lick you and touch you, I will have you begging. I will take that silly thing you've been told to protect your whole life, and I will destroy it. I will make you come. I will mark you with my body. And I will be certain you like every minute of it. *That's* what I'll do."

Her eyes were wide as saucers, her pupils dilated until there was almost no green left and her breath came short and fast. She stared at him, gape mouthed.

He smiled. "Is that a fair trade, Miss Shelley?"

He could see her considering it. See her wondering if she should just scream and bring the household running to save her. But then she nodded. "A very fair trade," she gasped out. "But you've already proudly declared that you are a thief and a liar, so I must insist on one thing in this exchange."

He nodded. "And what is that?"

"You give first."

His eyes widened at the brash demand, delivered without hesitation even if her hands were clenched at her sides, shaking like a freshly fallen leaf. That was all there was to it in the end. She was offering herself. He was going to take her.

There was nothing left to say except, "That's a bargain."

The words left his lips and then he tugged her forward, letting her collide against his chest as he ducked his head to kiss her again. This time there was only surrender, no hesitation as she lifted on her tiptoes, wrapped her arms around his neck and clung to him as she drove her tongue into his mouth.

She was aggressive in her desperation and he loved it, even if she was a little clumsy. Her ardor made him mad, his cock responded by easing to attention and throbbing in a constant code for him to spread her wide and fuck her hard.

But he ignored that. Ignored how she pushed him to that very end. He knew this wouldn't be the only time they did this. It was clear to him that once he touched her, he would want to do it until he'd squeezed every drop out of the pleasure. But it was the first time he'd take her. The first time she'd ever be taken.

He wanted it to be a happy memory for her, even when he was but a faint recollection of a dead man who had taken advantage of her desire. He wanted her to wake in the night with his name on her lips in pleasure, not as a nightmare.

So he stepped back, ignoring the part of him that screamed to press her against the wall and rut. He steadied her, then he unbuttoned his shirt and tugged it over his head to stand before her half naked. And just as he'd hoped they would, her eyes boggled.

Oh yes, this was going to be a great deal of fun. One last hurrah for Handsome Ellis Maitland.

Juliana wetted her lips as she stared at Ellis's half-naked form. Great God, but he was perfect. And imperfect. Both at the same time. He had toned shoulders, though they were marked with scars, not the least of which was the red mark left by the gunshot weeks ago.

"Does it hurt?" she whispered.

"Nothing hurts right now," he murmured.

She let her gaze flit lower to his broad chest, peppered with hair and a stomach that should not have had so many hard crests of muscle. It was as if he had been built out of her every secret fantasy and then dropped into her bedchamber.

He was...beautiful.

"No wonder they call you Handsome," she said, almost against her will. "No wonder love games are your bread and butter on the street."

"Were. And this isn't a love game," he assured her, his voice rough. "Because you are playing me as much as I'm playing you. Don't forget that, Juliana. You've broken my control, forced me to come to your bed, against all the very good arguments I've made to myself not to do it. I'm here and you are in control of me as much as I am of you. If you say no, I stop. If you say more..."

He trailed off and her eyes went wide as he winked at her.

"If I say more?" she whimpered.

He reached out and caught her nightgown strap between his fingers. He rolled the silk gently before he said, "Then I will give you all you can take."

With that, he flicked the strap down and tugged her nightgown to bunch at her waist. He'd seen her like this before, of course. Not that many nights ago at the Donville Masquerade he had stripped her entirely naked and licked her until the explosion of pleasure was undeniable. She wanted that again. She wanted so much more.

Was he telling the truth when he promised her the rest? It was time to find out. She shook her hips and slid the nightgown the rest of the way down.

He smiled at her, chuckling softly. "Always your own way, Juliana. Always in your own time."

"Not always," she corrected.

"Tonight, then," he promised. Then he pulled her against him again.

Her naked chest brushed his equally bare one, and she cried out at the sensation of flesh on flesh. That was a new one, and she liked the roughness of his hair against her sensitive skin. He closed his hands around her bare bottom and cupped her closer, his mouth finding hers as he ground her against him.

She lifted her mouth to his, drowning in him. For a moment, that was all the sensation her mind could process, but then her body began to awaken to other feelings. His fingers digging into her skin. The heat of his chest, the rasp of his whiskers as his chin abraded her own.

And the hard thrust of him bumping her stomach even through his trousers. It felt very strong, very big, and she shivered at the idea that she would soon see that thing she'd only ever imagined from crudely drawn pictures in a book. That it would enter her as she had dreamed of for months.

If he sensed her drive to rush, he ignored it. His kiss gentled, if anything. His fingers slid up her bare back, into her hair. He tilted her head back, he kissed her more deeply. She was lost in him and she never wanted it to end.

He slid a hand beneath her knees, and suddenly she was off her feet. She gasped against his mouth but never broke contact as he carried her to her bed and laid her against the pillows. Only then did he step away.

"Oh no, please don't," she protested, reaching out for him when she believed he would walk away from her again.

He shook his head. "Not even if I wanted to, angel. I'm here until the end."

She relaxed a fraction at that declaration and settled back, watching as he reached for his trousers. This was the moment. One she had feared and longed for and believed might never happen.

He unfastened the fall front of his trousers and let it drop away. She gasped, for his member—a cock, the book had called it—bobbed free. It was hard, curling toward his stomach at attention.

She leaned closer, trying to get a better look. He laughed and stepped in so that he was within arm's reach. And reach she did, brushing her fingers along the shaft and letting them trail over the mushroom head.

"The skin is very soft," she declared, mesmerized by this part that was so different from her own body. "Will it truly fit?"

He nodded. "Like a dream. Like I was made for you."

She wrapped her hand around him and stroked. To her surprise, he let out a garbled moan that sounded very much like her own gasp of pleasure when he touched her.

"You like that?" she asked, lifting her brows as his face contorted with pleasure. She stroked again and he cried out her name in the quiet room. She smiled, power filling her. "Shh now, Mr. Maitland. What was it you said about bringing the house down on us and we wouldn't get to…talk?"

"I very much want to *talk*," he gasped. "But if you keep doing that, the conversation will be over too quickly."

"Hmmm," she murmured, and stroked him one last time, eliciting a curse so salty that her ears burned. Then she let him go and settled back on the pillows. She opened her legs, thinking of the illustrations in the book, and sighed. "Come and show me then."

He wrinkled his brow. "That is the most unromantic invitation I've ever received. After I have licked you to completion and kissed you until you were breathless and promised you orgasms that would shake your legs to exhaustion—do you really think *that* is how it works?"

"I don't know how it works," she admitted with a roll of her eyes. "*You're* supposed to teach me."

Once again he laughed and her chest swelled. She'd expected this to be fraught, and it was. The tension between them was high, the future so cloudy that it was impossible to see.

But he also made it…easy. He made it fun. She never wanted that to end, even if she knew it would.

He crawled up on the bed, gliding over her like a cat the same way he had back in the Donville Masquerade. Only this time he was naked and his cock bumped her thigh as he lowered himself over her. His mouth found hers again and he kissed her, this time gently. Almost reverently. Like a bridegroom tending to his bride on the sacred night of their wedding.

She pushed that thought from her mind and wrapped her arms around him, and all but melted into the pillows. His hands moved as he kissed her, fingertips tracing her collarbone, her shoulder, down her side, her hip. She arched beneath him with a whimper, sucking his tongue a little harder in mute demand. He flexed his hips in response, his cock bumping her harder.

Then his mouth glided away, down the side of her throat. He sucked her flesh just to the edge of pain, but never beyond, nibbling as he made a lazy path along her shoulder, down her chest, to her breast. She was ready for him this time in a way she hadn't been the first time. When he caught her nipple between his teeth and tugged gently, she dug her hands into his thick hair and held him there so he could suck and circle and pleasure her.

He did all those things, taking his time as he set her body on fire. He repeated all those actions on the opposite breast and then moved lower, down the apex of her body. She shivered as his finger dug into her hips, holding her steady as he rubbed the rough whiskers on his cheek against her belly. Her breath hitched at the sensation and she whispered his name in encouragement.

Not that he needed any. The man seemed utterly focused and utterly certain of every move he made as his lips slid over her belly. Lower. Closer to her sex.

She wanted him there, so very badly. She wanted that intense explosion she'd been trying to replicate since almost the moment the ripples faded. She wanted him between her legs, those blue eyes watching her as he drove her mad with pleasure.

He grinned as if he could read her mind and pushed her legs wide with his shoulders as he settled between them. But he didn't put his mouth there. Instead, he gently traced her outer lips with his fingertips. Too gently. She wanted more.

"Have you touched yourself?" he asked, using his thumbs to peel her open and expose her to his gaze.

Heat flooded her cheeks, but she nodded. "Yes."

"Before I touched you?" he pressed, massaging gently.

"Yes," she gasped, for when he touched her just so her body reacted like it was flint to a dry piece of timber. "And since."

"Very good," he whispered, and bent his head, licking the length of her with one sweep. She hissed at the electric pleasure of it, but he drew back instead of repeating the action. "And have you ever put a finger inside of yourself?"

She lifted her head a fraction to stare down at him. She worried her lip as she shook her head. "N-No."

He arched a brow and reached up to catch one hand. He drew it down, pressed a kiss to her palm and then settled it between her legs so that her fingers tangled with his own. "Do it."

"Aren't you meant to—"

"I will, angel. I will," he promised, those blue eyes dilating as his smile grew even more wicked than before. "But I want you to understand your body. I want you to know what will happen. To help me make it less painful."

She swallowed. Yes, she'd heard all about the pain from grumpy female relatives who told her and her sisters to lay back and think of their duty. But her sisters had whispered far different tales when it came to what was about to happen. Stories of pleasure and bonding and a deepening of connection that changed everything.

Juliana chose to believe them. She brought herself up on one elbow and positioned her fingers at her entrance. It was wet already, both from Ellis's tongue and from her own increasing excitement, so when she slid her fingers over herself, there was only powerful pleasure. She ground against herself a little with a tiny moan.

"Great God," he muttered, shifting against the bed. "You'll unman me before I even put myself inside of you."

"How is that possible?" she asked, her tone garbled as she pressed her fingers harder to her clitoris.

"Because watching you do that is infinitely arousing," he grunted, his gaze focused on the show she was performing. "Now gently press a finger inside."

She nodded and pressed her index finger to her entrance. Slowly, she breached the entrance, wiggling her way into the tight channel. Inside was warm, wet, the flesh a little rough. It wasn't an unpleasant sensation, but it felt very tight. When she moved her finger, there was the tiniest flash of pain.

She glanced at him. "I can hardly bear this. How will I take that?"

He shrugged. "It will stretch. We'll go slowly." He leaned in. "May I?"

She nodded as his fingers tangled with hers. He pressed a thumb to her clitoris, swirling it there with expert pressure as he encouraged her to thrust the finger she'd put inside herself. As she did so, she dipped her head back. Oh, that was good. That felt very good. So good that she hardly noticed when he placed one of his own fingers at her entrance. Then he was inside and the channel stretched a bit more to accommodate. Their fingers touched and she opened her eyes.

He held her stare and smiled as she circled her hips against his hand, against her own. The pleasure increased as they ground together, dragging her to the edge of the cliff where she could feel what was about to happen.

And then she was flying. She bit her lip to muffle her cries as wave after wave of deep, powerful pleasure ripped through her. Her body rippled around her finger, clenching even tighter as her orgasm peaked. He moved his finger harder inside of her, his breath coming fast and sharp as her climax subsided in a series of twitching waves.

Only when she had let her hand fall away from her body did he do the same. He held her gaze as he lifted his fingers to his mouth and licked them clean. Her body shuddered at the action and she reached for him. He caught her hand, tugging her to an upright position as he swirled his tongue around her own fingers.

"Ellis," she whispered, her voice cracking. "I want this. Please."

He nodded and she saw the intensity of his desire was just as powerful as her own. That he was shaking as he shifted to return up the length of her body. He kissed the same path up as he had down, and by the time his tongue tangled with hers, she was mewling with pleasure, her body on fire for more.

He pulled away from her kiss and smiled at her. "This will be good, angel. I promise you that."

And even though she knew she shouldn't, she believed him.

CHAPTER 17

Juliana tensed as Ellis reached between their bodies and positioned himself at her entrance at last. The thick head of him bumped her slick sex and she shivered at the contact.

He didn't drive forward, though. He didn't take or claim as she'd thought he would.

Instead, he took a long, deep breath and met her stare evenly. "You still want this? Even though you know once it's done, it can never be undone?"

She caught his cheeks and drew him down for a kiss. He didn't resist as she tasted him—tempted him, she hoped. And when she drew away, she nodded. "I want to be undone, Ellis. I want you to be the one who gives me what I need. *Please.*"

He kissed her again, this time harder. This time with less control. She lifted into him, letting her moans and cries be lost in his mouth.

He pushed his hips forward and began to press inside. She parted her mouth from his, staring up at him in wonder as her body stretched to accommodate him. Yes, it stung, but the pain was not so terrible. The pleasure certainly made up for it because *that* sang through her veins at a much higher rate than anything unpleasant.

He was inside of her. They were one body, if only for a moment, and he was finding parts of her she hadn't known existed. New points of pleasure that only he could reach. She lifted against him, kissing his shoulder as he fully seated in her.

He leaned his forehead against hers, their rapid breathing slowly matching as the seconds ticked by. "Pain?" he whispered.

She shook her head. "Not much. I-I like it."

He jerked his head back, and when his gaze met hers, it was so dark and dangerous that a shudder ripped through her and made her tense her sex around him. He grunted out pleasure and then began to slowly move.

His thrusts mimicked those of their fingers earlier, only this time everything felt deeper. Harder. Certainly bigger. She lifted into him, meeting his rhythm out of instinct rather than understanding. And when they were finally in sync, she groaned. The pleasure was so good, so much. Waves of it seemed to work through her whole body as he slowly took her. They built with every thrust, different than every time before.

She rolled with him, kissing him, clinging to his shoulders. She dug her nails into his skin to find purchase, and he smiled against her lips as if he liked that little pain as much as she did. He slid his hand down her thigh, hitching it higher on his hip, changing the angle of his body as he took her.

That tiny adjustment sent a tidal wave of pleasure through her. She flexed her hips harder, faster, trying to drive toward the release she could feel around the edges of their coupling. Needing it like breath.

He didn't deny her. He ground against her, his hand snaking between them to flick against her clitoris. It was too much, it was everything. She gasped out his name as her body twitched out of control. She rocked against him, stealing every drop of pleasure, taking every hint of it until she flopped back, spent with it.

He slammed his hips against her a few more times, then groaned low and loud as he pulled from her and spent between them. He collapsed over her, panting and sweaty. She stroked her hand along his muscled back, crooning empty words against his skin as she licked and sucked his shoulder, his neck.

After a few moments had passed, he lifted his head to look down at her. "Did I hurt you?"

She shook her head. Although they had connected in the most intimate way she could imagine, now she felt shy as he stared at her so closely. He had been inside her body—she wasn't certain she wanted him inside her mind. And a man like Ellis Maitland could invade either one so easily.

"No." She didn't reach for him as he rolled off of her and onto his side next to her. "I'm sore, but not...hurt, if that makes sense."

"Perfect sense," he said, pressing a kiss to her neck that lit her on fire all over again. "A hot bath will ease the ache, I'm told."

She pursed her lips together. "By all those lovers you've deflowered."

He arched a brow. "Jealous, Miss Shelley?" When she didn't answer, he shook his head. "I think you are the first woman I've ever *deflowered*, as you put it."

The shock of that fact rocked her, and she stared at him in disbelief and a little pride, which she hoped she didn't show. "Oh," she said since he seemed to want an answer of some kind.

He chuckled and tucked her into his side, smoothing his hands over her sides. She relaxed at the touch of skin on skin and sighed. "And now you have what you wanted," he mused. "Your pesky virginity is gone. I hope you don't regret it."

"I don't," she said as she traced little circles on his chest with her fingertips. "But I suppose now that I have what I bargained for, you would like the same."

He leaned back. "That was our arrangement, wasn't it?"

He didn't sound particularly pleased by that reminder, but she ignored it. She was probably imagining that hint of wistfulness. A man like Ellis didn't give a damn about sex. He was versed in pleasure and it meant little to him beyond the moment certainly. She had to harden herself in the same way.

She cleared her throat. "That's fair. The Duke of Coningburgh lied to me when I asked after his family. Specifically, when it came to my supposedly innocent question about whether all his sons were in Town for the Season."

She quickly recounted her conversation with the duke and his daughter. The one her sisters and brothers-in-law had dismissed. But Ellis's gaze lit with interest with every word. As if she had truly contributed something to his cause.

When she had finished, he stroked his hand over his chin as if he were pondering the information. "Rook and Harcourt could be correct that he was simply avoiding embarrassment."

She pulled away from him a fraction as frustration replaced any pleasant emotions their encounter had created. "Then you think me a fool as well?"

"No, I think your explanation is far more realistic. If you say Coningburgh was afraid, then I believe you," he said. "You're certainly one of the most observant people I have ever encountered."

Relief rushed through her, followed by a flush of pleasure she knew she shouldn't dare feel, and yet...

"Thank you," she whispered. "You cannot know how much it means for what I've said to be heard, not dismissed."

"I know a little," he assured her as he took her hand between his own. "What about the daughter, Lady Lydia?"

"I have known Lydia a few years," Juliana said. "We aren't friends, but acquaintances. Still, she seemed confused by her father's lie. And angry when they got into their carriage. She...I think she may bear some of the weight of Leonard's bad behavior. She may have to clean up the mess and it is a frustration to her."

"What makes you think that?" Ellis asked, and seemed genuinely interested in her observation.

She shifted, for that answer was more revealing of herself than perhaps Ellis knew. More revealing than she wanted to be, given the transactional nature of their new arrangement. Did she want to give a part of herself to this man? More of a part than just her body?

The answer was a little terrifying. The answer was that she did want to share her mind and her heart. She wanted to so desperately, even though she knew the end would not go well. Maitland used others. He had declared that himself.

He would certainly be finished with her once this trouble was resolved, and he was ready to throw himself back into his underground life of sex and trickery. A place she most certainly did not belong.

"Juliana?" he asked. "What is it?"

She shook her head. "I…I saw something in her that I…I feel in myself. Perhaps we recognize kindred pains in others."

He stared at her a moment. "You are the one who cleans up the messes," he said softly.

She nodded, but the intensity of the connection was too much. She shrugged like it didn't matter. "Perhaps that is a way to wheedle more information out of Lady Lydia if I were to encounter her and her father again."

He arched a brow. "You think you could arrange that?"

She laughed. "You must know that those of the *ton* are creatures of habit. If the duke walked with his daughter today, that could mean it is a regular occurrence."

"Every day," he mused. "According to those who follow him."

"Then it would be easy to repeat the encounter if I wished to do so," she said.

"You think Rook would let you out of the house without a guard," Ellis said with a laugh she didn't feel contained much true humor.

She folded her arms. "You doubt me? I can surely convince my family that I have abandoned my interest in this topic. And in you. We had a row about it, after all. I pouted and locked myself away. I could tell them that reflection led to realization. And they would believe me. That would leave me much freer to move about the world, I think."

"Then perhaps you and I should encounter the lady and the duke tomorrow."

She stared at him. "Together? What would you say to explain that?"

"You would introduce me as your beau," he explained. "A rich merchant you met while in the country at your sister's wedding celebration. Then I'll be able to see Coningburgh's reaction for myself if we can maneuver the situation to our advantage."

Juliana considered the plan a moment. She certainly wanted her place in this investigation and Ellis was offering it. As a partner, even. Which felt a little different from the arrangement of quid pro quo they had originally discussed.

But not in a bad way.

"Very well. I'll find a way to break out of the prison I've been placed in by my well-meaning sisters and their husbands," she said. "And I will meet you in the park across the way tomorrow afternoon."

He nodded. "With that decided, it would probably be best if I left you," he said, and slipped from her arms. She couldn't help but stare as he rewrapped that beautiful naked body back into some semblance of propriety.

She also couldn't help but lament that this part of their bargain was over.

"I suppose I we won't, er...we won't be doing this again," she said, folding her arms as if she could protect the heart this man was beginning to touch.

He faced her with a look of surprise. "Of course we will. We have entered a bargain now, and that includes pleasure in trade for my assistance. I won't let you wiggle out of it."

"You'll be back?" she gasped, hating how much that meant to her.

He grinned as he backed up to her window and unlatched it with one hand behind himself. "My dear Miss Shelley. I promised you so much more than what I gave tonight in exchange for your help. We are *not* finished. And I will see you in just a few short hours."

Then he was gone, ducking out of the window with frightening ease. She rushed to look, unmindful of her own nudity. But he was nowhere to be seen in the inky dark of the night.

And she was left confused, concerned and wanting so much more. She couldn't wait to see what more entailed.

CHAPTER 18

When Juliana stepped into the breakfast room the next morning, her sisters were at the table, but not their husbands. Both leapt up at the same time, making twin sounds of relief and joy to see her.

For a moment, Juliana felt guilt at what she was about to do and say. But she pushed it aside. She was doing all this to help protect those she loved. She wasn't wrong to wish to do so.

"You look very pretty this morning," Thomasina said as she rushed to embrace Juliana. "You've a glow to you."

Juliana swallowed back a gasp and forced a smile. "I-I must have slept well."

A lie, of course. She'd spent half the night with Ellis and the other half staring at her ceiling, both reliving those powerful, passionate moments and planning for their next move together as partners. If she had a glow, it was from the excitement of those experiences.

"I'm glad you could," Anne said with a smile as she poured her tea and motioned to the sideboard. "I tossed and turned, wondering if you would remain angry with us."

"Anne," Juliana breathed, and in this, at least, she could be honest. "I *do* know that you, Thomasina, Rook and Harcourt all have my best interest at heart. You believe you are protecting me. And I appreciate it even if I might not have always agreed with the methods. Just as you didn't agree with mine." She moved to the sideboard and half-heartedly put a few items on her plate before she joined her sisters at the table.

"I'm happy you do know that," Thomasina said. "I realize things have…changed. For all of us, really. And that adjustment isn't easy. We're all finding our new place in the world."

Juliana flinched. Her new place in their world was alone. After an entire life with her sisters at her side, sharing a face and a connection more powerful than anything else…

Well, that was gone now. Her face wasn't the same anymore. And their connections with their husbands had eclipsed the triplet bond. Juliana was left out in the cold. Her only glimpse into that world a few stolen moments in Ellis Maitland's arms. Moments that would be over soon enough.

"You look far away," Anne said, reaching out to cover her hand.

Juliana forced another smile. The time had come to tell her lies and hopefully gain her freedom. "I suppose I do. After I went up to my room last night, I spent a good deal of time thinking about our… our situation. You are right that I've struggled to find my place now that it is clear I am no longer needed to soothe your wounds."

Thomasina shook her head. "We will *always* need you, Juliana."

Juliana smiled, but she knew it was a sad expression. "But not like before. My life will diverge from both of yours now. You two will eventually have children, probably. You'll take on your roles as wives and mothers, and I—" She choked on the words and it was not pretended. "I will be Father's secretary."

"We're going to work that out," Anne insisted, and the fierce determination on her sometimes reckless sister's face warmed Juliana's heart.

"I thank you for trying. But the best thing I can do for myself is to accept this. Stop fighting."

"What?" Thomasina breathed.

Juliana worried her lip. "My desperation did cause trouble. I shouldn't have tried to insert myself in the investigation Rook and Harcourt are conducting. I've only made it more difficult for you all. I wanted to tell you that I've given that up. I've decided to simply enjoy this time Father is allowing me to stay here. I'm sure he'll call me back within a week, if not sooner. I should revel in the remainder of my freedom with all of you."

"Do you mean it?" Thomasina asked, face lit up with relief.

Anne looked slightly more uncertain. "That is quite the shift from the past few weeks."

"We're all transitioning," Juliana said with a tight smile for Anne. "And last night I feel I was…changed."

Thomasina and Anne exchanged a look, and Juliana held her breath. She could see that unspoken communication they'd always shared flowing between the two of them. If they didn't believe her, she would never be given an inch to help Ellis. But at last they both smiled.

"I'm glad that your time here has allowed you to think more clearly," Anne said. "We should celebrate this! Thomasina, didn't you receive an invitation to tea at Miss Winifred Wallington's house for this afternoon?"

"I did!" Thomasina said. "My first invitation since our return to London. I am very pleased, as I've always liked Winifred. Won't you come with us, Juliana?"

Juliana shifted. There was a part of her that wanted to go to this tea and support Thomasina as she shifted back into Society as a countess. But it also offered her an opportunity.

She lifted her hand to her scarred cheek. "I-I don't think I'm ready," she said, and sought the closest thing to truth there was. "Yesterday in the park, I felt people staring at my face. Heard them whisper. I'm just not comfortable yet. You two should go, though. Enjoy yourselves. I'll stay here and read my book and eat too many biscuits. It will be heavenly."

Anne wrinkled her brow. "Are you certain?"

"I am. But I do want to help pick your outfits." She leaned forward, and now her excitement was true. "Thomasina, do you think the blue silk?"

Thomasina hesitated a moment, but then she laughed and the three began to talk about gowns and hairstyles and who else would be at this important tea. Juliana loved every moment of it, for it was a taste of something more routine after months of anything but.

She only hoped that if she and Ellis could catch and stop the man who threatened all of them, normalcy would be permanent.

E llis shifted his weight as he stood behind the bush outside the servant entrance of Harcourt's home. It was almost two, the exact time Juliana's missive had told him to come. He still had the paper in his pocket and found himself reaching in to touch it from time to time.

The paper was heavy and expensive, her hand flowing and elegant. He had memorized how she wrote his name, *Ellis*, not *Mr. Maitland,* as would be more appropriate. The very act of it was like a caress. And he certainly had more than one memory of those.

He'd sworn so hard and so long that he wouldn't claim her. He had every reason not to ruin her for the future she believed would never come. But he wanted her. More than he'd ever wanted any other woman. So he'd found a way to justify what he'd done, claiming it to be for quid pro quo in their bargain to work together to find Winston Leonard.

The reality was that he knew his time was running out, like desperate sand through an unyielding hourglass. Being with Juliana was a deathbed wish. A final meal before he was marched to the gallows. And because he was exactly the villain he'd always been, he was going to savor that last bit of pleasure even if he knew it was wrong.

The servant entrance opened, and he ducked back into the bushes to keep from prying eyes. But it wasn't a maid or footman who exited. It was Juliana, herself. He caught his breath as she stepped into the bright afternoon sunshine. She was exquisite, from the crown of her blonde head to the tips of her slippered toes. His body went on edge the moment he saw her.

But there was another reaction that struck him as she pulled the door shut behind herself and lifted up on her tiptoes to search the back courtyard for him. His chest stirred with...feelings. Emotions he had carefully trained out of himself over the years he'd performed tricks against ladies of her class. He cared about her. When he looked at her, he didn't just want to touch her and make her shiver with pleasure. He wanted to talk to her. Be near her. He wanted to know her and let her see into what was left of his shriveled heart.

Which made her the most dangerous creature in his life.

"Ellis?" she whispered.

He shook off the unwanted thoughts and stepped from the bushes with his best false smile. "Miss Shelley, fancy meeting you here."

A smile broke over that lovely face and it was brighter than the sun on a cloudless day. "You came," she breathed as she stepped up to him and caught his hand in both of hers.

"Of course I did," he said, trying to ignore the tug on his heart as he tucked her hand into the crook of his arm. It felt far too comfortable there, and he cursed himself. This wasn't good. He needed to distance himself from her a little. For his own good as much as hers. "I need your help—I had to come."

He felt her stiffen at the wall he'd placed between them, but she didn't address it. Instead, she said, "My sisters are at tea. I haven't seen Harcourt or Rook all day."

"They're at Harcourt's club," Ellis explained with a frown. "Trying to use some of Harcourt's connections to get information about Leonard. The house isn't busy with everyone out, but there is a little garden exit back here..." He guided her down and around a few secret paths to the same gate he had used to enter the property not a quarter of an hour before.

"I didn't even know this was here," she admitted as she followed him through and into a back alley behind the house.

He shrugged. "A whole life goes on in this city that you don't know about. Servant entrances and pathways are my specialty, angel."

"We can go around to the park this way," she said, drawing him forward toward the street where they fell into the walking couples and faded into obscurity in a moment. A place he had always been both comfortable and restless. "Are you jealous of Rook and Harcourt?" she asked.

He jolted at the unexpected question and glared down at her. "That's ridiculous. Why would I be jealous?" he snapped, perhaps a bit more sharply than he intended.

She drew a little breath, as if she were considering whether or not she should push. He waited to see what she decided, recognizing she would only pursue an uncomfortable topic if she gave a damn. He didn't know which answer would make him happy, if any.

"You and Rook are family," she said slowly. "You were partners in your endeavors. He credits you for saving him from a fate worse than even a life on the street. When you said he was with Harcourt, I heard that tension in your voice. I'm afraid I recognize it from my own tone."

He glanced at her, surprised by how plainly she could read him. How she could shine a spotlight on a topic he tried to ignore the existence of regularly.

He cleared his throat. "*You* are jealous of Harcourt and Rook?" he teased, trying to break the tension as they entered the park.

She hesitated and stepped off the path to look up at him. "Er... yes. Not of their relationship to each other, as I think you are. But... but the one between each of them and my sisters." She blushed from her hair to the fetching inches of skin that disappeared into her gown's neckline. "I have never admitted that out loud to anyone."

"Things have changed for you in these last few months," he said softly.

She nodded. "I always knew that when we each married, it would be different. We wouldn't be together all the time. But I thought we wouldn't...perhaps we wouldn't care about our husbands that much. Arranged marriages are often loveless, and our father never looked out for our hearts as much as his own designs on elevation. I thought we would still turn to each other for support and friendship. But..."

"But the new couples are in love," he encouraged as gently as he could, since he could see the tears that had flashed into her eyes.

"Deeply," she said with just a touch of bitterness. "And I keep telling everyone who will listen how happy I am. And I am, for they deserve to be in love. But I am...jealous. Both of the fact that they don't need me as much anymore, and of the lives they will live that I will never get a chance to experience. You must think very ill of me."

He chuckled even as he brushed away the single tear that had escaped those beautiful green eyes. "I could never think ill of you," he promised. "No matter what."

Her little smile was so lovely that his heart ached. Then she shook her head. "At any rate, I recognize the emotion because it's so close to me. Things changed for you, too. And I think you are a little jealous that Rook is now working alongside Harcourt. That they are becoming...friends."

Ellis shifted. He hadn't allowed himself to put it so succinctly but there it was. "Rook and I used to talk about 'those fops.' Couldn't understand 'those fops.' Never wanted to be one of 'those fops.'

Wasn't it fun to fool 'those fops.' And now he…I can see he respects Harcourt. And yes…in my darkest hour…when I let myself get maudlin…I suppose I do…feel…a little…jealous."

He drew the last word out and met her gaze. She was nodding, and then she caught his hand. "Rook loves you. It is evident in every word he says about you. Things may change, but the Earl of Harcourt will never truly take your place in his life." She smiled. "We are quite the pair."

"Yes," he said with a sigh. "Aren't we, though."

She looked as if she would say more, but her eyes went wide. "I think the Duke of Coningburgh and his daughter just passed by over there."

Ellis shook his head. He had been so caught up in the grace Juliana had offered him that he had all but forgotten why they were here together. Like a fool, he'd lost track of everything that could kill them both. He glanced over his shoulder and saw a gentleman and lady walking in the opposite direction. "That's him?"

She nodded. "Yes. Now we will approach. You are dressed very nicely. I meant to compliment you earlier. But be very careful in your address and—"

He held up a hand with a grin. "Angel, I have been training for these moments for years. Trust in me."

She tilted her head in disbelief but didn't resist as he guided her forward toward their quarry. The duke and his daughter had stopped by the side of the path to examine a rosebush planed on the perimeter, and as they began to pass by, Juliana put on a false smile and called out, "Lady Lydia, we seem to be making a habit of these meetings."

The two turned, and Ellis watched their reactions. The young lady smiled at Juliana, but there was obvious concern in her gaze. The duke's mouth grew tight. Annoyance. Was it because they were being interrupted? Was it for some more sinister reason? He couldn't yet tell.

"What a pleasure," Lady Lydia agreed. "Wouldn't you say, Papa?"

"Your Grace," Juliana said with the slightest of curtsies. "And may I present my friend, Mr.—"

"Mr. Francis Pettigrew at your service," he said, putting on an American accent.

Juliana stared at him as if he had sprouted a second head, but she rallied admirably. "Er, yes. The Duke of Coningburgh, Mr. Pettigrew. And his daughter, Lady Lydia."

Coningburgh was looking at him with increased interest, and Ellis stifled a smile. Good. "A pleasure to meet you both."

"And how are you acquainted with Miss Shelley, Mr. Pettigrew?" the duke asked.

"I'm in shipping, Your Grace," he said with another boisterous laugh. "And was passing through Harcourt not that long ago. I was well met of Mr. Shelley and his lovely daughters and decided to forgo my travel back home in order to spend a little more time taking in the countryside and all its pleasures."

Lady Lydia tittered. "How lovely."

"Yes, my lady. Very lovely." He lifted his eyebrows toward her and she tittered again. God, some of these women made it too easy. A few well-chosen words and he knew he could have that pretty necklace off without her even caring she'd been taken.

Of course, when he looked at Juliana, she seemed less than impressed at that. She tilted her head at him with pursed lips. He squeezed her hand a little harder and said, "Perhaps you're looking for some endeavors to invest in, Your Grace?"

The duke looked a bit taken aback by the uncouth and direct statement. One Ellis could get away with in his character of American Shipping Magnate. "Er, well, I don't really—"

"Or perhaps your sons might take an interest," Ellis pushed. "I've heard of their daring from many corners. Especially the younger. He is rumored to be interested in endeavors outside of the usual."

Juliana's fingers tightened on his elbow, and he felt her fear just as much as he saw Coningburgh's as Ellis mentioned *Lord* Winston.

"I would not be able to speak for my son, sir. You would have to arrange a meeting with him yourself."

"That would be jolly good," Ellis said. "Perhaps I could press you to help me with the introductions."

"I think it would be best if you sent a card around," Coningburgh muttered. "I could…I don't really know where he is at present, but mayhap he could be found. Now my daughter and I have another appointment. Good day."

He caught Lady Lydia's arm and dragged her away. As they exited the park on the opposite side, Juliana let out a long sigh. "I'm afraid that wasn't very fruitful. Do you fear you pushed too hard?"

Ellis chuckled. "Not at all. I obtained a great deal of information from that encounter. Let's go to my carriage and we shall discuss it."

He led her out the way they'd come and up the street a little where his carriage was waiting. He helped Juliana into the rig, gave the direction to his driver and off they clattered.

She stared at him. "What in the world could you have gotten from that conversation? Coningburgh only looked annoyed."

"No, he looked afraid, just as you said he did. I saw it in his eyes, around his lips. The same was true with your friend, Lady Lydia. Both of them are wound tight as a children's toy, ready to pop. And it only got worse when I made reference to his youngest son."

"His shoulders did tense," Juliana conceded. "But we already knew that he is afraid of Leonard. Everyone knows that."

"When I asked if he might know how to reach him, his hand clenched, he glanced at his daughter ever so slightly. He said no, but there was a slight nod he gave. Do you know how people win at gambling, Juliana?"

She shrugged. "Luck?"

"No." He smiled. "They learn what we call tells. Little actions people make when they're lying. And Coningburgh has a great many. He knows where Leonard is. I'd go so far as to guess he's hiding his son."

They rounded the corner onto Ellis's street, quick and efficient thanks to his driver's knowledge of back roads. "Do you really think we'll be able to find him then?" Juliana asked, her gaze lighting with both excitement and fear. A reflection of his own heart, truth be told.

He nodded. "I do. And once that is done, then everyone in my life will be safe again. This will be taken care of, once and for all, and you'll never need to fear Winston Leonard again."

CHAPTER 19

J uliana watched as Ellis paced the narrow parlor, his minions circled around him, waiting on his every word. "The Duke of Coningburgh has had mistresses, of that I am certain. Find all their hideaways. Find every nook and cranny that fop has created in this world and search them all. *That's* where we'll find Leonard, I would almost guarantee it."

"He'll have some places not on the books," said his right-hand man, who had been briefly introduced to her as Golden. "All the toffs have them."

"Good, use your ways and my money as best you see fit. No stone unturned, do you understand?" Ellis said, and there was a crack of desperation to his tone that made Juliana's eyes go wide. "No expense is too high."

Golden held his stare a moment, then glanced at Juliana. He nodded, then ushered the group out of the parlor, giving orders in the distance until the door closed and she and Ellis were once again alone. Ellis paced to the sideboard and poured himself a drink. After he'd downed half of it, he eyed her furtively. "I don't suppose you want whisky."

She wrinkled her brow. "It's a bit early for whisky for me." She drew in a deep breath and took a step closer. His pupils dilated as she did so, and that gave her a bit more courage. She edged nearer, wishing her hands didn't shake as she lifted them to take the glass from his hand. "But then again…"

She took a sip from his tumbler, and immediately the alcohol burned her throat. She coughed, staring up at him with a red face and tears in her eyes.

"That…" she said through coughs. "…seemed far more…confident in my head."

He laughed as he took the glass and set it behind him on the sideboard. His arms came around her, and he leaned in until his lips were just a hair from her own. "It was fantastic," he reassured her before his mouth found hers.

She tasted the whisky again, this time on his tongue, but it didn't choke her now. Not when it was tempered by his flavor. One she wanted to drown in forever. She wound her arms around his neck with a muffled sigh and lifted herself tighter against him.

He whispered something against her lips, but she was too foggy to understand the meaning. Too lost to focus. And wasn't that what she needed to do? To talk to him about his plan?

She pulled back a fraction. "Ellis—"

He cut her off with another kiss. "Not yet," he murmured against her mouth.

Perhaps she should have pushed the issue. Perhaps she should have demanded they speak further about what drove him so hard to catch Leonard. Why he looked so…lost…when he told her that everything would be over once he did.

But she couldn't demand. Not when he tilted his head and the kiss deepened. Not when his fingers bunched in the silky fabric of her dress and lit her on fire.

The tenor of the kiss shifted slowly. It had started out gentle, explorative, but the need in it shifted the longer they stood there. His lips grew rougher, more insistent, and she met him with her own pulsing desire. He grunted out pleasure as she clutched his lapels and tugged, smashing herself tighter against him.

He pivoted, spinning her so that her back was to the sideboard. Leaning into her so she felt the length of his body and his cock pressed firmly to her stomach. She wanted them both so very badly.

She snaked a hand into the tight space, letting her palm stroke over him through his trousers, feeling him shudder when she did so. He yanked away and stared down at her. His expression was fierce, no longer the playful lothario with all the time in the world to seduce and pleasure.

No, this Ellis was a man driven. A man who feared to lose. A man who needed to forget, and she was willing to be the one who helped him do just that. He leaned in, his mouth finding her throat, sucking there, biting gently, and she arched at the unexpected flash of pain amidst the pleasure.

Pain she actually liked, given the way her sex throbbed in response. He smiled at the jolt of her body, licking where he had nipped, and then his hands came to her hips and he lifted her up onto the sideboard.

Glasses rolled away, the bottle of whisky rocked, and she squealed at the unexpected movement. "Ellis, we're making a mess," she protested.

"Not yet we aren't," he grumbled, and then he cupped the back of her head and drew her down for another kiss. She grabbed his cheeks, her fingers fanning across the rough evidence of beginnings of a beard. She lost herself in full lips, a rough tongue, the way he whispered her name as he reached down to unfasten his trousers with one hand even as he cupped her head with the other.

The front fall dropped away and she broke the kiss to look down at him, already hard. Already waiting. She could see now the value of being placed on the sideboard. It aligned them perfectly.

She worried her lip before she parted her legs, before she gathered her skirt into her fists and slowly pulled it up. He shook his head, his cheeks bright with color, his eyes dark with determination.

He stepped into the space she'd created and placed his hands on her thighs. He slid them upward and the fine fabric glided up, revealing her stockings and her drawers.

"Wider," he ordered.

She didn't have to ask what he meant. She pushed her legs farther apart and the drawers gaped at the slit. He nodded, his gaze transfixed on the pink of her sex as it peeked out from the fabric.

He cupped her hips and dragged her forward, sliding her to the very edge of the table. Then he leaned up to kiss her as his hand came between her legs. His fingers tiptoed into the fold of the fabric of her drawers and brushed her sex.

She was wet. She already knew that, but he smiled against her mouth as he discovered it. He maneuvered her a fraction more, matching the head of his cock to her entrance, and then he surged forward.

She was still a bit tender from the first time, but the pain was gone as he seated himself in one wild and reckless thrust. She gripped her thighs around his waist with a cry and clung to his shoulders.

That seemed to be the permission he needed because he began to move in earnest. He thrust, circling his hips on every movement, grinding against her so that the pleasure mounted and mounted every time. She dipped her head back and he took advantage, tracing patterns on her exposed skin with the tip of his tongue.

And he took. His fingers dug into her body through her dress, the table creaked and the bottles shivered with every hard, powerful thrust. Harder and harder, building them both toward release. She reached for it, rising to meet him, gasping for breath as the waves of pleasure built in her. And just when she felt she might not be able to take anymore, he pressed his hand between them again and circled her clitoris with his thumb, 'round and 'round, harder and harder.

She cried out his name, jerking against him as sensation overtook reason. Pleasure tore through her, out of control and wild, and she chased it, surrendering as he dragged her into madness. But at least she wasn't alone. His face contorted as he watched her come, his fingers digging harder and the cords of tendons in his neck tightening as he reached his own edge.

When he fell, he roared and jerked from her body to come into his hand. They were gasping together as he rested his forehead on hers, wordless and soundless except for the sharp intake of their breath that slowly matched.

She wanted this to last forever. This abandonment of the rules she had followed her entire life. She wanted to chase him into oblivion, to stop worrying over all she had to change and repair and instead give into all the pleasures the world had to offer. Chiefly the man who was now stepping away from the circle of her hips.

He stared down at her as he wiped his palm on a handkerchief and then rebuttoned his trousers. "Too much?" he asked, his voice rough from passion.

She shook her head as she smoothed her dress back down and carefully pushed down from the edge of the sideboard. "Exactly what you promised me, I think," she said. "And exactly what I wanted, Ellis. You didn't take advantage."

He rubbed a hand through his hair as he walked away. "Angel, I have been taking advantage from the first moment I laid eyes on you. Let's not pretend otherwise."

"Why do you do that?" she asked, and all the old habits rose up in her.

He pivoted and speared her with a glare she supposed was made to make her nervous. It didn't. She saw it for the shield it was now. "Take advantage?" he growled. "Because I'm a bad person, Juliana."

Her lips parted. "No, do *that*. Talk about yourself so meanly. You have certainly done some lamentable things, I won't pretend you haven't. But you clearly aren't a bad person. I've heard how you protected Rook as a child. A bad person would have simply left him to his fate. You are a man who did the best he could with the circumstances he was thrust into."

"And why do *you* always try to make me into a hero?" he asked, folding his arms across that wonderful broad chest. "I'm not one of your projects, angel."

She flinched at the harshness of his tone. "Then what are you? If not a villain and not someone who can be helped, what are you, Ellis Maitland? Why are you so desperate when it comes to finding Winston Leonard? Why are you so driven?"

He stared at her and briefly she thought he might simply kick her out of his house. Send her home in his carriage to explain herself to her angry family. Prove that he was the bastard he so desperately wanted her to believe he was.

But then his expression softened a fraction. She saw the real man behind the mask. The one she liked so much when he allowed her a glimpse. The one who she knew instinctively could be and *was* more than what he pretended to be with his false smiles and lies.

She saw Ellis, not Handsome.

"Do you know I have a brother?" he asked.

She swallowed because she hadn't actually thought he would open up to her. Now that he was, she feared moving too quickly and scaring him away from this moment.

"Yes," she said softly. "In fact...I've seen him."

"What?" he gasped his eyes going wide. "When would you have seen him?"

"At the Donville Masquerade," she admitted. "The night you first kissed me. I was storming across the room, ready to tell you to leave me alone, and a man stepped up to you."

His brow wrinkled. "And how could you know he was my brother?"

"He looks a little like you and Rook, for one," she said. "But also there was something in your demeanor. Although I'd seen glimmers of the real you before, that night when you spoke to him, you weren't Handsome Ellis Maitland. You were just...you. That connection was real. Later, Rook mentioned your brother. And I put it together."

"You are almost too observant," Ellis muttered. Then his frown turned down. "Rook told your family about Gabriel. Of course he did. It seems all my secrets belong to the Shelley Sisters and Harcourt now."

"Not all," she said. "I want you to tell me about him."

Ellis let out a long breath and crossed to the settee. He sank into the cushions and shook his head. "My father died when I was very young. He was in trade, just a man who delivered ale to the inns and taverns. My mother was a barmaid in one. They married when she got with child. Me."

"Were they…happy?"

"They survived," he said with a shrug. "That was something. Until he didn't. There was an accident. He was crushed when a rope holding some barrels broke."

She jerked a hand to her lips. His tone was even and breezy. His eyes, though. That empty, haunted look was something she would never forget.

"How old were you?" she whispered.

"I was eight," he said. "And I mourned him. Perhaps she did too, but she had to eat, didn't she? Had to live. She found herself a new husband within a few months. The man who owned that same tavern she worked in. A bastard named Young. They became the Young family, and I…well, I was a Maitland. A reminder to that bastard that my mother had once been with someone else. He hated me and he let me know it."

Her brow wrinkled. "Ellis," she whispered as pain flowed through her. Pain on behalf of this man as a child. On behalf of him now as he sat on the settee and stared straight ahead like he was in another world. Another time.

Perhaps he was.

"I could see the writing on the wall as he got more hostile to me.

I started running the street to avoid him. And by nine, I was out entirely. On my own."

"You want to sound proud of that," she whispered as she slowly moved to him and took a spot perched on the other side of the settee. He glanced at her as she took it, his gaze haunted. "But you never should have been put in that position. Did your mother not fight for you?"

The corner of his lips tilted slightly. "My mother was built to fight for herself, not me. She was happy to have peace in her home, I suppose. I visited from time to time when *he* was out. And I don't regret it. I met Marcus Rivers on the street. He was working for a true bastard, one who almost killed him. But he helped me learn the ways. I was good at pickpocketing and running the game."

She frowned. "You're clever. I'm sure you were very good at it."

"Then Rook had to run, too," he said, his lips pursing. "So I took him in. I was ten by then. We started organizing. Doling out work to the other boys, making a real place for ourselves, so we didn't have to depend on men who had just as bad intentions as my mother's husband or Rook's mother's 'protector.'"

"You educated yourself," she said as things became clearer.

"Got that street accent out by force," he agreed with a slight smile. "It made it easier to slip into *their* world when we needed to. Rook taught me to read. I devoured everything I could steal. And I brought myself up in the world, out of the shit. And I *am* proud of it."

She saw that was true. He *was* proud of what he'd overcome, and rightly so. But there was also regret there, deep in those glittering eyes. Regret and loss and a tiny wish that he hadn't had to escape so much.

"So how did the brother enter the picture?" she asked.

He blinked as if he'd forgotten how this story began. He worried his hands in his lap. "I was sixteen when I came home one day to slip my Ma some funds and found her swollen up with a baby. I was so angry. So angry she would make a new family with a man who—"

He pushed to his feet and stalked off to the fire. He stood there, his shoulders ramrod straight, his hands clenched at his sides.

"A man who hurt you," she whispered. "Who didn't give a damn."

He nodded. "Yes. It was a slap in the face of everything I'd told everyone that I was over it. That I didn't care. But there it was. Things were bad, she needed help. She cried and begged, and what could I do?"

She flinched, for that was the same way she'd justified smoothing over all her father's messes over the years. What could she do but help?

And yet when Ellis said it, she wanted to save him from that notion. To take away guilt that his mother hadn't earned. To take away pain.

"I kept coming back, sneaking her money and things I stole for this horrible baby I hated. Except when you see a baby...how can you hate him? To keep hating him would have made me as bad as his bastard of a father. I looked into his eyes, Gabriel's eyes that are just like mine, and I..."

"You loved him," she whispered as she thought of how many times she'd looked into her own sisters' eyes over the years and felt that swell of love and connection and adoration.

He nodded slowly and his expression crumpled. "It was the damnedest thing." He sighed. "I kept coming back. Visiting when Gabriel's father wasn't around. Bringing him gifts and money for what he needed when that bastard she married couldn't or wouldn't provide. I paid for his education."

She smiled. "When I saw you, it was obvious you two are still close."

"Not too close," he murmured. "Being near me could be poison. He already had a brief time when he got ideas. He wanted to run with Rook and me, but I wouldn't let him. No, he's going to be a barrister. Or a merchant. I'm making sure he has anything he needs. I'll do anything that will give him a good life."

"Anything," she repeated slowly, for the way he said it was so forceful. She saw the way Ellis's chin hitched up, like he was ready to defend that desire for his brother's future to the death. A fissure of worry made its way through her. "What does that mean, Ellis? Because I don't like the way you say it."

Ellis turned his face, and the fire glowed against his skin as he stared down into the flames. "When Harcourt's brother Solomon and I double crossed Leonard a year ago, his rage was palpable. He killed Solomon. He has chased me across England, threatening and destroying anything in his path. Rook was safe, since he bolted the moment he knew a man had died due to my bad decisions."

"When did Leonard find out about your brother?" she asked, clenching her hands in front of her as she stood.

He looked at her, and there was the desperation, only this time it wasn't a fleeting moment of the emotion. No, all of it was utterly alive and utterly terrifying on his beautiful face. She saw his deepest fears and his most painful regrets. She saw his guilt. His shame.

And all she wanted to do was comfort him. But when she moved toward him, he held up a hand to stave her off.

"A few months ago," Ellis whispered. "It took him a while because we don't share a last name. Once he knew, he had my brother roughed up by his lackeys. And he told me if I didn't get him what he wanted, he'd do worse. Worse than what he'd done to Solomon even."

She flinched. Torture. The monster was talking about torture before he killed. "Oh, Ellis."

"I want to be clear," Ellis said, his jaw clenching. "*That's* when I went after your sister. I went after Anne to get to Harcourt because I would rather hurt them than let Gabriel suffer for the crime of being my blood."

Her lips parted at the way his voice broke when he said those terrible words. He bent his head, and now she couldn't help but go to him. She clasped his hand between hers gently and lifted it to her lips.

As she brushed her mouth against his knuckles, she sighed. "You didn't hurt them, not really. You freed Harcourt to marry Thomasina, who is the one he truly loved. And you took Anne…that was wrong. But if you hadn't, she never would have met Rook, and both of them would be lonelier and emptier for it."

He shook her hand away. "I don't want your false absolution," he snapped. "Don't you see? You cannot make me into a hero. I'm the villain of this piece, Juliana. Even if I make you come."

She flinched. "You think it's because of the pleasure that I have empathy for you? I can make myself come, Ellis. I've been doing a perfectly good job of it for a while now."

His eyes widened, but he folded his arms and she felt the wall come down between them. The one she knew now was a way to protect himself, and to protect her. But she didn't want the wall. She didn't want to be protected because what he was turned out to be exactly what she wanted.

She recognized, in that moment charged with frustration and desperation and pain, that she loved this man. She loved Ellis Maitland, despite all he'd done and because of all he was. She loved him.

And she didn't want to lose him. Not now, not in a week, not ever. She wanted a life with him that was like the one her sisters had found with their husbands. She wanted the private smiles and the gentle support and the loving whispers.

She wanted to save him, not just because that was her nature, but because he was worth saving. And so was she, or at least the version of herself she had found when she spent time with him.

"I feel for you," she continued, this time gently, because she realized she was dealing with fear now, disguised as anger, and one had to be careful with fear. Tender. "Because I understand the drive to protect those around you at all costs. I've done it all my life. You and I are so alike."

He held her gaze for a moment, his nostrils flaring, his fingers flexing like he wanted to reach for her. She thought he might. Then he clenched them at his sides and turned away.

"No, we aren't," he said.

"Yes, we are," she insisted, and moved to catch his arm and turn him back to face her. "We are. And now everything is changing for us both. Everything is threatened, and we are drowning because neither one of us knows what to do." She felt the tears in her eyes and didn't fight it as one slid down her cheek. "I don't know what to do and I am *lost*, Ellis. I'm lost."

He reached out and his fingertips crested over her cheek, tracing the line there, catching the tear that had fallen and wiping it away with his thumb. She leaned into his rough hand and prayed he could feel all the things she couldn't say.

"I'm not the one to find you, angel," he said, his voice rough. Then he backed away a long step. "I've always been lost."

She pursed her lips at how he retreated. Then she let out a long sigh. "You're only lost if you don't want to be found," she said. Then she turned away and paced across the room to the sideboard where she began to absently tidy up the flipped glasses and spilled whisky from their earlier encounter.

He chuckled, and she glanced at him over her shoulder. He still looked tense, but the smile was real. "You just can't help yourself, can you?" he asked with a shake of his head.

She shrugged. "I don't *want* to help myself," she corrected. "There's nothing wrong with trying to fix what is broken in the world. If no one bothers, everything stays the same."

His smile fell. She could see all the arguments he might make to keep the distance between them. But she didn't want to hear them. Not now.

"I should go back," she said. "I'm likely already in trouble if my sisters returned from their party. But I must ask you if you intend to break away from me."

He frowned. "Do you want me to?"

"No, but I'm not a fool. You got information about the duke today that you needed me to easily obtain. Perhaps that's all I have to contribute."

He moved closer. "You and I made a bargain, angel." He reached out and took her hand. His thumb smoothed over the skin between her thumb and forefinger, and she shivered at the intimacy of that touch. "And I still...need you. Need your help."

He added the correction swiftly and released her when he said it. But even as he walked away, she smiled. He needed her, and she refused to believe that was only something that came with this investigation they were performing together.

And if he needed her, then perhaps that meant he could care for her. *That* made the future a little less cloudy than it had been when she started her day.

CHAPTER 20

E llis sat at a table in the Donville Masquerade, nursing a drink as he watched the cacophony of pleasure drift by him. It had been a few days since he last returned Juliana to the safety of Harcourt's home. Since then she had written to him, lovely letters with little snippets of information she had spied off her hosts. And also glimpses into her day. Into her life.

They ought not have meant so much to him. And yet they did.

He frowned and took a sip of ale. He'd come here to remind himself who and what he was at his core. A man who belonged in a place like this when she did not. But coming here only served to remind him of the time they'd spent in this den of sin.

He moved to get up and go talk to Marcus in the hopes he could clear his head when a lady sat down at the table across from him. Her mask was elaborate, brocaded and feathered and bejeweled. It instantly identified her as a woman of the *ton*, come here to fuck her boredom away, no doubt.

"I beg your pardon, my lady, but I fear I am not available for entertainment," he drawled.

She tilted her head. "I realize that. I believe you are taken by a friend of mine. Should I say her name out loud to prove it?"

Ellis froze. He knew that voice. From the park with Juliana a few days before. "Lady—"

She shook her head. "No, no, sir."

"Lady L?" he pressed.

Lady Lydia smiled in acknowledgement. "Indeed. You have determined my identity. That is correct."

He arched a brow. "What is a duke's unmarried daughter doing in a place such a this?"

She shrugged, a delicate lift of slim shoulders as her gaze darted away. "The same thing *anyone* does at the Donville Masquerade. I come here to be myself, my true self. Sometimes we must hide those true selves in public. As I think you are, *Mr. Maitland.*"

He straightened in his chair and felt the blood draining from his cheeks. She knew his name. His *real* name, not the false one he'd given in the park a few days earlier.

"You needn't worry," she said with another dismissive shrug. "I have no intention of unmasking you here or out in the world. I just wanted you to know I was on to your game."

Ellis folded his arms and leaned back in his chair to examine her. Her body language was meant to be casual, but he saw the tension in her shoulders, around her mouth. There was more to this approach than a mere polite acknowledgement. Or a threat.

"And just what do you think my game is?" he asked.

Her smile thinned. "I think you are known as a lover in many circles."

He tilted his head. Her tone held a modicum of disgust. "So you think I am using Juliana Shelley, your friend? And you don't have anything to say about that?"

"Juliana Shelley is an *acquaintance,*" Lady Lydia corrected, with a snippiness to her tone that made Ellis a bit more protective than perhaps he should have been. "And if I thought your goal involved stealing something from her, using her as you have used others in the past, I suppose I *might* consider letting her know she was a fool.

But despite your reputation, that isn't why you've tangled yourself in her life."

"Do tell, I'd love to hear your theory," he said, keeping his tone carefully neutral.

"You are after my brother, Lord Winston. Winston Leonard, I suppose he is known as when he is slumming amongst people like you."

Ellis's eyes went wide. He'd seen her reactions in the park, but he'd been more focused on her father. But it was evident Leonard's behavior and reputation were as known to her as they were to anyone else. She hadn't been protected from them. Or perhaps she had just been investigative herself.

"And what if I am after him?" Ellis asked carefully.

She leaned forward. "I think it is a good idea. It's time someone eliminated him."

His lips parted at the harshness of her tone. "You would wish me to exterminate your own flesh and blood?"

She shook her head slowly and let out a long sigh. "Although I am ten years younger than my wayward brother, I have always been aware of his sadistic cruelty. I watched him wield it over my brothers, over my father and my mother. He tormented servants, he destroyed lives. And no one has ever checked him, no matter what damage he did. His power and his influence and his ability to get what he wanted at any cost grew over the years. No one in our family has been left untouched by it."

"I am sorry," Ellis said, and meant it.

She met his gaze evenly. "You needn't patronize me. His bad behavior outside the walls of our family homes was just as bad, if not worse. Because of his lack of decorum, he has destroyed the reputation of my elder brothers and harmed my own. My father is utterly weak, too weak to protect anyone, even himself. And Winston is an animal. I hate to say it, but putting him down is the only way this will stop." She shifted. "Are you the man to do it?"

Ellis steepled his fingers on the table. This could be a trap. This woman could be as cold as her brother, working in league with him. But there was something in the spark in her stare that made him wonder if he could risk it.

"My intention is to be that man," he admitted.

Her breath hitched. "Even though you know there will be consequences? He is the son of a duke, no matter how far he has fallen."

"The consequences to allowing him to continue down this path of destruction are far worse," he said.

She considered that a moment. "I can lure him to you. But he wants that gem. It is all he rants about. He is incensed that it was taken and is willing to do anything to get it back."

"I know. Where is he staying? I could take care of the problem quietly."

She shook her head. "He's on the move, property to property here in London. His paranoia is at a peak. And so is the danger. Get the gem, Mr. Maitland, and I can get him."

Ellis took a long breath. For weeks he had been strategizing and planning and trying to get to the man this woman had offered to him on a platter. Now he was being offered the end game. He just had to get one thing. Of course Juliana was the key to it.

"I'll get it," he said softly.

She seemed to sag with relief. "Good. Send word to me at my father's house when it's done. I'll take care of the rest and make the arrangements."

"Good." Ellis got up. "I can imagine turning on your family isn't easy. Thank you for your assistance."

"He isn't my family," she said as she pushed to her feet and headed into the crowd without a goodbye. He watched her walk over to the closest handsome gentleman, wrap herself around him and lift up for a kiss. It was clear how she intended to soothe her fears.

His mind shifted to Juliana. If this was the end, if he could truly get to Leonard and end the danger to those he loved…that meant it was the end for them, as well. He would be lost after he murdered his enemy. Hanged, transported or shot in the attempt to kill Leonard, the result was the same.

Even though he had been prepared for that, had always known it, he regretted it. Regretted the fact that he would never see or touch Juliana again. Hear her voice. Feel her skin against his. He ignored what that desire meant.

This was the only path now. And he had to stay on it so that everyone would be safe, including the woman who had turned his dark and dangerous world on its head.

~

Juliana walked down the hall with Anne, the two of them laughing at a joke Rook had told in the parlor after supper that night.

"You two are so well-matched," Juliana said as they reached her door. "It's lovely to see."

"Thank you." Anne leaned in to kiss her cheek. "I *hate* that Father is insisting you return home to him tomorrow. Despite all the danger still out there."

"We both know he doesn't acknowledge danger to anyone but himself," Juliana said with a long sigh. "He is entirely selfish. But I doubt I am in danger. After all, I am not related in any way to anyone Winston Leonard wants to destroy. I worry more about you. About Thomasina."

Anne worried her lip. "And what about Ellis?"

Juliana froze, hand on her door, as she stared at her sister. "What about him?"

"I think you two must have gotten close, given that you…you chose to spend time with him at the Donville Masquerade. I cannot ignore the fact that even though you hide it, you might be communicating with him still. Sometimes you get a faraway look in your eyes. It's the same one I see on Thomasina's face and feel on my own."

Juliana sighed. "You needn't worry yourself, love. I'm being smart and careful."

"I know you are." Anne shifted. "But I also know that Ellis can pretend to be whatever a lady desires, whatever she needs in that moment. That is how he got so far with so many and never got caught at what he's done."

"Including you?" Juliana asked softly.

Anne frowned. "He sensed I didn't want the life I was being forced into. He offered a different one. Full of adventure and fun. He wasn't wrong. That is exactly the life I've found with Rook. I don't hate him for what he did anymore...but I can't trust him."

Juliana nodded slowly. "I-I understand that."

Anne squeezed her hand. "I just hope you aren't being used and convincing yourself it's something more if you *are* still connected to him."

Juliana frowned. She was in love with Ellis, she knew that as strongly as she had a few days ago when the realization had first hit. But she wasn't a fool. Their bargain was, in a great many ways, still skewed in his favor. He got what he wanted from her when it came to assistance. And he certainly wasn't sad about the physical pleasures they shared.

That he might be using her, playing her, even if she did sometimes catch a glimpse of the real man he was had occurred to her.

She released Anne's hand with a smile she hoped appeased her wary sister. "I'll consider it. Good night."

"Good night," Anne returned, but she still sounded concerned. She worried her lip as she turned and left Juliana at her door.

The door she opened with a sigh and stepped into her chamber. She moved to close it and gasped. Ellis was standing behind it, leaning against the wall, a finger pressed to his lips to shush her so she wouldn't cry out in surprise.

She couldn't help her smile, despite the conversation with her sister in the hallway, and shut her door quietly before she stepped into him, lips lifted for a kiss.

He didn't deny her. His arms folded around her, hands splaying across her back possessively as he devoured her lips. She groaned at the sensation of his fingers against the silk of her gown, rubbing the soft fabric along her skin as he deepened the kiss even more.

She was lost to him. Lost forever. She never wanted to be found. She broke the kiss to look up at him and drink in the sight of him in the firelight.

He was so exquisitely beautiful, it was almost difficult to retain focus. His hair was slightly mussed and fell around his forehead in disorganized waves. His blue eyes were dark now, dilated with desire for her that still felt so strange to see and understand. He was not wearing a jacket, nor a cravat, and the top button of his shirt was undone, revealing a little chest hair that she wanted to glide her fingers through.

"Good evening," he drawled with a smile that popped the dimple in his cheek and made him even more irresistible.

"What are you doing here?" she whispered as she lifted her hands to his shirt and slid the second button free.

He chuckled. "The exact same thing you seem to be doing," he said. "I came here to just..." He leaned in and nuzzled his nose along the curve of her neck. "...breathe you in."

She shivered as his lips traced her throat and dizzied her mind. "I missed you," she admitted, even though that was a dangerous thing to do. "Three days is a very long time to only satisfy myself with smuggled letters."

He drew back and gazed down at her, the tension in his stare sudden and dark. "You ought not put so much stake in me, angel," he said softly, and lifted his hands to cover hers and keep her from unfastening the third button of his shirt.

"You keep trying to warn me off," she said, leaning in to kiss his knuckles instead of unbuttoning him. "But you must know by now that I am entirely stubborn and accustomed to getting my way. I will have it, you know."

He chuckled, but the sound was strained. "You are that. I wouldn't have you any other way."

She stepped away and smiled. "You may be the only one to feel that way, I fear. My sisters are becoming concerned about me."

He shifted slightly. "Yes. I, er, heard some of your conversation with Anne in the hallway."

Heat flooded her cheeks. "I see. Well, then you know what I'm dealing with."

"She's worried about you," he said gently. "And she should be. We already know I'm no good bargain. I'm a thief in the night and I've taken so much I never should have touched."

"I offered what you took," she reminded him as she reached for him. She folded her fingers through his and they both stared at their clasped hands. "Enthusiastically. More than once. I can do it again if you'd like to revisit whether or not you have stolen something from me."

He squeezed his eyes shut and shook his head. "You were sent here to test me. It is the only explanation. An angel from heaven sent to tempt the devil. And I think I'm failing."

"Only if you judge the test by hell's standards," she whispered, and wished she could make him see himself through her eyes.

His smile grew sad and he lifted her hand to kiss the top. Then he let her go and paced away. "I heard something else in your conversation with your sister. Is your father insisting you return to his home?"

"Yes," she admitted on a groan. "I've been here too long according to him. He wants his secretary back, as he is planning some little gathering with his cronies. Trying to repair the social damage done by my sisters' marriages, no doubt."

Ellis ran a hand through his hair, mussing it further, making it look like he'd just rolled out of bed. Her bed. That sent a shockwave of desire through her that had her clenching her legs together.

"I don't like it, Juliana," he said, his sharp tone pulling her away from pleasurable thoughts. "He knows the risk, doesn't he? He's aware of what Winston Leonard is and what he could do?"

Juliana sighed. "He was at Harcourt from the beginning. He was part of Anne's disappearance, he heard the stories of Harcourt's brother and he knows I was taken and injured by Leonard. But despite all those things he...he doesn't care."

His jaw tightened. "How could he not?"

"Oh, Ellis," she said with a sad smile. "You know how."

He frowned, and she could tell he was thinking of his own past, far more fraught than hers, far more dangerous, but when it came to abandonment? When it came to a lack of parental love or protection?

Well, that was another thing they shared.

"He's a bastard," Ellis growled, pacing away from her to the window where he stared out into the inky night.

"Yes. He is that. But I'm accustomed to him. I can accept what my future is when it comes to him. And I know my sisters and their husbands will take pity on me and draw me out as often as possible once all...all this is resolved."

He pivoted back. "Yes. I suppose the best thing we can do is resolve this. It's the best way to protect you from Leonard...and from...from everything." He straightened his shoulders. "Back in Harcourt, my cousin discovered a code that likely leads to the gem Leonard wants so much."

"In the statue, yes," Juliana said with a shiver as she thought of that day in Harcourt's study when she and Anne had found the shards of the statue and the note from Rook...the day she was taken.

"Rook and Harcourt still have it, don't they? They're determined to turn it over to Leonard and think that will end this. I know better. Do you know where it is? Can you retrieve it or take me to it?"

Juliana stared at him across the room. He didn't look like her attentive lover anymore. Or the flash of genuineness she sometimes caught. He didn't look like the false mask of Handsome Ellis Mait-land either.

No, he looked like something else entirely. A darker, more dangerous Ellis. The kind of man who had found a way to survive on the street. The kind of man who looked out for himself and didn't care who he hurt in the process. And her sister's words to her in the hallway suddenly echoed again.

"That's what you came for, isn't it?" she asked. "Is…is the rest of this just using me?"

CHAPTER 21

Ellis drew back at the question, spoken so softly but with enough power to rock him back on his heels. All his life, the answer to anyone who would have asked that question, *are you using me*, had been yes. To survive, he'd had to use others. To win, he'd done the same. Relationships were a currency to him. They'd had to be because letting them be anything more was only a threat to himself. Look at how Leonard could leverage his bonds with Rook or Gabriel even now.

But in this moment, staring at the woman across the room, the one worrying her hands before her and refusing to meet his gaze, he recognized something terrifying.

He wasn't using her. He couldn't use her. Because he was in love with her.

For a moment, the thrill of that realization nearly gave his heart wings. But then, the reality set in, as it always must.

Love was only pain. Especially in this case because within hours, days at best, he hoped to be facing off with a murderer. When it was over, he would be dead or transported. Either way, he would be gone. So loving her was only pain, and he could hardly bear it.

Part of him wanted to push her away because of it. To declare that he was, indeed, using her. It would be better for her, even if it broke his own heart. If he removed any inkling she had that he cared for her, when he was gone she would recover from the betrayal all the faster.

But then there was the other side. The side of him she had woken so gently and carefully and beautifully. The side that didn't want to leave her feeling used and broken by him. The side that wanted her to know she mattered. She had *always* mattered, from that first moment on the hill in Harcourt when he'd folded his arms around her and tried to comfort her. He hadn't wanted what he felt when he did that. He'd pretended it away, but it had been there, making him question every decision he'd ever made.

She would matter until the moment when he kissed her for the final time and walked away to save her and everyone they both loved so deeply. The second side won out, because she had given that side life.

"Ellis?" she whispered.

He moved toward her in three long steps and caught her hand. He drew her back as he sat down on a chair before her fire and tugged her into his lap. He cupped her cheeks, holding gently, forcing her to look into his face so she would see. So she would know the truth.

"I may lie about everything else," he said, hearing the roughness of his voice. The broken hitch of it that reflected his equally broken soul, his newly broken heart. "But not this. Your sister was wrong when she spoke to you in the hallway. I am *not* using you, Juliana. Yes, I came here because I want to end this madness with Leonard. I want to protect my brother and my cousin, but also to protect you and your family. But I also came here because..."

He trailed off and stared up into those green eyes. He could read her because he could always read people. He saw the flicker to her gaze, the gauzy sparkle of tears. He felt her soft in his arms, but also taut with waiting. With wanting.

What he saw, to his great shock and deepest awe and gratitude...

was her love for *him*. Juliana Shelley, who was worth ten of him, fifty of him...loved him. Despite his past. Despite his mistakes. Despite everything he'd ever done. She loved him. In this moment, she was his, truly his.

"Why did you come here, Ellis?" she asked, her voice shaking.

He stroked his thumbs along her cheekbones, tracing the scar his actions had left behind. Ones he had been forgiven for, even if he hadn't earned it. He had to earn it. And he would...soon.

"I came here because you have become the center of my world," he whispered. "And I can't resist you, no matter how I try. No matter how I know I should."

"Then don't," she murmured back, and dropped her lips to his.

When she kissed him, he was lost. Except no, that was wrong. They'd both confessed to each other that they were lost. But together they were found. He could see a life stretching out ahead of them. A happy life filled with adventure and atonement and joy and pleasure.

But it was a life he couldn't have.

And with his heart breaking, he tilted her head and kissed her more deeply. This was the last time he would ever make love to her. He knew that in his heart. And he was going to savor every moment. He was going to make sure she did the same.

He stood, gathering her into his arms as he did so, and she laughed against his lips as he carried her to her bed. He laid her out across the pillows, remembering the first time he'd done this. The last. Remembering every time he'd ever been so lucky as to touch her.

Then he stepped back and stripped out of his shirt, tossing it over his shoulder. He toed off his boots and removed his trousers. She stared at him, forever reverent when she looked at him like this. Forever anxious if the way she licked her lips was any indication.

He joined her on the bed, sliding one slipper from her foot and letting it fall to the floor. He massaged her foot, pressing a thumb into her arch, and she shivered as she whispered his name. Yet again he'd found some new place to explore, and soon he would not have that option anymore.

He pushed that maudlin thought aside and removed her other shoe, repeating the massaging action. He slid his hands over both her ankles, tugging gently to pull her closer on the bed. He let his fingers play over the fine bones there, memorizing even this tiny detail. He wanted every one.

Her calves were next, encased on white stockings with a blue filigree stitching through them. Could he steal these once he'd made her shake beneath him? Stuff them in his pocket? Touch that fine silky fabric any time he wanted to remember her? He could, but he wouldn't. That would be torment.

When his hands curved behind her knees, she arched. "Ellis," she moaned. He laughed, pushing her dress higher as he splayed his fingers across that sensitive place, let his thumbs crest over her knee bones.

She parted her legs and tugged at her dress, lifting it to bunch around her stomach. He groaned and leaned in to press a kiss to her inner thigh. She hissed out pleasure, her fingers coming down to dig into his hair, holding him in place there as she lifted against him to force what she wanted.

Not that she needed to. He had every intention of giving her just that. But first...

He pulled away from her hand and smiled up at the love of his life as she writhed in anticipation and scowled at him in accusation. He said nothing as he untied her garters, rolling her stockings down the same path he'd just traveled and traveling it back a second time. He caught the edge of her drawers and yanked those, bringing the delicate fabric down. She kicked them away, opening wider for him, giving him the prettiest glimpse of her slick sex.

He wanted to glide home in her. Deep as he could go. Come inside of her and mark her forever. He wasn't going to do that, but oh, the temptation.

Instead, he settled between her legs, pushed her thighs farther and then licked her from the rosette of her bottom to the hard nub of her clitoris. She let out a gasp that all but echoed in the room and then blushed as she clapped a hand over her mouth.

He chuckled and went back to work. She tasted earthy and sweet, his favorite flavor in the world. He never wanted to forget it, so he took his time, teasing and tasting, nibbling and stroking. For a while, he didn't focus on her clitoris, but every other inch of her. But at last her breath was rasping against her fingers and she was snaking her opposite hand between her legs to touch herself as he licked her.

"Always so demanding," he grunted as he let his tongue join those seeking fingers. Together they stimulated her clitoris, and he loved it. Loved that she was taking what she wanted, demanding what she needed. Loving even more than he could give it to her. He pushed her fingers aside at last with his chin and then he sucked her.

She jolted and began to quake. He repeated the action, once, twice. Steady pressure, suction and a swirl of the tongue, and in a heady rush she came. He tormented her through her release, letting her muffled cries become a symphony as he took and took and took, gave and gave and gave until she pushed him away, her body twitching with powerful aftershocks.

Only then did he climb over her, covering her, reveling in the feel of her softness beneath his hardness. She wrapped her arms around his bare shoulders, drawing him into her kiss, provocative as she licked the remnants of her release from his mouth. He shifted against her and drove home as she cried out against him.

He kept his eyes open, watching her face as he took her. Her head was dipped back, cords of tendons visible along the delicate column as she writhed under his thrusts. He loved how her lower lips trembled, how her fingers pressed into his skin, how her hips lifted to grind against his own.

He increased his pace, loving the tight clench of her pussy around his hard cock. Loving how it sent fireworks of pleasure up his length to explode through his entire body. He was close, but he wanted to feel her grip him one last time in release. He nudged a hand between them, stimulating her clitoris with his fingers as he circled deeper and slower.

She gasped, her fingers digging into his forearms as her gaze met his. He held there, watching her, pouring all his love into her as she began to quake around him, gripping and releasing with a second orgasm. He held out as long as he could, reveling in the feel of her pleasure, but his seed was moving, his balls tight, and at last he pulled out of her with a grunt and came harder than he'd ever come before.

He collapsed down over her, pressing kisses to her mouth, her neck. He would never forget this moment. This last time they were one. The last time she was his.

~

Juliana reached for Ellis's hand as they crept through Harcourt's quiet halls. Something had changed between them, but she was trying not to face that. Trying not to recall the pain that had been mingled with his pleasure as he made love to her. Tried not to recall that as he helped her fix herself as they readied to come downstairs, he had been quiet. Not comfortably, but as if he were at peace with something terrible.

"Ellis," she whispered.

He smiled at her. "So you never really told me where we're looking for the code."

She worried her lip. He was trying to avoid her questions before she even asked them. And his smile wasn't real anymore. It was tight and false and part of his act.

"The others don't often discuss anything to do with Leonard in front of me. I suppose they are trying to protect me." She sighed. "But I did overhear Rook say something to Harcourt about removing the code from his safe and hiding it in a book because of…" She trailed off because she didn't want to repeat the rest of the sentence.

"Because of me?" Ellis supplied, so she wouldn't have to.

Her eyes went wide. "How did you know that?"

"Because my cousin knows me very well," Ellis said, his tone going distant again. "And I know him. He must have guessed I would come searching here eventually, and the safe would be the first place I looked."

They reached Harcourt's study and she tried the door. It wouldn't open. She pivoted. "It's locked."

Ellis didn't look worried. He motioned her aside gently and then bent, retrieving some kind of tool from his boot. He fiddled with the door a moment, and then there was a click and it opened.

Ellis got up with a shake of his head. "That wasn't even a challenge. Tsk, tsk, cousin."

He entered the room first, holding her back with his arm as his gaze moved from one side of the room to the other.

"Are you expecting an attack?" she asked softly.

He didn't look at her but motioned her in and shut the door behind her. "In my world, I'm always expecting an attack," he said.

She shook her head as she moved to the shelves. "I'm sorry."

He had gone to the fireplace to raise the light in the room, but now he jerked his head up. "You needn't be. I'm accustomed to it."

She wrinkled her brow. "You shouldn't be. It's not a way to live your life, never trusting anyone, always believing someone is coming to get you."

"I trust a few people," he said, holding her gaze evenly. Then he darted it away. "Now, let's see. What book would we look for…"

He moved to the shelves across the room from the ones where she stood. For a few moments, they were quiet, glancing at titles. She caught one and pulled it free.

"What about this?" She read from the cover. "*Conrad Madison's Crop Rotation Manual.*"

His eyes went wide. "Riveting. Why do you think so?"

"It was pulled out on the shelf a fraction and there isn't any dust on the top. I can't picture anyone reading this for fun."

"Harcourt's a bit of a bore, though," Ellis said, coming across the room to stand beside her.

"No one could possibly be this much of a bore," she laughed as she opened the book and gave it a shake in the hopes what they were searching for would flutter from the pages. When nothing did, she twisted her mouth in defeat.

He patted her arm. "Try, try again," he sing-songed as he went back to his shelf. "Though the lack of dust on the books is a good way to track, I think I will take a different tactic. My cousin was likely involved in hiding the code, so I have to believe he would have a heavy hand in the choices." He rubbed his chin. "Let's think about favorite authors."

"Hm, Anne is a fan of Byron."

Ellis pulled a face. "Met him once. Not an admirer."

Her mouth dropped open and then she laughed. "Are you sure you aren't just jealous that his skills at love games rival your own?"

He winked at her. "Perhaps. Look for Byron then. It's possible Rook had your sister's desires in mind. And what about Thomasina? Where would Harcourt hide something with her reading habits in mind?"

"She is more interested in Walter Scott," Juliana said. "And I saw a collection of his works on this shelf."

She pulled a handful of books from the shelf and began to skim through them, looking for the paper Ellis so desperately wanted. When she found nothing, she turned to find him shaking out a few books from his shelf, the Byrons, she assumed.

Their eyes met and she could see that as playful as he was being, he was frustrated and upset at not finding what he sought. There was desperation to his intent now. And that scared her.

"What else?" she said. "Shakespeare is always loved."

"By all. It might be a law of the empire," he said. "Where would that be?"

She circled the shelves, letting her fingertip glide over the spines of the books. And finally she found the collection. It filled three shelves and there were multiple editions of each play.

"Here!" she said. "Will you help?"

He rushed to her side and together they pulled the books down. Carefully they flipped through them, standing so close that their shoulders touched. She glanced at him with a soft smile. "You do not like Byron, but are you a reader of the Bard?"

"Indeed," Ellis said. "I learned to read when Rook introduced me to Shakespeare."

"Which play?" she asked as she pivoted to face him.

"*Much Ado About Nothing*," he admitted.

She clapped her hands together. "My favorite, as well."

They stared at each other for a moment, and then they both dove into the pile of books on the table before them.

"*Much Ado!*" she called out as she held up a version with a well-worn spine and cover.

He held up a finer copy, this one with gold filigree. "I hate to compliment the man on taste, but Harcourt must be a devotee as well, since he has two copies."

She shook her head. "You two might actually like each other when this is finished."

He said nothing, but she felt him stiffen at her side. They each opened their copy of the play. He finished first and let out a groan that showed his frustration. She was about to give up as well and decided to flip through the pages once more. And there, hidden in the pages of act one, was a folded sheet of paper.

"Ellis," she breathed as she removed it with shaking fingers and handed it over. He took it but continued to stare at the page where it had been lodged.

"Don John's speech in Act One," he whispered. "*Let me be that I am, and seek not to alter me.*"

His pain lined his face as he said the famous line, and her heart broke for all he concealed beneath that mask of casual frivolity and disregard. She knew better now.

"It is the first thing I memorized from the work," he explained. "Rook and I used to tease each other with that line. And he...he put the code here."

She nodded. "You were in his thoughts, I suppose, when he did it. Accepting you was in his thoughts."

He shook his head. "He ought not accept me. I don't deserve it."

"Ellis—" she began, but he held up a hand to silence her as he moved to the desk. He sat down, hunched by the candle and looked at the coded lines of letters. Gibberish, as far as she could tell.

"Anagrams," he breathed. "No wonder Rook struggled. His strategic mind could never unravel them—he despised them."

She moved to stand behind him and looked at the jumbled words. "I can see a half dozen words in the mix, but how to know which ones are correct?"

"It's a skill," he muttered, his gaze darting back and forth. "*Hare. Roar. Garden,*" he said out loud, and she saw the same words.

"A skill?" she repeated.

"*Honoria,*" he whispered.

She shook her head but saw the same name in the jumble before her.

"Harder when it is such a complicated set of letters," he continued. "*Fountain.* It's meant to confuse. And if the message was meant for one person, even the decoded version might mean little to a person who didn't know the signs."

"But you do?" Juliana asked. He didn't respond. "Do you, Ellis?" she repeated, resting a hand on his shoulder.

He glanced up at her, and there was a strange peace on his face. It should have made her happy to see it, but instead it terrified her. It was...acceptance. Surrender. And she didn't want to see either of those things on the face of the man she loved.

The only reason a fighter like Ellis would surrender was if he thought he had a fair trade for it.

"Ellis," she whispered.

He pocketed the note and pushed to his feet. He cupped her cheeks and examined her face closely, as if he were trying to paint her image in his mind.

"Please." She felt the sting of tears in her eyes.

He smoothed his thumbs along her jaw, across her lips. Then he leaned in and kissed her gently. Without possession, without aggression, without desperation. He kissed her like it was the first time. He kissed her like it might be the last.

Then he stepped away. "Don't be afraid anymore," he said softly. "There's nothing to be afraid of anymore."

Her breath caught as he backed away a step, an eerie calm in the room around them. Until, that was, the door to the study flew open and Rook Maitland stepped into the room.

"What the hell are you doing here?" he burst out, his brown eyes darker than she'd ever seen. And he was glaring at Ellis like he was ready to throw hands.

CHAPTER 22

E llis should have been preparing for an attack if the expression on his cousin's face was any indication. But he didn't. Instead he simply stared at the man who had been his friend, his blood, his partner for almost his entire life. He stared at him and felt the swell of love and regret.

"Answer me," Rook growled, and stepped toward him.

Juliana gasped as she threw herself between them, her arms up as if she could protect Ellis. His Valkyrie from mythology, except she was real and in the flesh.

"Stop," she burst out. "Stop it now. You won't hurt him."

Rook flinched. "Hurt him? I would *never* hurt him. But I won't let him hurt you, either. Anne would never forgive me for that. I'd never forgive myself."

"He isn't hurting me," Juliana said, and reached back to take Ellis's hand. Her fingers were warm against his. Heavy in his palm. A weight that reminded him of his love for her even as he watched her love in return being demonstrated.

Rook's expression crumpled. "Juliana," he said softly. "What have you been doing?"

"You all cut me out of your plans," she explained softly. "So I've been helping Ellis with his."

"You allowed her to do this?" Rook asked him this time, talking over Juliana's head. "Are you so far fallen that you would involve yet another innocent in your schemes, even after all the consequences the others have suffered?"

Ellis flinched. "I was selfish, as usual. But it's over now."

Juliana gasped and pivoted back toward him. "Ellis!"

He lifted her hand to his lips and kissed it. "It was always going to end, angel. And I'll never regret it. But now I *must* go." He let her hand go, his own fingers shaking as he backed away. "Don't follow me. Just let me do this. Let me do this one right and good thing in my life."

He was moving toward the study window, and Rook caught his breath. "No, no!" he cried out.

But it was too late. Ellis flicked his wrist behind him, unlatching the window with a burglar's skill. He flipped backward over the sill and toppled into the bushes below. Thankfully it wasn't too far a drop—he landed flush and bounded back to his feet.

Rook leaned over the window. "Don't go!" he called out, but Ellis ignored him.

Even though it broke his heart, he ignored his cousin's voice and Juliana's as he took off across the garden, toward the waiting horse that would take him to the end. Of the game. Of the danger. And of his life.

Juliana leaned out over the windowsill. If she could follow him, she might be able to catch him, stop him. But before she could make the same leap Ellis had just made, Rook caught her arm. He dragged her back as she struggled, away from the window and the vanishing figure of the man she loved.

"No!" she cried out as she spun around and glared up at Rook.

"How could you do that? He isn't doing something wrong! Not this time. He's trying to protect you and Gabriel and—and me. He's trying to be better and all you're doing is—"

"You're in love with him, aren't you?" Rook said softly.

She broke off in her rambling and stared up at him. There was no judgment on his face, no pity. Only a gentle knowledge that couldn't be denied. She didn't want to deny it.

"I do," she said. "I love him with all my heart."

He pursed his lips. "It seems you two have been very busy behind all our backs."

She shrugged. "We are both…lost. We found each other, and I won't apologize or explain myself when it comes to that. I'm sure you think me a fool and will tell me how he's only using me and isn't capable of doing anything else."

Rook shook his head. "I would never tell you that. I certainly don't believe it. My cousin has not always made the best choices. But he isn't a bad man at his core. I think him infinitely capable of love and even fidelity if he found someone who could melt the icy parts of him." He let out a sigh. "If you want to be together, you'll have to fight your family on him. They all have reasons to doubt he's true." His gaze flitted over her face. "But looking at you, his fierce protector, I believe you'll win. Because we both know Ellis is far more than merely Handsome."

She smiled at him. At that acceptance he offered not just to her, but to Ellis. He'd thought he'd lost Rook. She knew he mourned that. It seemed he hadn't.

She blinked as the moment passed. "Oh, but Rook, none of this will matter, not if we don't keep him alive. He's solved the anagrams on the coded message, but he wouldn't explain to me what they meant. And you saw his face when he moved out the window."

Rook nodded. "I did. His calm was…frightening."

"I think he's going to do something…something dangerous," she whispered.

"I agree. What were the words?"

"He only said a few that made any sense. *Garden. Honoria. Fountain.*"

Rook shrugged. "Gibberish as far as I'm concerned, but if Ellis understood, then it must be the answer. His mind always worked better on these types of puzzles than mine did. The person who might know the connection is Harcourt. Solomon Kincaid wrote the anagrams, after all. Harcourt is his brother."

"Then let's get him," Juliana said, grabbing Rook's hand and tugging him toward the door. "We can't waste a moment. Not with Ellis's life at stake."

Rook followed her without argument, though she felt his stare on her back. But she didn't care. What she cared about in this moment was Ellis and getting to him before his desire to save everyone else pushed him to do something reckless.

⁓

E llis paced the private room at the Donville Masquerade, flexing his hands in and out of fists at his sides. Where the hell was she? He had no time for this. He wanted to get to Winston Leonard, do what he had to do and accept the consequences. He was ready to do that, and the more time he had to consider it, the harder the decision was.

He would never see Juliana again. At best, if he did, it would be at an inquiry where he was sentenced to death or transportation. He would certainly never touch her again, never hold her or kiss her. He'd never get a chance to whisper he loved her as she slept in his arms.

He stopped pacing and braced an arm on the mantelpiece as regret washed over him.

"Don't *you* look sick."

He pivoted to find Lady Lydia had entered the room as he pondered his lack of future. She was wearing a different mask from the one she'd had on the night before. Red silk and satin this time, trimmed with black leather. She sashayed forward and looked around.

"A private room, Mr. Maitland," she all but purred. "One would think you're trying to seduce me."

He backed away from her. Once upon a time, she would have been the perfect mark for seduction. Jaded, experienced despite her unmarried status, moneyed. They would have had fun and he would have collected a few baubles she wouldn't miss and perhaps some gifts she gave freely, as well.

But the very idea now, even in jest, of touching her was an anathema to him. "I chose a private room so we could have a private conversation. Nothing more."

"Pity," she sighed. "Then what is it you want to say privately?"

"I have the answer to the riddle. I know where the gem is."

Her eyes went wide and all the teasing and malaise fled her face. "So soon?"

"I'm motivated," he growled. "And so is your brother. I have written down a direction. You get it to him. I don't care how you do it. He will meet me there at dawn."

He held out the paper, and she took it and put it in the reticule that dangled from her wrist. "You think I can get him there in such a short time? It's only a few hours."

"I think *you're* motivated, too." He moved toward the door. "And I don't want him to have too much time to plan for traps. Get him there, my lady. I'll take care of the rest. Good night."

He left without waiting for a response and stalked down the hallway. He was going to simply leave. He had arrangements to make, after all. Final preparations for the night and for his life. But as he passed by the bar, he paused.

"Just one drink," he muttered, and strolled toward the barkeep, who was chatting with a few patrons.

The man smiled at him. "What'll ya have, mate?"

Ellis paused. What did a man choose for his last drink? "Your best whisky."

"My best is awfully expensive."

Ellis glanced over his shoulder with a slight smile and found Marcus standing there. His friend slid into on to the stools pushed up to the bar and called out. "Two of those, Brooks."

The bartender gave a wave of recognition. As they waited for their drinks, Marcus watched Ellis closely. Too closely.

"Damn it, Rivers," Ellis muttered as the whisky was set down before them. "Don't sit there reading me."

Marcus shrugged. "It's hard not to when I'm worried about you."

Ellis sipped his drink. "Christ, spare me your playing nursemaid. I'm fine."

"Saw you go into the back, but I don't think it was with the lady you kept encountering here before. The one you insisted I ban. The spitfire."

Ellis stared at his drink. The remnants suddenly tasted sour. "You know me," he said at last. "A lady for every occasion."

"Hmmm." Rivers leaned back and took a sip of his own drink. "If you say so. If you don't want to tell me the truth."

"You already know too many truths, old friend," Ellis said with a sigh and another sip of his drink. "If I lie, it's just out of habit."

"Self-preservation, I think," Rivers corrected with a frown. "Handsome, let me help you."

Ellis considered it. He could tell Rivers what he was off to do and where. He could ask for his help and he knew, without a doubt, that his friend would. Only when everything fell apart, Rivers would be implicated. He'd lose everything he'd fought so hard to build. So few people got out of the gutter. Ellis wasn't about to drag his friend back in.

"No, I don't think so," he said with a pat of Rivers' arm. He downed the last sip of his whisky and stood to reach into his pocket for blunt to pay.

Marcus shook his head. "That one was on the house."

Ellis stared at him and Rivers stared right back. His friend's gaze widened a fraction, and Ellis nodded slightly. "Goodbye, Marcus."

He extended a hand for Rivers to shake, and his friend rose before he did so. "Goodbye, Ellis," Rivers said softly.

Ellis pivoted and walked away, eyes stinging. Now he had to shrug off all he was about to lose. He had to focus on what moves he'd have to make to ensure no one else would lose instead.

~

Juliana paced Harcourt's parlor, glaring at the gathering of her two sisters and their husbands. They were all arguing around her now, talking about what should have happened in the past. What they could have noticed to stop all this.

Rook had rung for the household to be woken, much to the dismay of Harcourt's butler. But they'd come, bleary eyed and wrapped in dressing gowns. Rook's quick explanation of what had transpired that night, him coming upon her and Ellis in Harcourt's study, had been what inspired this cacophony of discussion.

She lifted a hand at last. "Great God, will you all stop? This is pointless and it won't help Ellis." The noise in the room stopped and everyone stared at her in surprise. She folded her arms, a shield of protection. "I've already confessed it to Rook, so I won't deny it now. I am in love with Ellis."

Harcourt drew back, an expression of horror on his face. Her sisters just stared. Rook remained unreadable, just as he had when she first admitted that his guess about her heart was correct.

"Juliana," Thomasina breathed at last, breaking the silence of the room.

Juliana threw up her hands in frustration. "You can argue with me about it later. Right now Ellis has deciphered the code that tells him where the gem was hidden. He didn't tell me where he was going, but I'm terrified at what will happen once he uncovers it."

"He'll run, you mean?" Harcourt snapped, his dark eyes narrowing. "He'll take the gem and leave Winston Leonard to potentially destroy us all."

"No!" Juliana took a long step toward him. This was the fight against her family that Rook had meant earlier. A war that she realized now would have many battles. And if this was the first, she would win it. "I realize you don't like Ellis. All of you have reason to be angry with him. But I *know* him. He would not abandon us for money. He wouldn't abandon Rook or his brother to potential death. He—he wouldn't do that to me."

Rook cleared his throat. "She's right. My cousin has a great many faults. But I saw his face. It wasn't triumph I saw when he bolted out that window. It was determination. Surrender. I fear for what he'll do in order to protect us all."

"As well you should."

The group of them turned, and Juliana caught her breath. Marcus Rivers had entered the parlor. Harcourt's butler Willard was on his heels. "My apologies, my lord. He wouldn't—"

"Mr. Rivers," Juliana breathed as she stepped up to him and looked into dark green eyes that were lined with the same concerns as her own. "He went to Donville, didn't he?" she whispered.

"You may go, Willard," Harcourt said. "Mr. Rivers, I presume."

Rivers looked past her at the crowd. "Lord and Lady Harcourt, Rook, Mrs. Maitland. I apologize for barging in at so late an hour. Though I'm happy to find you all gathered. I assume to discuss the same thing I came here for."

"Ellis went to you," Juliana repeated.

Rivers dropped his gaze back to her. "He did. He met with someone, a woman. Now, normally I protect the identities of the members of my club religiously, but I'll make an exception provided this remains between us."

"Who?" Rook pressed.

Rivers met his gaze. "Winston Leonard's sister."

"Lady Lydia?" Juliana gasped, and saw her sisters looked just as shocked as she did. "She is a patron of your club?"

"A great many *ladies* are, Miss Shelley," Rivers said with a slightly arched brow in her direction. "They met very briefly and then departed separately. I waylaid Ellis temporarily and I saw…" He turned toward Rook. "I want you to understand, Rook. Handsome is…he's on a suicide mission."

Juliana buckled at those words and Rivers reached out, catching her elbow so she didn't collapse onto the floor under the weight of that suggestion. He guided her to a chair and helped her into it. She stared up at him, blinking at tears, fighting around the lump in her throat. "A suicide mission. How?"

"He talked to me about it weeks ago," Rivers said, his mouth a thin, hard line. "About failing everyone he cared about. About how his only option was to sacrifice himself in order to end Leonard."

"End him?" Rook repeated, the color exiting his cheeks. Anne slid to his side and wrapped her arm around his waist as if to shore him up. "He's going to *kill* Leonard?"

Rivers nodded. "That was his intention recently. After tonight, I believe to still be."

"Why the hell didn't you send for me?" Rook cried out, marching up on Rivers, his hands in fists at his sides.

"Because Handsome wants you out of the life," Rivers said, never flinching even at the implied threat. "And to be honest, I hoped he would talk himself out of it." He glanced at Juliana. "Because of you. You were giving him something to live for."

"Not enough," she whispered, and now one of those tears she'd been fighting slid down her cheek. "Not enough to fight his urge to protect us all."

Harcourt had been strangely silent during it all but now he stepped forward. "Enough people have died because of the mistakes Ellis Maitland and my brother made. Juliana, you said Ellis solved the anagram. What did he say exactly?"

"Three words that stood out, that he reacted strongly to, and I hope they're enough. *Garden. Fountain. Honoria.*"

She expected Harcourt to be as confused as she had been by the answer, but instead the color fled his cheeks. "Honoria," he repeated, and his cheek twitched.

Thomasina reached for him, taking his hand. He glanced down at her, and for a moment, their connection was powerful. "Who is Honoria?" she whispered.

"My brother's mistress," Harcourt said softly. "The only woman he ever loved, I think. Solomon had a house for her here in London. When he died, she was devastated. She boarded it up and left for the continent. It has a garden with a fountain. She loved it."

"That's where he hid the gem," Rook breathed. "Because he and Solomon were friends, my cousin must have known about her, known about the fountain…so he would understand the reference as much as you did."

Harcourt nodded. "I'm getting dressed. Rook, do the same. Mr. Rivers, I hope you will accompany us. We're going to need all the help we can get."

"I've already sent word to Handsome's men. My man of affairs, Abbot, is gathering a few more. We'll have an army to save him."

"I'm already dressed," Juliana said, smoothing her gown. "I could change into more serviceable boots but that will take but a moment."

The men stared at her, and Rook shook his head. "You can't go. It's too dangerous."

Juliana barked out a laugh. "As your cousin has learned, Rook, I am not one to be argued with. The man I love is being threatened and is willing to kill and to die in order to protect me and all of you. I'm bloody well coming, and if you don't allow it, I'll break out of any chains you try to put me in. I'm not abandoning him because he wouldn't abandon me."

Anne drew back. "You—you *do* love him."

She faced her sister, the one of them Ellis had hurt most. And she prayed there could be forgiveness in the future. "I do. And I think he does love me. He is more than what desperation had him do. More than what any of you know, save Rook. I want to give him a chance to prove it and himself."

"It seems he's already proving himself," Thomasina said, and squeezed Harcourt's hand again. "He would die to protect us. That means something."

"It does," Harcourt said. "Juliana, you may ride with us. But you'll stay back."

"All of us will stay back," Anne said, patting Rook on the cheek and heading for the door. "Because we're all coming."

Harcourt and Rook exchanged a weary glance as Rivers laughed. "I understand the attraction now. Ready yourselves. I'll go gather the men at my disposal and meet you. You only need to provide me the address of this house."

Harcourt motioned him into the hallway. "I'll give it to you now."

Once the men were gone, Juliana faced her sisters. She expected resistance and argument despite their words in support of her plan to go with the men. Instead, she saw two faces that were a mirror of her own and expressions of only support and love.

"If he has earned your love," Anne said with a smile, "then I will choose to believe he deserves it. And pray I'll get to see that myself, soon."

Thomasina nodded. "I think we all know that a bad beginning doesn't mean a bad end. If you can be happy, we'll never do anything but support you."

Juliana felt the urge to buckle again at their words, but she forced herself to remain strong. For Ellis. "I'll need it. Now let's get ready, before the men talk themselves out of allowing our help. I can only hope we won't be too late. I can only hope we can save him...and ourselves, before this terrible night is over."

CHAPTER 23

The near dawn of a new day in the garden behind the fine little house just off Bond Street was truly beautiful.

"A fashionable address for the most fashionable lady," Solomon Kincaid had often said. Ellis hadn't understood his attachment to his mistress then. Now he did.

But the house was abandoned now. Left behind by a broken-hearted woman who had been settled well enough to flee the past and whatever pain it brought up in her. Ellis envied her that. His way to deal with the past was to destroy the future. Before that hadn't mattered. He'd always known a man like him died young. There wasn't anything to lose. Now? Well, his mind went to Juliana and all there was to feel was regret.

"Enough waiting around," he muttered, and marched across the garden with the shovel he'd brought with him in hand. He could only pray he was right about the anagram he'd solved, which gave this location, but also a few words to describe where to dig for the prize.

He moved to the location, facing the pair of cupids that would be squirting water out of their adorable little mouths, had the pump not been disabled and the fountain drained over a year ago upon Solomon's death.

With a sigh, Ellis began to dig in the spot he thought most approximated the direction. Shovelful after shovelful of dirt piled up before the fountain. But nothing inside. Had he guessed wrong? It didn't matter, he supposed. Whether he had the gem or not, Winston Leonard would come. Ellis would kill him and—

Before he could finish that thought, his shovel thudded against something more solid than mere dirt. He leaned in, searching in the dim light for what had stopped his progress. A box. His heart throbbed as he tossed the shovel aside and dug instead with his hands, loosening the box and drawing it out. He brushed off the dust on the lid and then opened it.

Inside was the thing he'd sought for a year. An emerald the size of his fist, cut to perfection. Worth…he couldn't even guess how much. Thousands of pounds at minimum, and many favors to a collector that were worth even more. He and Solomon had taken it on a lark when they felt Leonard took advantage of them.

How he hated this…*thing*. Even if it put him to mind of Juliana's eyes as he cradled it in his hands. What kind of life could he give her with this? If he crept into her room and spirited her away and they ran? A life of beautiful gowns and homes, of security.

Of course, he would doom everyone else they loved in the process. She would hate him for that. He'd hate himself.

No, he had a plan. He had a debt to pay with his life. There was no going back.

"Handsome Maitland."

He froze and stared harder at the gem in his hand. The one he'd sacrificed so much to find. The one that was his bait. Except the prey had come sooner than expected, and now all those plans dissolved.

He turned slowly and found Winston Leonard standing a few feet away, a pistol trained on Ellis's chest.

"*Lord* Winston," Ellis drawled, knowing how much Leonard

hated being called by that courtesy address. He felt it made him sound like a dandy rather than a dangerous criminal. "You're early."

"Normally I try for fashionably late, yes." Leonard motioned him to come closer with a waggle of his gun. "But I had a feeling the party might start a little earlier than my invitation indicated."

Ellis didn't respond but watched Leonard. There was a slight tip to his stance, the tiniest bit of off-center lean, but it would be enough if Ellis moved just right. He edged forward a little, sideways into the lean.

"You were always a clever one," he said, hoping that talking would keep Leonard distracted. "And a bastard."

That elicited a cruel smile. "Being a bastard is fun. You know that, Handsome—you've been one plenty in your life. Look at you even now, running around with that Juliana Shelley."

Ellis froze. "I don't know what the hell you're talking about."

Leonard shook his head. "Still lying. Still trying to pretend to be some hero. I saw her with you at the Donville Masquerade, where I can only assume you were properly debasing her."

"Shut up," Ellis growled, knowing he shouldn't let his emotions get to him, but struggling when Leonard brought Juliana into this.

"I wondered who she could be. And then I figured it out." Leonard chuckled. "You just can't help yourself when it comes to spreading the legs of anything with a smile and a giggle. But this is…very unexpected. Do you think she slummed with you because I cut up that pretty face? You should thank me."

Ellis drew in a breath. He would not lose control. He would not ruin all of this because of a taunt. He knew what Juliana was to him. He didn't need to prove it to a killer with no soul.

"Maybe I will," he said. "After you put the gun down and we take care of our business."

"We don't have any business," Leonard said with a shrug. "I'm going to shoot you because you stole from me and you lied to me and you made me wait. No one makes me wait. And when you're dead on the ground, I'm going to take the gem, and that's the end of it. No one will mourn you, no one will miss you and the world will go on as it always has."

Ellis clenched his teeth. Not because he believed this man. No, he knew he was loved. More than he deserved. But because all his sacrifice would be for nothing if it ended this way.

"Oh, the world will *almost* go on as usual," Leonard corrected himself. "You see, I don't think your blood is enough payment for what you put me through. And shooting you in the heart is efficient, but it won't really pay for what you owe me. I want you to know that I'm going to carefully and painfully punish everyone you love. Your brother. Your cousin. And that very pretty girl you've fallen in love with. She'll be last. And best."

Ellis ignored the sadistic laugh. He let out a roar and lunged, swinging out a leg to kick Leonard's knee. It buckled, and the double-barreled flintlock pistol fired. The bullet whizzed by Ellis's ear as he tackled his enemy.

One shot down. And if he couldn't get to his own gun, he could use the other shot to finish this at last. Once he got the pistol away.

They rolled, struggling together, both straining as Ellis squeezed a tender spot in Leonard's wrist to get to him to release the weapon.

But Leonard wasn't weak. Raised as a gentleman or not, Leonard had worked hard to become a villain. He was well matched to Ellis. He shifted his weight and they moved slightly, Leonard half covering him, Ellis straining as the gun began to shift toward him.

Leonard laughed. "Did you think you'd end me, boy? There was only ever one way this would end."

"With you begging for your life. Put the gun down," came a voice behind them.

Both men froze, pivoting to face the intruder. Rook stood there, a gun trained on Leonard's head. Harcourt and Marcus Rivers flanked him, also armed and similarly aimed. To Ellis's shock and horror, it wasn't just the men there, though.

Juliana was standing behind the others, her sisters at her sides. And all she was looking at was him.

"Juliana," he breathed, shaking his head.

She nodded in response, stubborn as always. God, how he loved her, even though he was going to ring a few necks if he got out of this alive.

"Get off of Ellis," Harcourt said, his hand trembling slightly. "And look me in the eye, you bastard. You killed my brother—give me any reason to splatter you across the grass."

For a moment, Ellis felt Leonard's hesitation. Then he rolled away and set the gun down, before he got up, arms outstretched. "Oh, good. You'll take me before the magistrate, will you?"

Ellis saw Harcourt's jaw twitch. "Yes."

"Excellent. My father has such a good relationship with the magistrates. This will be swept under the rug before a week passes."

"He's right," Ellis said, brushing himself off and grabbing for the gun Leonard had dropped. "Step back, Harcourt. Step away and let me do this. For my family. For Solomon. He was your brother, but he was my friend. And I'll avenge him for both of us and keep this bastard from hurting another soul."

"You would throw away your life to protect us?" Harcourt asked, and his gaze shifted slightly to Ellis. "Your future? Your happiness."

"I owe you that." He looked past him to Juliana. "I owe her even more."

"No," she said, desperation cracking her voice. "You owe me the future we might have. You'll throw that away by doing this. Please don't. Please."

He pushed the gun against Leonard's skull. "Just look away."

But she didn't. Instead, her eyes went wide and then she marched forward, slowly, her hands shaking. It took him a moment to realize she wasn't doing it as some kind of challenge to his decision to kill the man who had caused them all so much pain. As she came closer, he saw that Lady Lydia was behind her. And she had a gun pressed into Juliana's spine.

"I think you'd best be smart now, Mr. Maitland, and put the gun down. My brother isn't going anywhere."

The press of the gun against Juliana's back was so cold and hard that she could barely breathe. One wrong flick of the wrist, one lost bit of footing, and she would be dead or badly injured.

"Lydia," she said as she was shoved forward none too gently. "What are you doing?"

"Protecting my own future," Lydia hissed.

Juliana tried to keep her voice calm. Soothing. "How does *this* protect your future?"

"The best way I know how. Winston said he would give me a portion of the proceeds when he rids himself of the jewel. Enough for me to run away and live my life as I see fit. Then whatever he does won't matter to me."

"Even if he kills?" Thomasina asked as Juliana was pushed past her embracing sisters.

There was a slight hesitation, but then Lydia continued moving her forward. "I'm not responsible for that."

"Yes, you are," Ellis said. His eyes were locked on Juliana's, and she held there. That blue gaze gave her peace, it calmed her fear. Just as it had all those weeks ago. Just as she knew it could for all her days if any of them survived this nightmare.

"Hand over the gem to my brother," Lydia said softly.

Ellis's expression was so filled with frustration that he almost looked as though he would howl. He didn't, though, and swept up the gem from where it had fallen in their struggle. He held it out, his hands shaking. Winston Leonard stepped forward and snatched it.

"Well done, sister," Leonard drawled as he backed away. It was a taunt. Ellis still had the gun, but it was clear he wouldn't fire it.

Because it would endanger Juliana.

"You have what you want," Ellis growled. "Now let her go."

"No, I think not," Leonard said as he sidled up to his sister and Juliana. Together they pulled her back toward the gate at the back of the garden. An escape route. "The moment we don't have her, your men will move. She comes with us. If you're lucky, you'll get her back in one piece."

Lydia's face jerked toward his. "You told me we'd let her go at the gate."

"Shut up," he snapped, and glared at her.

Ellis was moving forward, one long step at a time. Getting closer and closer, and Juliana longed to reach out. To have him pull her away to safety. But that wasn't going to happen. For the second time in a few weeks, the most dangerous man in London was taking her away from everything she loved.

And judging from the cruelty in his tone and his look, she didn't fully believe she would be released, even if that's what he'd told his sister.

Lydia. Yes, that was the key. It was obvious the young woman was hesitant about the violence her brother reveled in.

"I don't know what he said to make you do this, but he's *lying* to you," Juliana whispered. "Think of all the times he's done that in the past. All the damage he's done without even caring about you. He will do what's best for him in the end. He'll leave you worse off while he is free."

"Shut up," Leonard said. "Lydia, keep moving."

Juliana looked at the man whose brutality knew no bounds. And she saw the deeper truth of him. "I can see he has no intention of letting me go. But he won't dirty his hands. He'll force *you* to shoot me just to prove your loyalty. He'll put my blood on your hands so you'll *never* be free of him."

Lydia stopped moving and glanced at Leonard from the corner of her eye. "That isn't the bargain we made," she whispered. "You said no one else had to get hurt."

"It will be you with a bullet in your head if you don't move her out the fucking gate," Leonard snapped.

Lydia's hand shook against Juliana's back. She was distracted. This was the time.

Juliana threw her elbow as hard as she could, smacking it across Lydia's chin. She cried out and her grip loosened. Juliana dove for the ground as Leonard pulled out his own pistol. He aimed it at her and she crouched, ready to die, but when it fired, she wasn't hit.

Ellis hurtled himself forward, jumping between her and the bullet meant to destroy her. He screamed her name into the night, and then his voice was cut off. He fell beside her, his hand gripping at the wound on his thigh. Blood was gushing from it.

Rook was moving now, Harcourt too. Juliana rolled to cover Ellis and protect him just as he had once protected her. As she did so, Leonard grabbed for his sister, trying to throw Lydia in the way of any bullets that might be fired.

Lydia jerked away from him and pivoted, her gun pointed at his chest.

He smirked. "You won't dare, Lydia."

Her jaw tightened and her gun fired. Leonard stared at the circle of blood on his chest as he dropped to his knees. And then he hit the ground face first. Dead in an instant.

There was a great deal of movement after. People running and shouting, Lydia being taken away by someone as Rook dropped to his knees at Ellis's side.

Rook's face was pale enough that she knew the injury was bad. He tore off his cravat, applying it as a tourniquet to the bleeding wound. Ellis winced as it was tightened, but his face was so pure white.

"Stay with me," she whispered, stroking his hair back. "You're not leaving me now."

"That's my line," he said, his voice rough and far away. "I said it to you that day on the hill."

She nodded. "And I stayed. And you must too. I love you. You can't leave me because I love you."

His eyes drooped. "I love you too," he whispered. And then he was unconscious, and she screamed.

CHAPTER 24

Ellis opened his eyes and found himself staring at a gauzy canopy of white. The pillow beneath his head was comfortable, the sheets clean and crisp against his bare skin. This couldn't be hell. Perhaps he'd done enough in the end to earn heaven. It wasn't all bad.

Except…this couldn't be heaven. When his foggy brain began to clear a little, he could see it was just a chamber. A nice chamber, yes, but hardly heavenly. There were a shockingly low number of angels and not a harp to be seen.

Which meant…he wasn't dead. Somehow. Some way.

There was a woman standing at a table across the way, her back to him. "Juliana?" he called out, his voice rough from his dry throat.

She turned and his heart sank. Not Juliana. One of her sisters.

"You're awake," the young woman said as she approached the bed with a cold, wet compress. She pressed it to his lips and he exhaled a sigh of pleasure at the relief of water on his tongue. "Easy now."

"Anne?" he asked, guessing.

"Indeed." She sat on the edge of the bed, examining his face closely. "I will fetch Rook and Juliana in a moment."

He would have jerked into a sitting position but found he was too weak. "They're here?"

"Yes." She examined his face closely, as if she were truly seeing him for the first time. "You've been quite popular in the last ten days. Your brother Gabriel has been here every day, as well as Marcus Rivers. Even my father made a call." She frowned. "Although that was to demand Juliana back."

Ellis swallowed. "She refused."

"Of course. It was something to see. She's been forced into the position to soothe him so many times, but she made it clear in no uncertain terms that those days are over. The language she used... well, you've rubbed off on her. He left and I somehow think he won't return. My husband and Thomasina's will assure it."

"I'm sorry," Ellis said, carefully because he couldn't fully believe that Anne was engaging him in such casual conversation about such a personal matter rather than...say...scratching his eyes out. "But it sounds like he wasn't worth much as a father."

"He wasn't. Not worth a farthing. But you...*you* apparently are." She shook her head as if it shocked her. "And I know my husband and your brother and my sister will be happy to see you awake."

"Wait, did you say ten days?" Her earlier words had finally pierced and shocked his system into understanding.

She nodded. "You were in and out. You lost a good deal of blood. Harcourt's doctor thought you might even lose the leg."

Ellis moved the leg she referred to and a shot of heated agony moved up his entire body. He couldn't help but cry out, and she rested a hand on his to steady him.

"Yes, that *would* hurt. I wouldn't recommend it. You'll be down for another good while." Anne shifted slightly and took her hand away. "Rook called for your underground doctor after the earl's brought out a saw. He was the hero and somehow brought you through. But between the pain and the laudanum, you were not to be found. No matter how hard Juliana searched for you as she lay in this bed beside you, willing you to live."

Ellis shut his eyes as the pain faded slightly. "I'm not worth the effort," he said.

"Stop that." Anne's tone was suddenly harsh, and he opened one eye to find her glaring at him. Rather the same way she had when he'd abandoned her with the man she now called husband. A lifetime ago, it seemed. "If my sister believes you are worth something, if my husband says you are, then I will not hear a word against them."

He pursed his lips. "Even after what I did to you?"

She sighed. "I had my part in what happened. Running away was my lifeline. And you were, though not in the way I originally thought. You brought me to Rook."

"Does that make me good enough for your sister?"

"No." She smiled, and it softened the harsher response. "But if you were to make her happy, forgiveness would come easier."

"And Thomasina feels the same? Harcourt, who blames me rightly for my part in his brother's death?" he pressed.

"Thomasina is built to find the best in people," Anne said. "Harcourt can be earned, I think. Eventually. Your attempt at noble sacrifice impressed him." She pushed to her feet and walked to the door. "I'll fetch them."

She left the room and he stared at the ceiling again. He had prepared for the end. He'd known what it would bring. But now... he was here somehow.

The door opened again and Rook careened through. He came to a sharp halt and stared at Ellis lying in the bed. Then his cousin bent at the waist, his breath coming in harsh sobs.

"I thought you would die," he managed between the broken sounds. "Don't ever do that to me again, you bastard."

Ellis felt his own tears stinging and patted the bed bedside him. "I'll try. Though I have to say, I have no idea how I came to survive this trial. Can you help me with that?"

Rook wiped his eyes and took the place near Ellis that his wife had recently abandoned. He smoothed Ellis's forehead with as much love as a mother. "Jennings," he explained.

"I assumed so," Ellis said, "when Anne told me about an underground doctor. And where am I, exactly?"

"The same house where you were shot. It was too dangerous to move you. Harcourt made arrangements with his late brother's mistress. We've all been encamped here for over a week."

"And when I'm well enough to move, I assume there will be a cell awaiting me," he said. "Could you not have convinced Juliana to walk away to avoid seeing that second end for us?"

Rook snorted. "As if Juliana can be convinced of anything. Besides, why would you have a cell waiting?"

"Because the third son of a duke is dead," Ellis growled. "Don't be a fool."

"But you didn't kill him. His sister did. Harcourt and Coningburgh were locked away together for hours in negotiation. In the end, the duke seems just as happy to be rid of the son who threatened and abused everyone around him. The guard is useless. They only care about prosecuting those like us, not those with a shine to them. And Lydia? Well, she has seen fit to take a long holiday to the colonies where her mother's aunt apparently lives. I don't think she'll ever return."

"There's still the matter of the gem," Ellis said.

Rook cocked his head. "When it was brought up to him, Coningburgh didn't even know about it. His son had stolen it, Harcourt has been trying to work out from whom. But there won't be any trouble about that, either. Your life, as much as you tried to throw it away, seems to have been protected. Fixed, in part, by Harcourt."

Ellis broke his confused stare from his cousin and went back to examining the canopy. "Why would he do that?"

"For Thomasina, I think. For Juliana. Perhaps because he has a grudging respect that you tried to save everyone at the cost of yourself." Rook shrugged. "He isn't so bad, you know."

"Then it's settled," Ellis breathed.

"Except for one thing," his cousin corrected.

"Juliana," Ellis whispered, her name fearful and wonderful all at once. Because the future was suddenly wide open, and he had no idea what to do with that gift. If he should dare to take it at all.

"Juliana," Rook repeated. "May I offer you some advice, as a man who faced a rather similar choice not so long ago?" Ellis nodded and his cousin smiled. "If you love her, don't let her go."

"Even if it hurts her?" he whispered.

Rook's smile broadened. "I've spent a week and a half standing at your bed beside Miss Juliana Shelley. I watched her fight for your leg and your life. I watched her go to war with her father when he wanted to take her from you and ultimately sever a relationship that she has been tethered to her entire life. I will tell you, she is well capable of making decisions for herself. Trust her to do so." He moved to the door as he said, "The moment we were told you were awake, Rivers left to fetch your brother. Gabriel had gone home for a change of clothes. He will be gloriously happy to see you alive."

"Thank you," Ellis called out.

Rook turned at the door and smiled. "I love you, you great idiot."

Ellis laughed even though the shaking movement hurt his leg. But the laughter faded as Juliana shoved past Rook and stepped into the room. She stopped at the doorway, entirely oblivious to how Rook shut the door behind her with a smile. She simply stared at Ellis, her green eyes wide.

"I *told* them I didn't want to have a bath and change," she muttered. "I *told* them I shouldn't leave your side just in case you woke."

She crossed the room then and climbed into the bed without preamble. Her arms came around him, gentle so as not to jostle him, and her lips found his as their tears mingled.

He had no idea how long that lasted. He sank into it, glorying in her love for him and his for her. Glorying in the fact that she was safe now. If nothing else, at least he had managed to protect her from the dangerous situation of his own creation.

But at last he knew he had to pull away. This was not resolved, and they had to do that before he knew the next move of his life.

"Juliana," he began, tracing her jawline with his fingertips. "Angel."

She shook her head with fierce determination, and her chin lifted away from his touch in an act of pure defiance. "No," she said sharply.

"No?" he chuckled. "You don't even know what I was about to say."

"Of course I do," she insisted, and her scowl could have intimidated anyone to her will. "I *know* you. And I know you're about to give me a very long explanation about why we can never be together."

He blinked. She was right, of course. That was what he had to tell her. Those were the words hanging on his tongue. The ones he couldn't quite say even if that was the right thing to do. For her, at least.

She certainly deserved far more than a former thief and seducer with no future and a leg he had suspicions would never be the same again.

"I can't—" he made himself begin.

She pushed her fingers against his lips and forced the silence he would not give her. "No. I won't hear it," she said. "But you...you will hear *me* now."

J uliana had been practicing what she would say to Ellis if he woke up for days. *If* he woke up, because that had never been a guarantee. Doctors, healers, they had all looked at him with the grave injury and clucked their tongues and made her world implode upon itself.

To combat her terror, she had begun rehearsing what she would say when Ellis proved them wrong with his strength and his will and his glorious ability to fight. Now she was here, looking at him in the bed. He was alive. He would survive, that was evident.

She wasn't about to miss this chance to keep him with her forever. Even if the prospect of confession and demand was abjectly terrifying.

"For ten days I have fought to keep you alive," she said. "And I have no more patience for appeasing or being sweet or making it comfortable for anyone else."

He gave a weak mock salute. "Yes, ma'am."

She frowned. "Don't tease me. You were ready to *die*, Ellis."

He recoiled slightly, and she saw an echo of the heartbreak he must have felt when he decided to make that sacrifice. How desperate he must have been. "Yes," he said at last. "I knew as soon as Leonard attacked you all those weeks ago that I had no other choice."

She rested a palm on his cheek. "But you didn't tell me."

"The longer I knew you, the more I knew you'd try to stop me. Everyone would have. As you all did, actually." He forced a laugh even though she could see how much their rescue had meant to him, this man who'd told himself he had to go it alone.

"It's a good thing we did," she whispered, and pushed the blankets up a little to look at the dressing high on his thigh. The swelling had gone down, but the damage was great. It would take a long time for him to heal.

His fingers brushed her chin again and this time he turned her face toward his. "I'm sorry, Juliana," he whispered. "I am. For causing you pain. For causing you fear."

"Then stop doing it," she said, letting her hand cover his. "Stop fighting me. Fighting us."

He sucked in a ragged breath. "No matter your feelings, angel, no matter my own, you must know in your heart that I'm no good."

She moved closer, inching her way up the bed as she lowered her hand to cover his bare chest just above his heart. "You're *good* for *me*."

He squeezed his eyes shut, but she saw him wavering. He'd pushed her away so many times to protect her. But the danger was gone now. What he wanted to protect her from, she didn't fear. Their future. And she could see he wanted it just as she did. She just had to make him say those words.

"You know my past," he said, almost a pained moan.

"I do." She hesitated as his mouth turned down farther. "Please open your eyes. Please look at me."

It took him a few seconds, but he did as she asked. His blue eyes met hers and she could see he fought to keep them there.

"I *do* know your past," she repeated. "I love you for it. And there are parts of it I wish weren't true. But the future is something neither of us knows. I want to learn it together. I want to stand beside you as you repair the bond with Rook and your brother. I adore Gabriel, by the way. He is wonderful."

That elicited a small smile. "He is. A brilliant mind. I'm glad you've met him properly at last and that you like him. I have no doubt he adores you, as well."

"Because you see me as a far better version of myself than I do. And that's how it's supposed to be. I see the best in you, and hopefully I help you act in that. You do the same for me. There is so much to be done. I want to help you show my sisters and Harcourt the man you really are."

A shadow flickered over his face. More regret. "If I can."

"I have faith even if you don't," she reassured him. "I want to be yours, Ellis. I want to give my whole self to you and make you feel safe enough to give me the same gift. I want to laugh with you. I want to see the world with you. I want to have children with you."

"Juliana," he gasped, and in that moment she saw him picture the same. And he smiled. And she knew she would win.

"Do you love me?" she whispered. "Or are you going to lie out of some desperate fear and tell me I was just a game you played?"

He shook his head. "It was never a game," he said softly.

"Then *do you love me?*" she repeated.

His breath exited his lips in a long, unsteady sigh. "Yes," he admitted. "I love you. I love you with my whole heart. I love you in all your forms and expressions. I love you with all that I am. All that I wish to be. I love you for now and forever."

She couldn't help the wide smile that broke across her face, the first time she'd truly felt happy since the moment Ellis had slipped from Harcourt's window all those days ago. She also couldn't help the tears that fell down her cheeks. Because this man she adored was hers.

"Then you can't say no to me," she declared. "I won't allow it."

"Perish the thought that anyone could say no to you," he said with a laugh. "Marry me...even though I cannot promise to be perfect."

"You only have to promise you'll be mine," she said, and leaned in to claim his lips and the future they would share from this day until the end of their days.

EPILOGUE

Five years later

The children squealed as the cold seawater rolled up on the sand. They scattered up the beach toward their fathers, who were gathered together no more than an arm's length away from their beloved charges.

Juliana sat on the blanket farther down the shore, her sisters on either side of her, and she smiled at the picture the three men, three best friends, created. It had taken a long time to get there, but they were close now.

Rook stood on the far left, balancing Thomasina's youngest on his shoulder while her father, Harcourt, herded the other children nearer: his and Thomasina's oldest, a boy named Solomon, and their middle child, a little girl named Angelica. They were joined by Juliana's daughter, Violet, who rushed to her father at full speed.

Ellis was slow to kneel and leaned heavily on his cane as he did so. He had never fully recovered from the bullet that had nearly destroyed their lives, but he was whole and here and hers.

That was all that had ever mattered.

So much had changed since the events of the summer that had

changed all their lives. Harcourt had carefully invested Thomasina's dowry, building their fortune back through hard work and careful consideration. Their father, of course, had refused to pay additional dowries for Anne and Juliana. Their confrontation at Ellis's bedside all those years ago had been the last time they'd seen him.

But it didn't matter. That gem, the one that had nearly torn them all apart, had never been tracked back to a rightful owner. They'd sold it off, taking some of the money to support themselves and using the rest, the bulk, to start a school for foundling children. Supported by their family, as well as Marcus's in-laws, the Flynns and their friends and in-laws, the Woodleys, they took in children like Rook, Marcus and Ellis had all been. Offering them the chance those three had once been compelled to take by force. It gave Juliana such pleasure to see how much it moved them all to be a part of it.

Rook had turned his creative talent for woodcarving into a business. He and Anne split their time between their island and London, where he sold his wares.

For Ellis, it had been more complicated. Juliana had watched him struggle with his injury. Watched him struggle with losing the mantel of Handsome Ellis Maitland and his place in the underworld. But he had found his way, at last, thanks to Marcus Rivers. After Rivers himself had married, he'd asked Ellis to help him run the club. He had taken to it instantly and he, Paul Abbot and Rivers were a strong team. Juliana loved to watch him blossom. And loved the benefit that they could slip away to the Donville Masquerade any time they wanted and play a few love games with each other.

"Look at that little family." Thomasina's words drew Juliana from her musings. Thomasina laughed as she leaned back against the blanket. "How did we ever get so lucky?"

"Well, I take all the credit," Anne said as she poured a glass of wine for herself and Thomasina. Juliana shook her head when offered and reached for a container of tea instead, for she had been limiting herself as her second pregnancy blossomed.

She rested a hand on her swollen belly and laughed. "You mean because you ran away from home, you get to take the credit for everyone's happiness?"

Anne shrugged. "It's true."

For a moment, the three considered that suggestion. And then they dissolved into giggles.

"I cannot argue the logic," Juliana said. She caught up her tea and raised it. "To the Shelley Sisters. And to the very happy lives we somehow managed to build against all odds."

"To us," Thomasina and Anne repeated in unison. Then they clinked glasses, the joy of their futures far surpassing any sorrows of the past.

And so true love conquered all.

COMING SOON

Look for the next series from the mind of Jess Michaels, starting in June 2020. If you loved the 1797 Club, welcome back to their world, as we meet The Duke of Desire, Robert Smithton's bastard brothers and sisters. Wild as their brother, each will face love and danger and have to decide if a future is worth fighting for.

A series with beloved favorites, new heroes and heroines and stories that will make your toes curl. Turn the page for an excerpt of the first book, **The Love of a Libertine!**

Excerpt of The Love of a Libertine

The Duke's Bastards Book 1
Available June 9, 2020

He lowered his arm to find his half-brother, Robert Smithton, the Duke of Roseford, staring at him from outside the cell. He was dressed impeccably, just as he always was, not a hair on his head out of place. His expression was unreadable, though Morgan could tell he was irritated by the way his arms were folded tight across his chest.

"You look like shit, too," Roseford added and there was a hint of a smile that tilted one side of his lips.

Morgan slowly sat up and tried not to react to the searing pain that burned through his skull and into every joint in his body. God's teeth, how much had he drank?

"How did you know?" Morgan grunted. His mouth was so dry it was difficult to speak. "*I* didn't even know I was here."

That elicited a chuckle from Roseford. It was well known that Robert had lived a wild life, himself, for a very long time. Not recently, of course. Not since his marriage. "Do you actually need to guess?"

Morgan let out a long sigh. "Selina?" he asked.

Roseford inclined his head in the affirmative. Morgan slowly got up, hating the roil of his stomach as he steadied himself on the wall. Selina Oliver was another half-sibling shared by the two. They all had the same bastard of a father, along with God knew how many others. And while his relationship with Roseford was…strained and uncomfortable at times, his bond with Selina was much stronger. Perhaps because they were so much alike.

"I suppose she was there," he admitted.

"Yes," Roseford mused with a troubled expression. "Our sister is as wild as you are. Well, almost. But she isn't my problem. Yet. You are."

Morgan pursed his lips and dropped his gaze to the floor. "No I'm not," he grumbled, wishing there wasn't so much revealing bitterness in his tone.

He had only come to know Roseford recently. They'd been kept apart as boys. Their father, the last duke, kept his by-blows far from his 'real' son. Payments had come, to keep everyone silent, rather than safe. Ten years ago, when his father had died, Morgan had felt a genuine terror that those payments, which supported his education and his mother's small comforts, would dry up.

And yet they hadn't. Robert had continued to pay to support his father's bastards. He'd even managed to get doors opened for them in ways the previous Roseford hadn't tried. Morgan both appreciated his brother for making the effort...and resented him for wielding a power over him that Morgan couldn't make equal.

"We're only half-blood, Roseford," he muttered. "I'm not your problem."

"Yet here we are," Roseford said.

As he said it, a guard approached. At first Morgan thought he might be there to escort his brother from the premises, but instead the giant oaf of a man pulled a ring of keys from a chair around his waist. After a few seconds of fumbling, he opened the cell door and swung it wide, motioning Morgan from the unpleasant accommodations.

Morgan blinked at the offer of freedom and then glanced at his brother. "What?"

"Your debts are paid," the guard answered first and flashed a rotten-toothed smile toward Roseford. "With our thanks, Your Grace."

Robert sniffed his response and then turned motioning to Morgan to follow. "Come along, Morgan."

Morgan looked around but there seemed to be nothing he'd left behind in the nasty cell. He staggered after Robert, his stomach still rolling and his brain still a bit foggy from whatever had felled him last night. Normally he was capable of holding his liquor, so it must have been far more of a party than he recalled.

They weaved their way through the corridors, past men in cells in varying conditions. There were no words said until they exited the building at last and stood in the fresher air of the city. A cold rain drizzled down around them and Morgan pulled his jacket closer and hoped he hadn't lost his fine great coat in his foggy night of sin.

Roseford's carriage came along at last. Roseford motioned him in, then said something to his driver before he joined Morgan. They were off in a flash and Roseford sat, silently staring at Morgan as they rose along.

If his brother had railed at him, Morgan would have preferred it. But when he sat silently, arms folded, gaze held firmly on Morgan's, it made him feel worse than he already did. Like he needed to defend himself.

"You were just as bad as me," he said at last.

Robert tilted his head back and let out a full, loud belly laugh. Morgan couldn't help but stare. It made his brother look younger, more wicked. He could see the man he would have liked to run the hells with, rather than the stern duke who held the purse strings.

"I was that," Roseford said. "I never ended up in Newgate, mind you…but close. I have changed, though."

Morgan shrugged. Everyone knew that story, even if he and Roseford weren't that close. "Oh yes. Your *great love*."

Roseford's eyes narrowed at the dismissive tone to Morgan's voice. "Yes. Katherine changed me. Or made me want to change myself, which is better. And you may scoff, but I would wish you the same luck if you could find someone like her."

"Hm," Morgan said, staring out the window into the distance. "Not interested."

ALSO BY JESS MICHAELS

~

The Shelley Sisters

A Reluctant Bride

A Reckless Runaway

A Counterfeit Courtesan

The Scandal Sheet

The Return of Lady Jane

Stealing the Duke

Lady No Says Yes

My Fair Viscount

Guarding the Countess

The House of Pleasure

The 1797 Club

The Daring Duke

Her Favorite Duke

The Broken Duke

The Silent Duke

The Duke of Nothing

The Undercover Duke

The Duke of Hearts

The Duke Who Lied

The Duke of Desire

The Last Duke

~

Seasons

An Affair in Winter

A Spring Deception

One Summer of Surrender

Adored in Autumn

The Wicked Woodleys

Forbidden

Deceived

Tempted

Ruined

Seduced

Fascinated

The Notorious Flynns

The Other Duke

The Scoundrel's Lover

The Widow Wager

No Gentleman for Georgina

A Marquis for Mary

To see a complete listing of Jess Michaels' titles, please visit:

http://www.authorjessmichaels.com/books

ABOUT THE AUTHOR

USA Today Bestselling author Jess Michaels likes geeky stuff, Vanilla Coke Zero, anything coconut, cheese, fluffy cats, smooth cats, any cats, many dogs and people who care about the welfare of their fellow humans. She is lucky enough to be married to her favorite person in the world and lives in the heart of Dallas, TX where she's trying to eat all the amazing food in the city.

When she's not obsessively checking her steps on Fitbit or trying out new flavors of Greek yogurt, she writes historical romances with smoking hot alpha males and sassy ladies who do anything but wait to get what they want. She has written for numerous publishers and is now fully indie and loving every moment of it (well, almost every moment).

Jess loves to hear from fans! So please feel free to contact her in any of the following ways (or carrier pigeon):

www.AuthorJessMichaels.com
Email: Jess@AuthorJessMichaels.com

Jess Michaels raffles a gift certificate EVERY month to members of her newsletter, so sign up on her website:
http://www.AuthorJessMichaels.com/

facebook.com/JessMichaelsBks
twitter.com/JessMichaelsBks
instagram.com/JessMichaelsBks

Printed in Great Britain
by Amazon